Boy, Everywhere

Boy, Everywhere

BY A. M. DASSU

Tu Books
An Imprint of LEE & LOW BOOKS, Inc.
New York

TU BOOKS, an imprint of LEE & LOW BOOKS Inc.,
95 Madison Avenue, New York, NY 10016
leeandlow.com

Manufactured in the United States of America
Printed on paper from responsible sources

Edited by Stacy Whitman
Book design by Sheila Smallwood
Cover illustration by Daby Zainab Faidhi
Typesetting by ElfElm Publishing
Book production by The Kids at Our House
The text is set in Dante MT

10 9 8 7 6 5 4 3 2 1
First Edition

Cataloging-in-Publication Data is on file with the Library of Congress

For everyone who had to leave everything
behind and start again

Chapter 1

*I*t all started going wrong during English. It was the last lesson on Thursday before the weekend began, we'd just finished reading *To Kill a Mockingbird,* and Miss Majida stood at the whiteboard going through some comprehension questions. I was scribbling them down, my head resting on my arm, when Leila tapped me on my shoulder from behind and handed me a note.

Are you coming ice-skating tomorrow?

I'd started writing back when the door flew open and Mr. Abdo, our principal, burst into the room.

I shot up from my desk the second he entered and straightened my shoulders. Everyone's eyes were fixed on Mr. Abdo, their faces blank.

"Pack your bags. You're all to go home," he said, rubbing the creases on his tired, worn face. "See you back here on Sunday morning."

We didn't need telling twice. Everyone slapped their books shut and the room erupted into noisy chatter. My best friend, Joseph, turned to me and our eyes locked in confusion.

"Your parents and guardians have been called and are on their way to collect you," Mr. Abdo added, loosening the knot in his tie, his lips thin and tight, lines deepening across his brow.

"But why, Sir?" asked someone from the back of the class.

"There's been a bombing. This is not a drill, eighth grade. We need to get you all home. You know the protocol."

A collective gasp rose from the room.

Through the sash windows, the sky was a clear blue. I couldn't see any smoke. Everything looked normal. The old orange tree stood firm in the sunlit courtyard, the gold crescent moon on top of the mosque's minaret gleaming in the distance. Behind it the red-, white-, and black-striped flag on top of the church tower fluttered gently in the breeze, cars were hooting their horns, and the newspaper seller was still shouting out to people passing by his stall.

Where had the bomb gone off? Panic prickled through me as I thought of home. I wished phones were allowed in school so I could just call to see if Mama, Baba, and Sara were okay. I grabbed my bag to get my iPad, but remembered it wasn't in there. "Joseph, get your tablet out," I said. "Just want to check what's happened—I left my iPad at home."

"They won't have bombed anywhere near us, Sami. Don't worry," said Joseph, pulling his tablet out of his bag and swiping to log in. "What shall I type?" he asked, leaning in toward me.

"Google 'bombing in Damascus.'"

After a second, he pursed his lips and said, "Nothing's coming up." He showed me the error message—the internet was down for the second time that day.

My shoulders tensed. I quickly reminded myself that it was usually the outskirts of the city that were bombed. Most of Syria was torn apart because of the war, but no one had gotten close to Damascus.

"Your mama and baba are at work, right?" Joseph asked, his eyes focused on my forehead. I realized I was sweating and wiped my arm across my face.

"Yeah, Baba's at the hospital but Mama worked from home today because Sara wasn't feeling well. They *should* be at the mall now," I said, glancing at my Swatch. "She's picking up my football boots before the trials."

"Well, no one's ever bombed the center. The government's always on high alert. Just chill, bro," said Joseph, lightly pushing his fist into my shoulder before turning to put his tablet away.

He was right. But every time there was a bomb alert, I couldn't help worrying. *Damascus is safe*, I told myself. I took a deep breath, gathered my books, and packed them into my bag while Mr. Abdo spoke to Miss Majida. She had her hand over her mouth and looked like she was about to burst into tears.

A backpack pushed past my arm, followed by another—everyone was leaving.

"They're doing you a favor, Sami. You weren't gonna pass the English test later anyway." I turned to find George grinning at me, then pushing Joseph. "Neither were you, sucker."

Even at a time like this, George couldn't help being an idiot. Maybe it was his way of showing he wasn't nervous like me, but it was so annoying.

"You're the one that's gonna fail, loser," said Joseph, sticking his face into George's.

George sneered at Joseph. "Shut up! You're so fat, the only English letters you know are *K, F, C*." He turned to me, raising his eyebrows and running his hands through his hair.

So dumb, I thought. George still hadn't gotten over Joseph coming from a non-English-speaking school.

The class babble and sound of scraping chairs made it hard to think of a quick response, but I had to stick up for Joseph, whose cheeks were now the color of tomatoes. I rolled my eyes at George. "We'll see. *K, F,* and *C* are still three more letters than you know. Did you stay up all week thinking of that one?" His grin grew, so I added, "Should I use *smaller* words to make sure you understand what I'm saying?" It wasn't the greatest comeback but I couldn't think of anything else.

George's mini fan club, which consisted of exactly two friends, tugged him away.

"Loser," I muttered as they left.

Joseph and I joined the stream of kids leaving the classroom. Mr. Abdo was now speaking to Miss Majida at the door, but she stopped talking the second I drifted toward it.

Joseph clutched his backpack, his head lowered. He was unusually quiet. Ugh. George had gotten to him again.

"You want to go to Damer's for ice cream after the trials?" I asked to cheer him up.

"Yeah, of course, man!" Joseph said, his eyes sparkling with excitement. "Then we can go again tomorrow after ice-skating." He grinned.

Mr. Abdo marched past us. "Hang on," I said to Joseph and ran to catch up with him.

"Um, Sir, we're supposed to be going to football after school. Where should we wait?" I asked, wondering if Mama had collected my football boots.

He picked up his pace and strode into the classroom next door to ours and started talking to the teacher inside. I shrugged at Joseph as he caught up with me.

We rushed down the central stairway of the school behind the swarm of students and flowed into the large reception area, where our physics teacher, Miss Maria, was ushering everyone out of the side exit. I slowed down as I spotted Joseph's dad in a smart dark-gray suit, sitting on the deep-buttoned green leather sofa with his head in his hands. No one else's parents were inside, which was odd. The dark wood-paneled walls where the president's portrait hung made him look even gloomier.

"Baba?" said Joseph. His dad looked up.

"Ah, Sami, come here." Joseph's dad stood up and reached out to hug me first. *Weird.* I went to him, feeling awkward, and as he embraced me tightly my heart began to race.

He pressed my head against his shoulder and ruffled my hair, then released me and grabbed Joseph. I stepped back, feeling woozy from inhaling his strong aftershave.

"Right, let's get you both home," he said in Arabic, turning from Joseph.

"But what about the football trials?" I asked. "Our driver is bringing my boots. I have to wait for him!"

"Your baba asked me to pick you up. It's not safe to be out today."

"But Baba!" Joseph interrupted. "We were gonna get on the team today! This is so unfair!"

"Joseph, I already told you, it's not safe to be at the stadium."

Joseph tutted, shoved the carved wooden door open, and walked out.

"Thank you! I'll keep you updated," Joseph's dad

shouted at the school receptionist as he followed Joseph out. I ran after him, my stomach lurching. Baba wouldn't send Joseph's dad to pick me up unless it was serious. Maybe the bombing was really bad. Baba would know because of the number of casualties coming in at the hospital.

The street outside school was a tangle of gridlocked cars and beeping horns. Cars were double-parked across the sidewalk, leaving hardly any room to walk between them. The newspaper seller pushed papers and magazines into our sides as we walked past his stall, desperately trying to get them sold while the street was jammed with people. We all got into Joseph's dad's Honda CR-V, and I pulled the seat belt over me slowly, looking out at all the parents frowning in their cars. Joseph glanced at me and then pulled out his tablet.

"Can't believe they dropped a bomb today of all days. I've been waiting *ages* for this," he muttered under his breath.

"I know . . ." I said. "I bet Avraham's on his way with my boots as well. He's probably stuck in all the traffic now."

"What did you end up ordering?" he asked, pressing Play on a game.

"Can't get the Nike Magistas in Damascus. So I got the Adidas Predators."

"Oooh, nice." He looked out of the window and then said, "Thanks for sticking up for me with George." His cheeks were flushed again.

"No worries. I'd never leave you to face that thug alone."

George and his stupid gang had bullied Joseph ever since we started middle school. They thought they could do or say anything they wanted because they were ulad masooleen—kids of government officials. I'd never seen Joseph look so sad or alone as that first week of middle school, and I never wanted him to feel that way again. I'd always be there for him. It had always been Sami and Joseph. And it would be forever.

"Ignore him," I said. "He's just jealous of your skills—still hasn't gotten over last semester when you scored that penalty."

Joseph smiled. "Yeah, that was awesome. Do you think they'll rearrange the trials to next week now?"

"Yeah, probably."

As Joseph went back to his game, I stared out the window, checking out everyone's cars. Leila's mama was in her gray Lexus RX, but I couldn't see Leila through the tinted glass. *Oh man.* I realized I'd totally forgotten to reply to her note after Mr. Abdo walked in. I hoped I hadn't upset her. I'd message when I got home and tell her me and Joseph would be at the ice rink at three P.M. tomorrow.

It took twenty minutes to get out of the school street behind all the other cars, but when we got moving I could see the high-rise buildings were still intact, the roads were clear, traffic only building up near the checkpoints. There were a few fluffy clouds scattered in the sky. Something circled the blue far away, probably a helicopter. I still couldn't see any smoke in the air. *They probably bombed the outskirts of the city*, I reassured myself again.

On the way to Joseph's neighborhood, a crowd of people were gathered outside a big villa, the men in smart suits and the women in dresses, some wearing headscarves. But I was more interested in the cars they were standing next to—a black Bentley and a white Rolls-Royce parked on the road. Both Joseph and I sat up to get a better look, our mouths open, practically drooling.

"Whoa. What do you think they're here for?" I asked Joseph.

"Probably a wedding . . . or a funeral," he said, showing me his game score and smirking. "I beat you, right?"

"Hey! Give me that," I said, grabbing his tablet and pressing Play. We'd been doing this for weeks.

Joseph's dad parked outside their apartment building. As the car stopped on the smooth black pavement, we heard what must've been gunshots in the distance. I always thought it sounded like rain hitting a tin roof. But it wasn't raining. We jumped out, sheltered our heads with our arms, and ran through their black front gates. We raced straight up to Joseph's bedroom, throwing our bags down next to some dried orange peel he hadn't bothered throwing away.

I sat on the end of his bed while Joseph switched on his PlayStation and small flat-screen TV. "May as well play *FIFA* if we can't play the real thing, eh?" he said, his chin jutting out because of his grumpy face.

"Yeah, may as well," I said, wishing the trials hadn't been canceled and that we were showing off the skills we'd been practicing in the stadium instead.

There was a small knock on the door and it opened. "Hi, you two. Do you want anything to eat?" asked Joseph's mama.

"Nah," said Joseph, still facing the TV screen, waiting for the game to load.

"How about you, Sami?"

"No thanks, Aunty, but can I have a drink, please?"

Joseph's mama smiled. "Sure. What would you like? Coke?"

"Yes, thanks. Shall I call my mama to get Avraham to pick me up? He's probably waiting for me at school."

"No!" she said quickly in a strange high-pitched voice. "Your baba wants you to stay for dinner. Stay there—I'll be right back with that Coke!" She pulled the door tight and left.

I bit my lip and frowned. Even Aunty was acting weird. I grabbed the remote from Joseph's hands and put it on TV mode.

"Hey! What you doing?" shouted Joseph.

"Shhh, I just wanna check the news. See why Baba got us picked up. Don't you wanna know?"

"Not really. All they'll show is more dead people."

"Oh, come on, it'll only take a minute."

"Go on then," said Joseph.

I flicked through the channels one by one. Kids' cartoons, music, documentaries, news channel. My head started spinning as I read the headline flashing in red at the bottom of the screen.

DAMASCUS: CHAM CITY CENTER MALL REBEL TERRORIST BOMB ATTACK

I sat staring at the image on the screen. The once-shiny glass building was now partly rubble. The glass half of the mall was a broken gray shell, and the concrete half was just barely standing. There were no windows or doors left in any of it and people in high-vis jackets rushed through the smoke, debris, and rows of police cars and ambulances. I watched but couldn't move. My ears throbbed. I could see Joseph's arms waving around next to me. Everything had slowed down, the noise from the TV and Joseph's words muffled. I tried to say something, but nothing came out.

The mall had been bombed. Mama and Sara were there. Buying *my* football boots.

Chapter 2

A knock on the door broke my daze. I turned—Joseph's mama's head poked through the opening.

I leaped up from the bed. "I need to go!" I yelled. "You've got to take me, now!"

Joseph's mama took one look at the TV and rushed toward me, handing the Coke to Joseph. She grabbed my shoulders and fixed her eyes on mine.

"Sami, you can't go there. They'll be okay."

"NO!" I struggled under her firm grip. "You HAVE to take me, NOW!"

"Listen, habibi, your baba is there. He's finding them. They'll be fine. Please. Sami." She pulled me back to the bed and sat down beside me, holding on to the cross around her neck. Tears rolled down her cheeks.

"But it's my fault they went!" I jumped up again. "I have to go there!" I grabbed my bag and ran through the door, leaping down the stairs two at a time.

"SAMI, COME BACK!" Joseph's mama shouted after me.

I swung around the bottom of the staircase and into the hallway. As I neared the front door, Joseph's dad stepped in front of it.

"Let me go! I need to go!" I shouted, pushing my hands into his chest.

"You can't do anything now." He put his hands over mine. "Please, come and sit down and I'll explain what happened."

Pain stabbed at my heart and I slipped to the floor, sobbing. "I know what happened! I made them go. I killed my mama and sister!" I screamed.

Joseph's dad knelt down and put his arms around my shoulders, gently lifting me.

"Come on." He walked me through to the living room. Joseph and his mama stood on the bottom step, staring at me, their faces gray. I wanted the ground to open up and swallow me whole. I wanted the rebels to drop a bomb and crush *me*.

Joseph's dad led me to the sofa and sat me down.

"Why do you think it's your fault, Sami?"

I sobbed into my hands, thinking about this morning. *Why did I make them go?* I tried to picture Mama's face when I'd been pleading with her to pick up my football boots.

"Oh, come on, I really need them tonight!" I'd said in Arabic to Mama, trying to mimic Sara's wide-eyed look.

She took a sip of steaming coffee and put her mug back on the kitchen island, before logging into her laptop.

"Sami, I'm supposed to be *working* from home. I have got mid-semester reports to sign, and I'm not in the mood to trek through a mall looking for football boots," she'd said, still staring at her MacBook screen through her rimless glasses.

"But, Mama, you can sign your stuff in the morning, and then you can go to the gym at the mall, so you can easily pick up my boots," I said, dumping my cereal bowl in the sink and walking back toward her.

"I can't. I've got to get through two hundred student reports before lunch, and then I've got a charity benefit at the Four Seasons hotel."

I had put on my most desperate face. "Don't you want me to get selected for the team? Please, Mama, I ordered them to the store, so you don't even need to look around. You'll be straight in and straight out."

Mama sighed and picked up her coffee. "Oh, Sami, why do you have to be so disorganized? You could have bought them over the weekend. You knew you had the football trials. Avraham has a hospital checkup today, so he can't get them, and that means I have to drive myself *and* I've got Sara with me, so it won't be a quick in and out."

I had to try one more time. "Can't you *quickly* get them before your charity thing? Please? And then Avraham can drop off my boots at school after his appointment?"

She'd looked up at me, back at her screen, and then at me again with the faintest of smiles.

"Thanks, Mama! I already emailed you the collection receipt." I pecked her on the cheek, grabbed my backpack from the kitchen counter, and ran out to our Mazda 6 waiting on the drive.

"Sorry, sorry, Avraham. Are we going to be late?" I slammed the car door shut, blocking out the sound of our neighbor's lawnmower. "I had to convince Mama to pick up my football boots."

"No, we are okay," said Avraham, glancing at his watch.

"Will you have time to pick up my boots from Mama's charity thing and then bring them to me before the end of school please? *Please?*"

"Sami, Sir, you are a cheeky chappie. After my appointment, if your mama tells me to do this, of course I will."

"Thanks! Avraham, you're the best."

He'd tipped the front of his black chauffeur hat in the rearview mirror as the front gates opened slowly.

This morning, I couldn't wait for school to finish. Joseph and I planned to tear through the Under-15s football trials and make sure we got chosen to play for the school team. I'd thought those Adidas Predators would make me unstoppable. But what did I know? *Nothing*.

A phone rang, breaking the memory. Joseph's dad rushed to pick it up. "Tarek! How are they?"

It was Baba! I ran and snatched the phone from Joseph's dad.

"Baba! Come and get me. Please!" I blubbered.

"Sami, I can't. I need to stay with your mama and Sara. Give the phone back to Uncle Tony."

"I'm so sorry . . ."

"Why are you sorry? Please get Uncle—I need to speak to him and then get back."

"I shouldn't have made them go. They'd be alive right now . . ."

"Sami, *listen*, will you? This is not the time. They're alive, praise be to God. But I need to get back to them. Give the phone to Uncle Tony now."

I peeled the phone from my ear, handed it to Joseph's dad, and traipsed back to the sofa. "They're alive," I said, slumping back down next to Joseph.

"Huh?" Joseph turned to me, smiling. "Thank God for that!"

"But they might not be okay," I said, still looking ahead.

"What do you mean?"

"They might have no legs or something. Baba

said he had to get back to them. Maybe they're being operated on."

"Come on, bro, don't think like that. They'll be all right." He nudged my shoulder with his.

Joseph's dad put the phone down and turned around. Beads of sweat had formed on his forehead.

I jumped up. "You have to take me. Please, Uncle, I need to see them."

"Sami, they're okay—they're alive," he said, wiping his brow with the back of his arm.

"Then please just let me go and see them!" I slapped my arms on my sides.

He fixed me with his brown eyes and took a deep breath. "Get your shoes on. Let's go." He walked out of the room.

"Huh?" I looked at Joseph, my mouth hanging open. I didn't think it'd be that easy to convince him. Maybe he'd realized I wasn't going to stop asking. I ran for my shoes before he changed his mind.

○ ○ ○

I don't know how long it took to get to the hospital. Time seemed to freeze; each red traffic light seemed to take hours to change. Finally we were pulling up. As soon as Joseph's dad stopped the car, I opened the door and zoomed toward the hospital entrance.

"Sami! Wait!" Joseph's dad called after me, but I wasn't waiting for anyone.

An overpowering hospital smell of disinfectant and rubber hit me as I rushed through the double doors. Then came the stench of vomit, dust, and burned meat. It was mayhem inside, with doctors in blue overalls rushing from one place to the next, and people lying on stretchers in the hallways, their clothes and skin covered in blood. Most beds had their curtains drawn, and every few seconds a scream from a different place pierced my ears.

I ran to the reception desk and leaned over it, the fluorescent lighting flickering above me. "I need to find my mama and sister. Uh . . . um . . . Zeina and Sara al-Hafez."

"AAAAAAAAGGGGGHHHHHHH!" came another scream. I jumped and turned to see where it came from but couldn't tell. My heart felt as if it was beating twice as fast as normal.

"They're up in ward five, level two," the receptionist said, still staring at her computer.

"Thanks." I turned around and began weaving through the people sitting on the floor—some bandaged, all with zombie eyes, unseeing—trying to avoid the blood on the floor smeared with footprints. There was no sign of Joseph's dad yet. Two dust-covered children walked through the corridor accompanied by a nurse, peering into each side room as they passed.

"Is this your mama?" the nurse asked them.

I gulped and took a deep breath. It was like a bad scene from a movie. So this was what Baba had been working with for years whenever there was a bombing in the suburbs. It hit me that I didn't know if I could become a doctor like him. I couldn't deal with stuff like this! Right then I was wishing I could walk with my eyes closed. But I had to move forward for Mama and Sara.

A crowd of people waited outside the elevators, so I squeezed past them and headed for the stairs, leaving the screaming and crying behind. It was a relief to get away into the empty, cold stairwell. I ran up two steps at a time. By the time I got to the second floor, I had to bend over to catch my breath before pushing through the door into the ward.

A nurse sat behind a desk at the entrance. "Zeina, Zeina al-Hafez. . . . I need to see her. She's my mama," I panted, wheezing in a strong smell of antiseptic.

"You're Dr. Tarek's son! My God, haven't you grown!" The curly-haired nurse smiled and pointed to her left. "She's in bay three, your sister next to her."

"Thanks!" I ran through the ward, passing beds of people. It was quiet and calm compared to downstairs; men and women lay still, their arms by their sides. I didn't know if they were dead or waiting to die, but I shuddered just thinking about it.

I stopped under the sign for bay three, outside a blue curtain pulled around two bed spaces. "Mama?" I asked.

"Sami!" Baba opened the curtain fast. I slid in through the gap and froze. Mama and Sara lay next to each other on separate beds. Baba must've moved the cabinet between the beds to bring them closer together.

They both wore oxygen masks. Their closed eyes were swollen and bruised, as if they'd been beaten in a boxing match. I stood still and scanned the space, trying to work out what everything did. Each had a tube inserted into their arm, attached to a bag of liquid, and a monitor that beeped every second. Other than their eyes and a few small cuts on their faces, I couldn't see any injuries. I moved around to check that they still had their arms and legs.

Baba put his arm around me as I neared him. "They'll be okay, son. They'll be okay. . . ."

I looked up at him; his face was pale and his eyes swollen, but not like Mama's and Sara's, more as if he'd been crying a lot. Mama and Sara hadn't moved since I entered.

"Can . . . can I talk to them?" I whispered.

"They've been sedated, so they won't be able to hear you right now. I spoke to the consultant. It's best for them to stay here tonight, so the other doctors can monitor them." He turned to look at the curtains. "Where's Tony?"

"Um, he's coming." I shrugged, my shoulder still under Baba's arm, my eyes fixed on Mama and Sara.

What have I done? I thought.

Don't die. Please don't die.

Chapter 3

"*Sami, get ready! Your* baba just called. They're back home!" shouted Joseph's dad from downstairs.

Finally! I thought, jumping off the bed and dumping my PlayStation controller on the cluttered desk. I'd been waiting for him to call since I got back from the hospital last night.

"Oh, man! You're going already? It's the weekend— just stay a bit longer!" said Joseph as he stared at the screen, keeping his controller steady and his car on track.

I shook my head. "I can't." I picked up my school backpack and slung it over my shoulder. "I need to see them, Joseph. Anyway, we've been playing all morning!"

"See you tomorrow?" His car's engine roared as he sped up to pass the finish line.

"I don't know what's happening yet. I'll probably give you these back at school on Sunday, yeah?" I said, pulling at the T-shirt Joseph had lent me.

"Yeah, no worries." He dropped the controller into his lap and put out his fist. "Message me later?"

"Yup," I said, fist-bumping him before rushing downstairs. No one was in the hallway, so I wandered into the kitchen where I could hear pots clanking.

"Uncle?" The smell of meat cooking wafted up my nose.

"Ah, Sami!" Joseph's mama smiled at me as she chopped some parsley next to the sink. "They're home, praise be to God! I was up praying all night—I even went to the church to light a candle. God has listened to our prayers."

"Yeah, He has Aunty," I said, with lightness in my chest. I didn't often pray, even though Mama was always going on about praying every day and Baba took me to Friday prayers each week. Last night I didn't need to be asked. I begged Allah over and over again to save them. "Where's Uncle Tony? He just called me down." I pushed my hands deeper into my pockets.

"He's in his office getting something for your baba. He won't be long." She carried on chopping parsley.

Water grumbled as it came to a boil and the kettle clicked off.

"I'll just wait in the hallway. Thanks for having me, Aunty," I said, walking toward the door, hoping Joseph's dad would hurry up.

"Always a pleasure, Sami. Hold on—take this bag." She dropped her knife on the chopping board and rinsed her hands under the tap. She pulled a parcel wrapped in a knotted blue plastic bag out of the fridge. "Some maqluba for tonight. Don't forget to give it to your baba when you get in. I made it this morning."

"Thank you," I said, putting my hand under the bagged stack of tubs to keep them steady.

"You take care of your mama and sister. Okay, Sami?" she said, smiling and holding out the kitchen door for me. I smiled back and walked out.

The main apartment building door was open. Through it I could see Joseph's dad putting a brown leather bag in the trunk of his car.

"Right. You ready?" he said, slamming the trunk shut then walking round to the driver's side.

Joseph's dad stepped out of the car at the gas station. The smell of grilled chicken from a nearby restaurant drifted in with a gust of warm air before he shut the door. The cross hanging from the rearview mirror swung like a pendulum.

I lunged forward and turned on the radio, making sure I kept the volume low as I glanced outside, where Uncle Tony was staring at the rising digits on the pump display. I needed to know more about what had happened. Baba had explained that we had liked the president and his government to start with, but when people started peacefully protesting his presidency, he said his people were against him and attacked them instead of resigning. Baba said we wanted him out but couldn't do anything, and then rebel groups tried to remove him but in their attempts started killing ordinary people too. I didn't understand it all properly—I knew that everyone was fighting and the whole country was in a mess, but Damascus had been safe so far because the government controlled it, so how did the rebels get in? Maybe someone on the radio would have answers.

The news was on, and a reporter was interviewing people about the mall bombing. A woman spoke to him frantically, panic in her voice. I leaned forward to focus on what she was saying.

"I'd just finished shopping, my hands were full of bags," she said. Her voice quivered and she blew her nose before continuing. "I stopped outside Damascus Desserts—to have a quick rest before I left—and was looking at the iced cakes. . . . I was going to leave—" She started weeping.

"It's okay, take your time," said the reporter.

"As I stepped toward the shop door," she continued, "a bright flash like an enormous bolt of lightning shot through the mall, and immediately after it a thunderous boom. Everything shook. I was thrown into the air, debris raining all over me . . . I landed on my chest and skidded across the floor. I felt the explosion ripple right through my body." She went quiet.

"What happened then?" asked the reporter.

"I felt hot—there was a powerful heat . . . Everything was still and soundless; I wasn't sure what had happened. I lay in a daze for a few minutes, then opened my eyes, but I couldn't see a thing. My eyes burned from all the dust. I was suffocating, gasping for air, but it felt like someone had sucked all of it away and replaced it with smoke. Everything stings, even now." There was silence for a few seconds. I wondered if they'd gone off air. I looked out the window and saw Joseph's dad walking toward the cashier.

"I'm sorry . . . It's okay . . ." the reporter consoled her.

The lady sniffled and took a deep breath before continuing. "I thought I was in a nightmare. I couldn't hear a thing, except the ringing in my ears. Then someone grabbed me by the arm and dragged me into the dusty shop. Probably to get me to safety, but I was in a lot of pain. I don't know when I managed to swallow, but my ears popped. And then all I heard was people's screams. Loud, loud, piercing screams." The lady started sobbing again.

My chest felt tight and a lump rose in my throat thinking about what Mama and Sara had been through because of me. If this woman was thrown by the force of the bomb, little Sara would've flown through the air and landed harder. Mama and Sara were alive, but what if they were now blind or deaf?

Joseph's dad was approaching the car. I jumped forward to quickly switch off the radio, rubbed the tears out of my eyes, and sat back in my seat.

"Right, let's get you home," said Uncle Tony as he sat down and pulled the door shut.

The front gates to our apartment building took an eternity to open. As soon as we were through, I saw the iron door to our backyard had been left open and Baba was crouching looking through some boxes. His tennis rackets and empty boxes from things we'd bought were scattered around him. *What is he doing?* I wondered.

As the car tires crunched over the gravel, Baba looked up and walked toward us. His eyes were still swollen, but not as much as the night before. His hair was a mess, and he was still in yesterday's scrubs.

"Sami, son . . ." He opened my door and pulled me close as I got out. I fumbled with the stupid bag of food tubs, wanting to hug him back but unable to.

"You get inside. Go and see your mama. I'll come in a bit. I just have to finish off some stuff here." He glanced at Joseph's dad, who was now around my side of the car, standing next to me holding two brown A4 envelopes. They obviously wanted to talk without me, so I went around to the front of the building and up the steps, breathing in the comforting smell of jasmine from the yard. *Home*.

I dumped the bag of food on the side table in the hallway, next to the tall vase of roses, then threw off my backpack and tugged off my school shoes. "Mama?" I called, looking around the hallway and up the stairs as I stepped on to the cool marble floor. "Sara?" The house was silent.

I ran into the living room, where the curtains were still drawn. Now I could hear sniffling coming from somewhere. I squinted in the gloom and saw Mama, sitting on the floor by the bookshelf, surrounded by boxes, one of our photo albums open on her lap. She had her mobile pressed to her ear.

"I can't come back—you'll have to step up until you can recruit someone else." She paused, then added, "I know principals are supposed to give longer notice, but I can't stay. I'm sorry . . ." Her voice broke with her last words.

Was she leaving her job because of what happened to her? Couldn't she just take some time off?

"I can't get the sound of the sirens and screaming out of my head, Sabah. . . . I can still hear the metal scratching the rubble as the rescue workers tried to dig people out of the wreckage. I can't stop the noise—" She started to cry and then stopped herself.

I bit my lip, thinking about how me making Mama pick up my football boots had ruined her life.

"Sabah, please listen. I'll send in my resignation letter tomorrow. I'll put together a handover document too. I'm sorry." She pulled the phone from her ear, tapped the screen, and put the handset down on the rug.

"Mama?" I said softly.

She jumped, looked at me, and struggled to get on her knees to stand up.

"Ohhh, Sami! My boy!"

I rushed over and she hugged me tight, putting her face in my hair. I closed my eyes and rested my head on her shoulder. She smelled of vanilla and orange blossom. "It feels like years since I saw you." She wept.

Don't cry, I told myself, trying to hold back my tears. "I'm so sorry! I shouldn't have made you—"

"Hey." She took my face in her hands and I looked into her eyes, barely open, only slits. I could hardly make out their hazel color. Her face was wet from tears. "You have nothing to be sorry about. Don't you go blaming yourself." She wiped a tear from my cheek with her thumb. "It was fate. We were supposed to be there at that time." She let go of my face and put her arms around me again.

I didn't know what to say. I wanted to let everything out and bawl like a baby, but I stopped myself. I had to be strong for her.

"We're going to be okay. We've got some scratches and cuts, but they'll heal, Sami. The bomb was in another part of the mall. Some debris hit us, but we managed to get into the back of Costa until someone came to get us out. We were mainly covered in dust— it was nothing compared to others. God willing, we'll be okay."

I looked up at her face. Tears streamed down her cheeks.

"Go and see Sara and Tete. Your grandma's giving her a bubble bath." She released me and turned back to the bookshelf. She was probably packing up the books that belonged to the school. Was she really going to leave her job? Maybe Baba would talk her round.

"Shouldn't you be in bed resting?" I asked as I headed for the door.

"I'm okay, Alhamdulillah. I have a lot to do," she said, putting books into an empty box.

I nodded. I wanted to ask her why she was resigning from her job if she was really okay, but I couldn't. I knew it was my fault.

The moist heat from the bathroom hit me as soon as I opened the door. It was as hot as a greenhouse.

Tete sat on a wicker chair by the side of the bath, holding my sister on her lap. Sara's eyes were still swollen and bruised, and I spotted a cut on her upper arm, which was scabbing over. She clung to Tete's arm, still in her dress. I took a deep breath. I had to sound normal.

"As-salaamu alaikum, Tete. You okay, Thumbelina? Why aren't you in the bathtub?"

Sara flinched.

"Shhhh . . ." Tete raised her finger to her mouth. "I've only just managed to settle her. She didn't want to get in and wouldn't stop crying."

"Didn't miss me, then?" I asked, kneeling next to them on the warm tiled floor. Sara didn't move. Her eyes looked blank. I leaned back—normally she'd jump on me in her cute five-year-old way, wrapping her arms around my neck and poking her knees into my stomach, pecking at my cheeks.

"She's not talking, Sami," said Tete. "I thought a bubble bath might help—you know how much she loves them—but she just looks out into space. God help habibti."

"Oh . . ." I didn't know what to say.

"I'm glad you came to see me. Come. Yalla." She patted the foot of the chair and shuffled it nearer the bathtub to make room for me next to her.

"Will she be okay?" I asked, watching Sara, who was still staring ahead.

"I hope so . . . If the bomb had gone off just five minutes earlier, they would've been right at the center of its destruction. Praise be to Allah, He saved them."

I shuddered at the thought of them being beside the bomb when it went off. Tete stroked my hair along its gelled parting. Then she took something out of her cardigan pocket and her eyes welled up.

I recognized it immediately—Jiddo's precious ring. My grandad used to wear it on his little finger. The stones in it twinkled as Tete held it out to me.

"I'm giving you this, habibi, because you are a special boy and your jiddo wanted you to have it. I was going to wait until you got married, but who knows how long we will live?"

She saw me cringe and grabbed my shoulder. I

wanted to run off before she went on. I didn't want to think about marriage or death.

"Sami, you keep it safe and with you everywhere you go. *Don't* lose it. It's been passed down for generations. I want you to give it to your son when you have one. It must stay in the family. Okay?"

I felt my cheeks flush and shuffled my feet. "Yesss, okay, Tete. Shukran." *Ugh*. Why did she have to keep talking about marriage and kids?

She dropped it into my hand. I felt its weight for a moment and then slipped it over my left index finger. It glided along it smoothly, as if it had been made for me. I moved my hand and watched the stones glimmer in the light from the fluorescent tube above.

"Now go. Go and help your parents and be strong." She closed her watery eyes and put her arm back around Sara, who was still staring into the room.

But I couldn't leave without finding out why Sara wasn't speaking to me. She could still hear—she reacted to me when I came in. Had she forgotten me? "Did something hit her head at the mall?" I asked. Maybe she had a concussion.

Tete brought her face closer to mine and whispered, "She saw a man's head and arm on the ground as they took her out of the mall. It was awful. Ohhhh, habibti." Tete squeezed Sara tighter as I tried to get the image out of my mind.

A head! I thought. *What have I done? That would've traumatized anyone, even an adult. Poor Sara.*

I got up off the floor, feeling dazed, my mind numb. "I'll just go and get showered and changed," I said, tingling with guilt. I couldn't sit and look at Sara's little blank face a moment longer.

In the hallway, the cooler air made the hairs on my arms stand up.

"Come here." Mama was walking out of her bedroom with a box in her hands and ushered me to follow her downstairs.

"Bring me your iPad with its charger, please."

"My iPad?" I said, confused.

"Yes, your iPad, Sami. I need it."

"What about your MacBook?" I rushed after Mama, trying not to fall into her as she stepped off the stairs.

"Don't argue, just go and get it," she said, irritated. She put the box down beside the side table in the hallway. The blue bag of food still sat there. "Take your backpack up as well." She handed it over without looking at me.

Maybe her MacBook was damaged at the mall, I thought. *But she could easily use Sara's iPad instead. She never asks for mine.*

I trudged back up the winding staircase to my bedroom and hung my bag on the back of the door. My iPad was on the desk. The screensaver flashed on as I picked it up—a photo of Joseph and me pulling a stupid face at Leila's last party. I swiped right to log in and sat down on my bed and began to message him.

> So I'm home. Mama's fine-ish but being weird :|

The iPad pinged right away:

> Same here, man. Mine keeps hugging me : \

> Lending mama my iPad. Don't send anything dodgy! Think she lost hers.

> Good thing u told me. Was gonna facetime later.

> Ha! I don't wanna see how many fries you can get in your mouth in one go again! That's getting old! Will message u when she gives it back.

I pressed the Home button, grabbed the charger, and ran back downstairs. Mama took both from me and put them on top of a pile of books on the living room rug. I frowned.

She wasn't even going to use it!

But looking at her thunderous face, I didn't dare ask why she wanted it. I just slouched out of the room, hoping she'd give it back soon so I could FaceTime Joseph and tell him about poor Sara.

Chapter 4

*T*he front door *was* wide open as I walked down the stairs on Sunday, tightening my school tie and tucking it under my blazer. Four men dressed in gray overalls were struggling to carry our marble dining table through the hall. I gasped as I watched them maneuver through the door, then ran along the hallway, inhaling the sharp smell of fresh bleach that seemed to fill the entire house.

"Where are they taking the table?" I asked Mama. She was in the kitchen scrubbing an already spotless counter. "Where's Rima? You've already done the bathrooms this morning. Why are you cleaning again?"

"She won't be coming anymore. We let her go. Avraham too." She pulled down the spray kitchen tap and began washing the sink with it.

My chest tightened a little. "Huh? Why? You've been cleaning all weekend. I thought it was because Rima was ill."

"We're moving," she said, grabbing a mop and swiping it over the sparkling white marble tiles.

"What?! Why?" I stepped back.

"We can't live here any longer. We need to be somewhere where Sara has the best chance to heal and start talking again. And someone recommended a psychologist who has been successful with children like her."

Poor Sara. She hadn't said a word since the bombing, even when I skipped the latest episode of *Top Gear* so we could watch her favorite princess movie, and I'd danced around like an idiot to make her laugh.

I looked down at my gray school socks and shuffled my feet. If only I could turn back time and never ask for those stupid new boots.

"Go upstairs and get changed. I need you to help me pack up yours and Sara's stuff."

"But what about school?"

"You're not going. We've got a lot to do." She adjusted her headscarf.

"But I have to hand in my science project today! I've been working on it for days!" Mama squeezed the mop in the bucket and picked them both up. "I won't have to change school, will I? We won't go too far, right?" My chest tightened again and bile rose in my throat.

Mama turned and walked into the utility room. "Stop asking questions and be helpful, Sami!" she shouted. "Just don't let Sara see you packing her toys—it'll upset her."

I heard men arguing and walked to the hallway to see what they were doing. Two men were carrying the big TV from the living room, while a third shouted at them to hurry up. I wondered where they were taking the TV and what our new house would look like. I looked back into the kitchen, but Mama was still in the utility room. Probably scrubbing something else that didn't need cleaning.

As I passed the living room, I saw Baba packing the iMac into its box. He always kept the original packaging for all our devices. Next to him were two empty iPad boxes that still looked brand new, even though the iPads themselves were almost as old as Sara. I wanted to ask him for mine, but it didn't seem like the right time. *It's my fault that Sara's traumatized,* I told myself. *Be helpful and do what's best for her.* I could live without it for a few more days, and I'd just call Joseph from the landline later when he got home from school.

I took off my blazer and loosened my tie as I climbed the stairs, then turned into Sara's room. A row of empty brown boxes stood lined up against the hallway wall ready to be filled, labeled BOOKS, TOYS, and CLOTHES.

Tete was reading Sara a story on her bed. She must've come to our house really early. I hadn't even heard her arrive. I wasn't expecting Sara to be in her room—since she came home from the hospital she'd been sleeping with Mama and Baba. Now I had to somehow get her downstairs so I could pack.

"All right, Thumbelina?" I said, walking to her bed.

The bruising around her eyes was a lighter shade of purple and the skin less puffy. I wished I could fix her speech just as quickly.

She startled and grabbed Tete tight, burying her face in Tete's shoulder. My stomach dropped like a brick. "Come on, Sara, let's play 'Teacher Teacher' downstairs—you love that, don't you?" Her face remained in Tete's shoulder. "You can be the teacher," I tried again, "and I'll let you boss me around. You can teach me how to read, okay? I think I forgot how to!"

She didn't move. I sighed. Mama was right. She did need real help.

"I'll take her downstairs," Tete said, struggling to get off the bed with Sara still clinging to her. "She's not ready to come to you. Have you come to . . ." Tete nodded at the boxes outside the room.

"Yeah," I said, picking up one of Sara's teddy bears from her bed and looking at its big, sad eyes.

I spent most of the morning in Sara's room, packing away all her toys. Going through her things reminded me how loud and silly she usually was—constantly running around, her toys scattered everywhere. I used to have to tell her to be quiet. By the time I got to my room, I was convinced we had to move for Sara. I'd still see Joseph at school and on weekends, I told myself. It wouldn't affect me too much, and if Sara started speaking and being her lively self again, it would be worth it. Still, sadness crept over me as I looked around my room, filled with memories of my life.

I slumped down on the rug, not knowing where to

start. My desk was cluttered and the bookshelves were bursting. I spotted my Meccano car in the corner under my desk and crouched low to pull it out. I had built it on the afternoon of my ninth birthday. Baba came up to help me fix the engine to the chassis, and then we'd taken it downstairs into the kitchen and watched it shoot across the smooth marble floor and crash into the patio doors, both of us grinning. Mama yelled at us for marking the doors and banned it from the kitchen.

Dust fell off the metal plates onto my sleeve. I raised it above my head to look at its wheels and smiled. Good memories. We'd made so many in this house. I swallowed and put the car in a box—I couldn't get rid of it, even if I didn't play with it anymore.

My helicopter drone sat on the windowsill. I picked it up and closed my eyes. Tete had bought it for me two years ago, but I hardly got to fly it. I wondered when I'd be able to go outside and fly it again without worrying about jets or missiles soaring over us. I couldn't even go fly it in Tishreen Park with Joseph because of the president's ban on drones. I pulled a T-shirt from my drawer, wrapped it around the helicopter, and put it in the box beside the car.

It wasn't going to be easy to pack away my whole life in this house. I turned to the shelves and started taking down my books and PlayStation games. They held fewer memories and would be quicker to pack, and I figured if I cleared my shelves before dinner, Mama would see how productive I'd been and hopefully be less irritated with me.

"Sami! Come down for dinner!" Tete called. I closed my favorite *Guinness World Records* book and glanced at my Swatch—it was already six o'clock. The day had flown by.

Tete had brought over some fried kibbeh and lentil soup. We ate it in silence around the kitchen island. Baba had only eaten half his portion when he left to continue packing. I ate as quickly as I could so I could call Joseph. He'd definitely be back home from school now.

About ten minutes later, I sat on my bed, waiting for Joseph's mama to get him on the phone. My stomach lurched seeing how empty my room now was. It felt different. As if it wasn't mine.

"Where were you today, man?" Joseph asked, out of breath.

"We're moving, so I had to help pack," I said, looking out my window. It was a clear black night and the moon seemed to float in the sky, dazzling in the darkness. In the distance, I could see bright orange flames. Something was burning.

"WHAT?!"

"Yeah, I know. I've been dying to tell you all day. It's for Sara. She's still not speaking. We need to be closer to this amazing psychologist that can help her."

"Oh, right. But you're not leaving school, are you?"

"Nah. I think they're just selling to get some extra money to get the best treatment for her. I think the next place will be smaller, though. At dinner, Baba told Tete he can't get any of his money out of his bank accounts in Lebanon and he's hardly kept any cash here. He sold the dining table and the big TV!"

"Oh, right. How'd he sell the house so quickly? It took ages for us to sell our last house."

"Tete said our neighbor in the smaller apartment upstairs wanted it for his son who's getting married next summer."

"Wow."

"Mama said it's fate. But I have no idea what the next place will be like. Mama and Baba are being so weird, I don't wanna ask. Anyway, what happened at school, man? Did George give you any more grief?"

"Nah. I stayed out of his way."

"Have they reset the date for the football trials?"

"Not heard anything yet. You're coming to school tomorrow, right?"

"I dunno. I'm just doing what they say at the moment. I don't want to make things worse, especially after last Thursday."

"Yeah, I know what you mean. That's why I didn't come round yesterday after you called. Baba said you guys needed family time."

"Joseph, give me the phone!" Joseph's elder brother yelled in the background.

"Uh . . . hang on, Sami. I'm talking!"

"I need it now! Give it here. You can talk to him tomorrow." His brother sounded much closer now.

"I'm gonna have to go . . . Message me, yeah?"

"I—I can't. I still don't have my iPad. Baba packed it."

"Oh maaan . . . what for?"

"Hang up NOW!" screamed his brother.

"I gotta go. I'll chat to you later." I heard a click, then the dial sound. Joseph had gone.

I should've been getting ready for school on Tuesday morning, but instead was lying in bed listening to the pigeons cooing outside when Mama came to my bedroom. She stood silently watching me, her hand on the door handle. I didn't say anything. After all, she'd been acting weird all week and completely dodged my questions yesterday.

After about a minute, she spoke. "Sami, Baba and I have decided to leave Syria today."

"Huh?" I couldn't have heard her right. She didn't just say Syria.

"Get up. I said, we're leaving Syria today."

"What?!" I shot up from my pillow. They'd gone mad. "That's impossible! We can't! What about my English test on Thursday? I need to beat George!" I searched her eyes for some kind of emotion, but they were still. "I thought we were just moving to another house! That's what you said!" I sprung out of bed and paced the floor. "What about Baba's work? What about

Sara? What about my school and Joseph and my other friends? We can't just move to another COUNTRY!" My arms flapped all over the place, while Mama stood calmly by my bedroom door.

"Baba has canceled all his surgical operations and I've left the school. We'll start again, somewhere safer."

"You told me we were moving house. I even helped you pack stuff up! I can't believe you lied to me!"

"Sami, show some respect! We didn't lie to you. It takes time to sort things out." Mama tucked her hair behind her ear. "A few days ago, we didn't know if it would be possible. We couldn't risk anyone finding out. We *are* moving to another house—it will be in a different country, that's all."

"I'm not coming. I'll stay with Joseph."

"Don't be silly. They'll also have to move. We can't live here any longer. It's not safe. You know that. The rebels have found a way in—and we're not waiting around to find out if the government will start attacking our neighborhoods to root them out, while they live amongst us. Or if they'll force your baba or even *you* to enlist and fight them. We can't wait till Damascus ends up like Aleppo."

I took a breath. How could Damascus end up like

Aleppo? I had to fight this. "But Sara needs help. That's why I thought we were moving, to be closer to a good psychologist?"

"She does, and we're going to get her the best. But I can't risk her seeing or even *hearing* another bombing." Tears swam into her eyes. "I'm going to clean the bathroom," she said, opening the door wider. "Get dressed and pack the last of your things into those." She pointed at some more boxes she'd left by the door.

"What's the point of cleaning the already clean bathroom when we're not going to use it anymore?" I grumbled.

"You can't leave a dirty house for someone else. We wouldn't like it, would we?"

Mama left, and I flung myself back on my bed. My mind spun. How could this be happening? We couldn't just leave! I didn't want to leave! They couldn't make me. I looked around my room and decided I wouldn't go. I'd get away so they couldn't take me. I'd go to Joseph's.

I ran down the stairs as quickly as I could in my flip-flops and slammed the front door behind me, rushing down the front steps. The Mazda wasn't in the yard; Baba must've gone out. I'd made it halfway across the gravel when I heard Mama shout after me.

"SAMI! COME BACK HERE, NOW!"

I continued to march toward the front gate, trying to ignore the loose stones pinching my feet, my face burning, my ears throbbing.

"Don't you think we've been through enough without you behaving like this?"

So she did blame me! I stopped and turned to her, standing a meter away from me on the drive. Her face was pink and her eyebrows furrowed.

"I can't believe you didn't tell me! I'm thirteen, not a kid like Sara! I'm not coming!"

"Yes, you are!" she screamed, closing the gap between us and pointing to our house. "Get back inside, NOW!"

"You should've told me so I could've gotten ready for it. *You've* had time to get used to the idea. How can you expect me to leave today? This is so unfair!"

"We couldn't tell you," she said, putting her hands on my shoulders. "We did it to protect you. No one knows. We couldn't risk anyone finding out."

A jet roared across the sky. I put my hands to my ears and Mama ducked under her elbow. We stayed still until it passed over our heads, leaving a trail of white smoke behind it. In the distance there were five or six lines of thick black smoke billowing into the sky.

"Let's get back inside. Please." Mama rubbed her upper arms. "Sara's inside. Don't do this to her."

My face tingled with guilt. Sara. I'd forgotten about poor Sara. I couldn't leave her after what she'd been through. After what I'd done to her. I had to be there for her. I had to make sure she talked again. I took a breath and slouched slowly back toward the house.

Inside, although the big bits of furniture remained, it was bare. No pictures, no vases; the side table in the hallway and the grandfather clock had gone too. Everything had been moved out the day before. Now I wasn't sure whether they sold it all or put some in storage.

Swallowing painfully, I went back upstairs as Mama rushed to check on Sara, who was crying somewhere in the back of the house. I must've scared her when I slammed the door. Everything made her flinch now.

"Mamaaaaaa!" I shouted from my bedroom. A few seconds later the door opened.

"What is it? Are you okay?" Mama rushed in, pulling off her yellow rubber gloves.

"Sorry, I just wanted to know where my suitcase was. I want to pack a few things to take with me."

She sat on my bed and dropped her hands on her lap. "Sit down," she said, fixing her eyes on mine. I flumped beside her.

"Son, we can't take anything. We'll be traveling with a lot of people and there won't be much space at times. You need to be free of things so that you can run if we need to get away."

My mouth went dry. "Run from what? Where are we going?"

"Nothing. Don't worry. We're going to England. Your baba says it's the best place for us. But there aren't any direct flights from here, so we'll go through Istanbul and some of Europe. We have quite a journey ahead."

"Oh, wow . . ." England was so far from here. It would take ages to get there.

She frowned. "Sami, this is not an adventure holiday—"

"I know that!" I interrupted. *Which adventure holiday required running from people?* I took a breath.

"We're not coming back. We're trying to do something we're not allowed to do. Syria isn't seen as safe anymore, so we can't travel easily to England as we normally would. You understand? You need to follow your baba and me—you must stick with us and listen to *every* instruction we give. And you must stay quiet—don't ask too many questions."

"Why not?" I asked, my knee bouncing up and down. This all seemed so dangerous.

"Shhh, everything will become clear. Just do as you're told like the good boy we've raised you to be and, God willing, we will all make it. I love you. Just remember that, okay?" She stroked my hand, then heaved up from my bed and left the room.

I looked at my half-full wardrobe, the dark-blue velvet floor-to-ceiling curtains, and bare shelves. All my books were gone but I hadn't packed away my football and English speech competition trophies because I liked looking at them. Three little gold trophies, lined up like soldiers. If I left them behind, no one would know what I'd achieved.

What would my new school be like? The thought sent shivers of dread into my stomach. I wouldn't have Joseph by my side. I'd be a loner. I couldn't imagine making new friends in a new country. And how would Joseph deal with George all alone? He needed me.

But I had to go. I had to listen to Mama and Baba and help them fix Sara. I wished Joseph was home so I could call him. I needed to talk to him.

I ran out of my room and rushed downstairs to Baba, who was stacking heavy boxes against the wall in the hallway. "Can I borrow your phone?"

"What for?" he asked, wiping his brow.

"I want to take photos of my trophies and my room to remember them, but I don't have my iPad. I could take some photos of the rest of the house too?"

"Okay, but be quick and don't answer the phone if it rings—I don't want anyone to suspect we're leaving today. We can't talk to anyone until we've got out," he said, tapping in his password to unlock the phone.

"Thanks." I grabbed the phone, ran back up to my room, and started taking photos of my bed, with all the extra pillows on it, my dark cherrywood desk, my trophies, my empty shelves, the view of the yard from my balcony, and then the whole room from the doorway.

I went next door to Sara's bare room and took photos of it, then Mama and Baba's room and the guest room.

It was a shame I hadn't thought of this when the

house was full of all our things. Although I couldn't quite remember what those missing things were at that moment.

I went down the curved staircase and took photos of the living room, kitchen, and Baba's office. Everything.

I stood in the dining room where the huge marble table once sat and rubbed my feet into the dents it had made in the plush rug. Inside, I felt emptier than the room looked.

I headed back upstairs and took photos of the yard from Mama's bedroom. I zoomed in on her favorite flowers—the white jasmine that bordered the grass—and then the small orchard where Baba picked fresh olives and apricots.

"Sami!" Baba shouted. "Bring my phone—you've had it long enough."

"I just need to take a few more."

"Bring it, NOW."

I traipsed back downstairs and handed it to him.

"All right, we've got a lot to do. Put all the leftover things from your room in a box and bring it down. Go shower and get dressed. Try to do a number two."

"Ugh! Baba! I don't need to go!"

"Trust me, Sami, it could be a while before you can do so again. Just go and do it!"

I turned back up the stairs, my shoulders hunched. Why didn't they tell me before? If I knew we were leaving Syria even just a few days ago, I could have packed my trophies or put them somewhere safe. I could have said goodbye to Joseph. We could have taken selfies together.

We'd been best friends since we were four years old. His dad and my baba had studied, then worked together, so our families had always been close. Joseph was like the brother I never had.

It's so unfair, I thought as I reached the upstairs landing. Adults thought they were in charge of everything. As if only *they* had feelings and things to finalize. They should've asked me how I felt about leaving.

My thoughts were interrupted by the sound of the doorbell.

"As-salaamu alaikum!" called Tete as she entered through the front door. She sounded tearful. I realized I had no idea if she was coming too.

I turned around and crept back down the stairs until I could see Tete and Baba, but they couldn't see me.

"Tarek, my boy, my beloved, God protect you. Allah protect you." Tete hugged Baba tight and sobbed into his chest. She looked at him and stretched up her crinkly hands to hold his face. "If I'd known this day would come, I would've asked God to take me with your father."

Baba pulled her hands away and took her by the shoulders.

"Shhh, Mama, don't say that. As soon as we are settled, we'll arrange for you to come and be with us. I'm not leaving you here. In the meantime, please lie low and don't go out too much. Uncle Habib will drop off your groceries each week—I've left him enough money. Just call him if you need anything."

"Tarek, I don't want to come. This is my land. Its soil is in my body, its water runs through my veins. I was born here and I will die here. I want my bones laid next to your father. Not in some Western country."

I leaned hard on the banister as it hit me she wasn't coming with us.

A cold hand rested on my shoulder. It was Mama, her eyes narrowed, her forehead furrowed with lines. "Get back to your room. You shouldn't be listening in on other people's conversations. How many times have I told you?" she whispered.

I rushed back up the stairs without saying a word, ashamed I'd been caught.

All I heard for the next half an hour was Tete and Mama wailing and crying.

I wanted to call Joseph and tell him what was happening, but he was still at school. I felt as if I was on a plunging rollercoaster all alone, with no way of getting off.

The tears wouldn't stop and my insides quivered. I didn't know exactly what was to come, but I knew it scared me more than anything ever had before.

Chapter 5

We left on Tuesday at two P.M., straight after lunch and the afternoon prayer. We all stood on the back steps in the warm sun waiting for Baba to check the house over. I looked through the wooden double doors and wondered when I'd see it again. The scent of jasmine enveloped me. The gentle breeze made the silver-green olive leaves shiver on the potted plant next to us. The water fountain had been turned off, the pool below it rippling in the mosaic basin.

I realized I didn't have a photo of the front of our big stone apartment building, but I knew I couldn't ask for Baba's phone again.

Sara snuggled into Mama's legs and clung on to her. I wasn't sure if Mama had told her what was happening, but she must have known it was something big.

Baba came out of the house with his backpack in his hand. "Get in the car. It's open," he said, shutting the back door and locking it.

Mama got into the back with me, because Sara wouldn't let go of her. "It's okay, Sara, I'm here," she said, trying to push Sara into the middle of the cream leather seat.

I watched Baba leave the door keys under the plant pot as I pulled my seatbelt over me.

"I've arranged to sell the car in Beirut," Baba said as he turned on the engine. My stomach churned. He was selling everything.

"The car?" I asked. "Can't we drive to England?"

He glanced at me quickly in the rearview mirror before turning back to the road. "The bombing's getting closer now. We have to leave while we still can. All my money's tied up in Lebanon. I had to sell whatever I could to get the money we need to get out of here quickly. I had no choice. Please don't question me, Sami."

My legs twitched. I didn't say anything. What could I say? I looked at Sara staring blankly as she sat between Mama and me, and then turned to the window.

● ● ●

We stopped behind a minibus trying to get in the long line of cars attempting to enter the gas station. A man sat on a bench reading a newspaper. The front page showed a photo of a street of shops that had all been destroyed. One looked like Mr. Elyas's shop, where Joseph and I used to go and buy chewing gum and *Football Plus* magazines whenever we'd go to visit his dad's friend in al-Zabadani—back when we used to actually leave Damascus for day trips.

Everything was a mess, and I suddenly understood why Baba wanted us to leave. The war had got to us too. I looked at everything with fresh eyes: the debris, the bombs, the sirens, and the noise I'd seen on the news for years was now coming for us.

It's strange how we'd gotten used to the war in Syria and thought it wouldn't affect us in our safe little bubble. But then, everyone in Syria thought the war wouldn't affect them—until it did.

We got used to the electricity blackouts several times a day. I couldn't remember the number of times everything switched off in the middle of a *FIFA* game, or during a YouTube video, or I had to use the flashlight app on my iPad to finish off homework. I'd almost cried when the power went out and I lost my physics assignment on the iMac, and I still remembered that time I had to go to school without a hot shower.

We were now used to the army checkpoint outside school each morning to search us—we just made sure that we left home earlier to get through it. We didn't protest, even when some of the soldiers shouted and pulled us into line. As much as we wanted to talk back, we didn't. We couldn't risk getting locked up. And as frustrating as it was, it sort of made me feel safer too. You never knew who was going to attack.

We understood when all the British and American teachers left after the car bombings started, even though the government tightened security and nothing happened inside Damascus after that.

We got used to hearing about friends of friends getting killed or injured by a stray missile launched from Ghouta. I now remembered when Joseph's big brother's coach and friends from judo class died.

We got used to Baba working through the day and night. Sometimes, after a bombing in the suburbs, we wouldn't see him for days and he'd just fall in a heap on the sofa when he got home. I didn't ask him about work. I didn't think he'd want to talk about what he'd seen.

We all knew someone who'd been affected by the war, but I had stupidly thought it would never *really* affect me.

After picking up some work papers from the hospital, Baba slowed the car down as we approached al-Hejaz train station in the city center. Cars were backed up all the way from the university and museum area. Maybe there was an event today. The road looked blurry as the sun seeped into it. Cars and buses beeped their horns, as if the sound would suddenly make us move faster. Baba took a left to bypass the traffic. We soon came to some wooden barricades painted to look like the Syrian flag. The road had been closed, and soldiers in camouflage stood around it, holding guns. I could feel my heart pumping as Baba rolled down his window and showed our IDs without being asked.

A soldier wearing a black cap leaned into the window and said in Arabic, "Turn the car around and take another route. This road will be closed all day."

Baba didn't question it, just nodded and put the car in reverse.

● ● ●

We passed the Mezze air base in the distance as we finally got on the Damascus-Beirut road. We passed a huge painted poster of the president on a billboard. *Thanks for nothing*, I thought.

Tete once said when we were watching the news that the problem in Syria was we were attacked from all sides. If it wasn't our government attacking us, it was the rebel groups, and if it wasn't them, it was a foreign government that had nothing to do with us. We weren't safe anywhere. And now not even in Damascus. But even though I knew that, I still wished we weren't leaving.

We traveled quickly on the straight, fast highway before getting stuck in traffic at the border with Lebanon, where Baba stopped to show our IDs and plane tickets, and get our papers signed. "We're just going to Beirut airport to fly to Istanbul," Baba told the armed guard scowling at us at the checkpoint as he handed him a few extra dollar notes.

"Take the slip road right and follow the signs. The road's closed. There's a diversion for road works," the guard said, shoving the money in his back pocket. We were ushered through and I breathed out.

"Argh, this will add over an hour to our journey." Baba bashed his hands on the steering wheel and passed his phone to Mama. "Text him and tell him we'll be late."

He must've meant the guy he was selling the car to. I closed my eyes. I wanted to go back to Joseph, or at least tell him I'd return soon, that I wouldn't leave him for long. But how was I going to do that now that we were on our way to the airport? I should've forced Mama or Baba to let me go see him, but they seemed so stressed, it didn't feel right to ask for anything. I had no choice but to listen to them. I don't know what kids in England were like, but in Syria we couldn't do anything without our parents' permission. It was an unwritten law.

After what felt like ages of driving through countryside toward the Bekaa Valley, the road took us past a large area covered in tents, all sizes and colors. It went on for miles. The white tents looked sturdy, but a lot of the blue and green ones were hovering at angles, as if they might collapse with a strong gust of wind. I saw children playing in the mud and dust, all barefoot and some topless. Their hair and skin were caked in dirt. I couldn't look away. This was a refugee camp, like I'd seen on the news.

Men sat on plastic white chairs or the dusty ground, their faces in their hands, looking fed up. Some stared at our car as we passed by, not moving a muscle.

A bony woman in a black-and-white flowery dress squatted as she bathed her baby in a red plastic tub, using an empty yogurt pot to pour water on him. A girl who looked about ten was hanging baby clothes on a wire attached between two tents.

We passed an old woman covered from head-to-toe in black, crouching in mud over a fire made out of bits of wood.

I remembered Joseph's dad praising Lebanon for all of the help it had given Syrian refugees. But this didn't look like much help. They looked thin, sick, and dirty. Life was definitely better back in Damascus compared to this.

I peeked at Mama, rolling her prayer beads between her index finger and thumb while Sara slept beside her, her head leaning on Mama's arm.

The newsreader on the radio was talking about America wanting to bomb Syria. I knew they had the power to destroy the whole country in one go. Everything could be gone in a day.

A weight tossed in the pit of my stomach as I looked out at the sky to check for jets—it was clear and blue.

I didn't want to leave, but I guessed I just had to trust Baba. His younger brother, Uncle Bashir, had left Aleppo a year ago when the fighting between the rebels and the government had gotten really bad. He fled with only the clothes on his back when rebels with black flags told him he had to fight with them or be killed. He was so scared they'd kill him that, instead of coming to Damascus, he fled to the Turkish border with no money. Nothing. He, Aunty Noor, and my cousin Mohammad were split up on the boats crossing the sea from Turkey. Uncle Bashir's boat had capsized, but he'd been wearing a life jacket and the coastguard rescued him. Aunty Noor and Mohammad had made it to shore, but it took Uncle Bashir a week to find them, all the while each thinking the other was dead. There was no way I'd get on a boat and risk that. It was too dangerous.

We worried they would end up in France in a jungle—not a real jungle with overgrown plants and wild beasts, but a camp, called that because some people said the refugees lived there like animals. As far as we knew, Uncle Bashir, Aunty Noor, and Mohammad were still at a border in Europe trying to get into England.

It'd all seemed so far away back then. I didn't think it would ever happen to us, living in our gated neighborhood. I thought the fighting would stop and we would never have to leave like Uncle Bashir did.

"How did the rebels get into Damascus?" I asked Mama. "And why did they hate the president so much they started fighting?"

Mama dropped her prayer beads on her lap and blinked hard. I don't think she was expecting this conversation.

"Um . . . well . . . lots of Syrians weren't happy with the government and officials misbehaving. They were also unhappy with joblessness and not being able to choose who governed us." She looked around as if someone might be listening and started whispering like she did at home when discussing the government with Baba.

"You were only eight when the war properly started. Almost five years ago, some school children were arrested and apparently tortured for writing anti-government graffiti on a wall. People peacefully protested, asking for the kids to be released and for more freedom in Syria." She glanced at Sara, who was still asleep. "But the government shot and killed protesters and then shot people again at the funeral of the victims that they'd killed the day before. People across Syria were so shocked and angry at this, they protested for more freedom and for President al-Assad to resign. Of course he refused, and this made people angrier." She looked at me and then ahead at Baba driving.

"Then what happened?" I asked.

"Well, basically, pro-government people and rebels started fighting in areas where ordinary people live. As the violence got worse, the rebels tried to get rid of the security forces, and everything spiraled out of control into a full-blown civil war across Syria. The rebels who are against the government must've been trying to get into Damascus for years and have finally succeeded. I'm not sure . . ." she stopped and took a breath, "not sure how they did it." She picked up her prayer beads and turned toward the window.

So a war began and millions of people became homeless all around the world because some kids wrote some bad stuff about the government. Insane.

I glanced at my Swatch. We'd left home more than four hours ago, but we were finally in Beirut, the capital of Lebanon. It usually took us two hours to get here. Beirut was modern and lively, like Damascus. Cafes, shops, and restaurants buzzed with people. Horns beeped nonstop in front of huge, shiny towers and older buildings. It looked like a mixture of many cities, each building in a different style of architecture to the next.

Everyone was well-dressed and tidy. I thought back to the refugees, living in dirt just a few miles away from this beautiful city.

We passed through the capital, and soon the planes flying overhead looked bigger. The Holiday Inn's glass building reminded me of our mall before it was bombed. It was unbelievable how something so strong-looking could be destroyed within minutes.

Baba turned around to look at us and smiled as we approached the airport, but I could tell from his tight face that it was forced. He reversed into a space in the outdoor parking area. As the car stopped, Sara woke up, her round eyes wide.

"You okay?" I whispered to Sara as Baba made a phone call. I lowered my head to hers, and she looked at me and gave me her small hand to hold. I took it in mine and squeezed it.

Something in me relaxed. This was progress. *Everything will be good again once she gets better*, I told myself.

A few minutes later a tall, well-built man wearing a beige baseball cap strode toward the car. He opened the door and sat in the front passenger seat.

"As-salaamu alaikum, brother. Let me take a look at it?"

"Walaikum as-salaam," said Baba, pulling the lever to open the hood. The man stepped out and examined the engine for a few minutes, then walked around the car, studying it closely.

The man nodded and handed Baba a brown envelope. Baba took out a small wad of cash and started counting it.

"It's hardly been used. I should be getting a lot more for it," said Baba.

"Yes, well, you need the money quickly so you can't be fussy. I can leave it here if you'd prefer?" The man smirked and started to walk away.

Baba's shoulders dropped. "No," he said and handed him the keys.

"Thanks." The man smiled, walking around the car toward the driver's seat.

Baba then gestured for us to get out as he opened the trunk and lifted out two luggage bags. When Mama opened one to put away her prayer beads, I saw our winter jackets, hats, and clothes in the bags.

Doors slammed shut and a car fired up somewhere in the distance. I turned round to see the man driving our car out of the parking space toward the exit.

That was it. We had nothing now. I closed my eyes for a long second. Everything had gone.

We walked through a passenger tunnel and entered the airport terminal. We didn't even need to check any bags in, since ours were small enough to carry on board.

Sara squeezed and pulled Mama's hand. "She needs the toilet," Mama said, looking around for bathroom signs.

Baba and I waited outside.

"Sami, you okay?" asked Baba, wrinkling his brows.

"Yeah." I didn't know what else to say. There didn't seem much point telling him I wasn't. I looked down at my Air Jordans and noticed the mud I hadn't wiped off from last week after Joseph had tried to tackle me and I'd fallen. I tried to scrape it off with the sole of my other shoe.

I looked out at the runway. One plane was preparing to take off and another one was coming in to land in the distance. The sea behind them was sparkling blue, the sun's rays reflecting off it like diamonds. The Tannoy blurted out some announcements in English and then French as people rushed around.

The door behind us opened and Mama and Sara emerged.

"Ready?" Baba knelt down to Sara and cuddled her. She put her small hands on his eyes. "Habibti, everything will be okay," he told her gently. "You're safe. Baba is here. Don't you worry."

A lump rose in my throat as I watched. *You can do this for her,* I told myself. *You've got to be strong.*

Chapter 6

Two hours later, we landed in Istanbul, Turkey. Already today we'd been in three countries and left two, which was pretty mind-blowing. I wondered what Joseph would think of that. He was probably doing his homework in his bedroom, completely unaware of what we'd just done. I wished I could call him and tell him where I was. As soon as I got to England, it'd be the first thing I'd do.

I'd never been to Turkey before. Istanbul airport was massive and bustling with people. It reminded me of the one in Dubai, with designer shops, a Burger King, and a Starbucks. My mouth watered seeing the juicy burgers on an advert. I wondered when we were going to eat, but I didn't ask. Baba had just sold his beloved Mazda—I guessed he probably couldn't afford to buy me an airport-priced burger right now.

As we headed outside, Baba got a handbook out of his backpack and flicked through it. He took out his phone and made a call, picking out words from the book in a different language I couldn't quite understand. *Turkish?* I guessed, wondering where we'd be going from here.

I wrapped my arms around myself as we walked toward the airport's taxi rank. It was colder here. The wind bit into me, and my teeth began to chatter. Yellow cabs beeped as they rushed passengers away from the airport. Baba told us to sit on the low posts lining the sidewalk.

Mama took clothes out of the hand luggage and dressed Sara. She slid the bag across to me. "Put on your winter clothes," she said.

I pulled on a turtleneck over the gray long-sleeved top I was already wearing, then a thick-knitted cream sweater and my black padded jacket. Mama took the bag back and rummaged in it to find woolen hats, scarves, and gloves for all of us. I put mine on and instantly felt better.

She put the empty bag inside the other one, then produced two small tubs of Pringles chips, handing a tub to Sara and one to me. I had ketchup flavor—my favorite. Sara hated the smell. I still offered her one, but she shook her head and pinched her cute nose before turning around to face Mama. I smiled, glad that she'd communicated with me twice in one day.

I looked at the night sky as I ate, my tummy gurgling as it digested the long-overdue food. The huge moon hung right above us, almost full and glowing white like a lamp in the sky.

Just as I'd eaten the last crumbs from my Pringles tub, a rusty old gray car pulled up, its exhaust spluttering. Baba got up to greet the scrawny man inside, then spun round to the car trunk and loaded our bag into it, keeping his black backpack with him. *From a Mazda 6 to a rusty old five-seater,* I thought. That said it all.

"Where are we going?" I asked Mama as I sank into the ancient dusty seat.

"I don't know, Sami. Shhh." She looked at me, blinked away tears, and then turned to look out of the window.

We left the airport, and I wondered if we'd drive past Istanbul's famous Blue Mosque. I'd seen photos of it looking grand in the night sky, lit up and outshining everything else around it. I wondered if we'd be going there to pray. Looking at Baba's face, it seemed unlikely; his forehead was creased with worry.

"Please drive safely," he said to the driver in Arabic as beads of sweat rolled down the side of his face. "We can't get caught."

My stomach lurched in ways I'd never felt before.

We'd been in the car for about half an hour when we drove into a small street in a village. The driver pulled up outside a terracotta house that stood alone at the end of the street, tucked behind some trees. There were no lights, and the darkness made my spine tingle.

"What is this?" Baba asked the driver. "You're supposed to take us to a hotel."

"Change of plan," said the driver, pushing his car door open. "It will be quicker to get you on the boats from here. Trust me."

I sat up. *Boats? Did he just say we'd be getting on a boat?*

Baba followed him and asked him something else I couldn't make out, but the driver walked ahead.

Sara clung to Mama as we shuffled out of the car. Outside, my fingers felt icy cold even with gloves on; I pushed my hands deeper into my jacket pockets.

We trudged through the muddy front yard and through a wooden side gate into the back. I could just make out some iron railings. Behind them was a stone staircase, which the driver led us down. Baba reached out for my hand and I took it, surprised to find Baba's was trembling. I held my hand out to Mama as she carried Sara, and we all moved down carefully, making sure we didn't miss a step and tumble. We walked through a creaky door and into a room full of people.

The driver went to speak to a tall, thin man in a language I guessed was Turkish and then nodded to Baba as he walked back out. He locked the door behind him, and the hairs on the back of my neck stood up. Why had he locked the door? What if there was a fire—how would we get out?

I looked around. Were we going to be staying in this one room with all of these people? There were no windows, just the locked door behind us, the only light from candles dotted about on the floor.

We followed Baba between groups of people, trying not to step on anyone. Some lay on their backs and stared at the ceiling, while some slept. A woman rocked a baby back and forth. The room smelled tangy—of mold and stinky armpits. I tried not to breathe in with my nose, but I could still taste it in the back of my throat.

Baba stopped in a corner where space had been made for us. "Go to sleep for a bit," he said.

Sleep? There was no way I'd be able to sleep. I leaned against the cold wall, looking around the room. There were so many people, I could hardly see the floor—there had to be at least thirty of us. The people became blurry. I couldn't see them clearly anymore.

Tears spilled down my chin and splashed onto my jeans. For the first time since we left Syria, what we were actually doing had really hit me. We had left home.

Home—where my bed was, my clothes, the fridge full of food, where the maid cleaned up our mess and kept everything in order. Now, I was in chaos. And I had no idea how long we'd be here. A day? A week? How were we supposed to get to England from this dump? What if the only way was on a boat? My mind raced with questions, even though I didn't want to think anymore.

I looked at Baba. He had his eyes shut. Sara lay on Mama's chest, her eyes closed tight as if to block out everyone and everything. Mama's fingers glided slowly over one prayer bead, then the next.

I wanted to shout and scream and ask why we were here. But I knew I couldn't. We were all in the same situation. I had to stay quiet—Mama said so. *You can do this, Sami,* I told myself. *It'll all be okay once* you get *to England.*

I thought back to what Baba said to the driver. What if we were caught and then taken back to Syria? What would we go back to? Baba had sold the house, the car, and all of our stuff. We had nothing. We'd probably end up in a refugee camp like the one in Lebanon.

I squeezed my eyes shut and prayed we wouldn't. I prayed as hard as I'd ever prayed in my life.

We spent the whole of the next day sitting quietly, huddled in a corner of the room, watching people leaving and being dropped off. I was so bored, but I just tried to pretend I was sleeping.

When the same driver that had brought us here appeared at the door and called for Baba, we quickly scrambled up, glad that we were leaving. He handed Baba a SIM card before starting the engine of his rusty old car. Baba thanked him, fumbling with his mobile to take out his Syrian SIM.

We passed field after field in silence before we got to the next building. It was an old, white four-story villa in the middle of nowhere, with countless windows stacked one above the other. All the windows on the bottom two levels had metal shutters covering them.

The driver stopped in front of an old flaking garage door and jumped out to lift it open. Insects murmured all around. I fiddled with Jiddo's ring as cold air rushed in, bringing the scent of rotting fruit from the trees surrounding us.

The driver got back in the car and parked inside. My heart thumped as we followed him out into the empty, freezing garage and through an internal door leading into a musty corridor. I stared at a spider building its web in a corner, then noticed Mama's face was paler than the peeling white walls. *Please let this be a better place than the last one,* I thought.

We went down some stone steps to a painted black door, where the driver opened a bolt, turned a key, and let us into a room. I blinked hard as the foul smell of drains hit me and pulled my arm over my nose. The driver closed the door behind us and slid the bolt across. He was locking us in *again*.

The room was candlelit, like the other place, and cold—I couldn't see any heating. But it had mattresses to sleep on. I wrapped my jacket tighter as I looked around. There must have been at least twenty people scattered about, including a few young children and some teenagers, who looked as fed up as I felt.

I guessed it was an apartment of some kind— maybe it used to be for the staff of the villa. On the wall to the left of the front door was a stainless-steel sink with a cupboard underneath. A doorframe with no door led to a smaller room on the right. A few meters from the kitchen sink was a small bathroom. There was no flooring in either room, just gray concrete. The walls hadn't been painted, just plastered a long time ago, and were covered in cracks. There was no furniture. It was an apartment full of only mattresses and people.

An old man with a white moustache and beard pushed himself off his mattress and went to the kitchen sink. There was a small boarded-up window above it. He picked up a smudgy glass, filled it with tap water, then came over to Baba and offered it to him with a smile.

Sara flinched and hid her face in Mama's headscarf, and I looked around the room for cleaner glasses. They were all filthy. There didn't seem to be anything to wash them with either. I felt sick thinking about it. And, there was no fridge to keep drinks in—there wasn't even a place to plug one in.

Baba offered me the glass of water but I shook my head, even though I was thirsty. I headed toward the bathroom, but as I neared the door, I stepped back. It stank. There was no toilet paper, no soap. It wasn't tiled, and there was dirt on the concrete floor.

But I had no choice. I had to go in. As I pulled down my jeans, I wanted to cry. I swallowed hard and made myself stop, reminding myself that the people we saw didn't even have toilets in their camps, and they slept in tents in the cold. At least we had walls and a roof.

Baba took Mama and Sara to the smaller room, which looked as if it was for the women, then led me to a spare mattress in the main room. "Just try to sleep," he said gently. I sat on a spongy mattress opposite the entrance and watched Baba walk away to his, which was pushed up against the wall adjoining the women's room.

I overheard a blue-eyed boy with dark blond hair on the mattress next to mine telling a man in a low voice that his house had been bombed. He was probably a year or two older than me.

"I lost my baba, sister, grandma, and uncle in one go," he said with a slight lisp. "My mama's legs were injured when parts of the house fell on her—she can't walk now. She wants me to get to England to earn some money. I'm just waiting to get a boat across into Europe. What about you?" he asked the man beside him.

My shoulders juddered thinking about what he'd lost, and my brain struggled to process what I'd heard. I couldn't imagine leaving my parents and going off alone across the world to get a job. I stayed quiet and didn't say a word. They didn't need to know what we'd left behind or who my baba was and what he did. The people here looked much poorer than us . . . not that we had much left now.

I lay down on my pillow and pulled the thin, holey blanket over me. I decided Mama was right—until we got to England and were safe, I would stay quiet and just listen. That would be the way I'd get through this.

Chapter 7

I lay on my mattress, hands under my head, staring at the cracked ceiling, wishing I had my iPad. Clammy fingers stroked my cheeks. I jumped away from them, hitting my head on the wall behind me. A woman in a pink headscarf stood over me, her eyes glazed. She mumbled something I couldn't understand.

I sat up, rubbing the back of my sore head and pulling my knees toward my chest. A girl, around nine years old with scruffy shoulder-length hair, ran up behind the lady and put her hand on her arm.

"Please. Let her touch you. You remind her of my brother," she said to me as she itched the side of her head.

My eyes widened but I couldn't speak. I didn't know what to say.

"I've tried to explain that you aren't my brother. But he looked just like you. He had light brown hair and eyes too."

The blue-eyed boy on the mattress next to mine sat up and muttered something quickly to the woman and girl.

The girl and her mother turned around and walked away.

"Don't worry, she's okay," the boy said, clearing his throat. "She's just confused." He shuffled across his mattress and sat on the edge nearer to mine. "They left Syria after their family was killed in an air strike. Then on the way to Europe her son drowned when their boat capsized."

I gulped at the mention of boats and drowning. I'd fallen out of one on vacation when I was seven years old and Baba had to pull me out of the water. I shuddered at the memory. I couldn't get on one again.

"Oh, right. Sorry to hear that," I said, after a couple of seconds of silence. I didn't know how to respond to his friendliness. I wasn't expecting it.

"The problem is, they keep overloading the boats," he said, shaking his head like an adult.

"But how come they're here and not in Europe?"

"I think they were taken back by the Turkish coast guard. They're trying to get across again to get to the woman's uncle in England."

I couldn't imagine trying to do the journey again after what they'd been through. *I just wouldn't,* I thought.

"How long have you been here?" I asked the boy, trying to change the subject. It was hard to stay quiet, when he was being so friendly.

"I got here the day before you, but I'm hoping I won't be here long."

"Me too. I don't even know why we're stuck here."

The boy raised his eyebrows. "It's like a halfway place. You know, where smugglers bring people till they get their fake papers and the boats are ready to take us across. I'm Aadam, by the way."

I had no idea what fake papers meant and didn't want to show myself up anymore by asking, so I just said, "I'm Sami," and watched him push his dark blond hair back with his palms. He couldn't have been more than sixteen. His eyes were the color of the sky. He could easily pass as an English boy, if he didn't speak in his southern Syrian dialect.

Aadam smiled, then moved to the other side of his

mattress as he saw Baba walking over. Baba nodded at him and sat down next to me, his weight making us sink closer to the floor.

I looked down at our knees and noticed the grime under Baba's nails. I'd never seen them so dirty.

"I heard what happened to that girl and her mama, but it doesn't happen often," he said, putting his arms over his knees. "Sami, don't worry. We're taking one of the *best* boats available to get to Greece. I've paid extra money for it. That's why we're having to stay in this place."

I shook my head as cold fear flooded my entire body. "I don't care—there's got to be another way. We can't get on a boat, Baba. What if it capsizes? It's too dangerous."

Baba knew I'd avoided boats since I'd fallen in the sea, except for a pedal boat that Joseph had persuaded me into when we were at a theme park, and even then, I'd counted the seconds till we got off. He wouldn't make me take a boat *all* the way across to Greece. He'd understand.

It was early morning the next day when the door handle rattled. Every single person inside jolted up in fear, hoping it wasn't the police or the Turkish government. We all relaxed again when one of the drivers entered, the men's faces falling when they realized he'd come to give bread to one of the families he'd brought to the apartment. My stomach groaned at the sight of the loaf, as if it was calling the bread over.

The dad from the family got up and walked over to the driver at the door. They had a brief conversation, the dad took the bread, and then he handed the driver some money.

"I don't have any more!" the father started shouting. "How much are you going to take? You told me last week it was the last time you'd be asking!"

Everyone in the room looked up. The driver grabbed the man by the throat and slammed him against the wall. I gasped and froze on my mattress as he squeezed tighter. The whole room was silent, staring in fear.

Finally, the driver pulled himself away and turned to look at us.

I sat up, worried he might attack us too. But he

walked out of the apartment, banging the door shut and locking it. The man the driver had threatened glared at the door.

"I've paid thousands and thousands for this damn boat trip and now he's saying he needs more money for the life jackets. I've got nothing left!" he shouted to all of us. Tears streamed down his stubbly face as his body scraped down the wall and fell in a heap on the floor.

I dug my nails into my mattress, trying to force back tears as I watched him. It was only then that I realized that the drivers weren't really just drivers, but criminals trying to make money out of desperate people.

The man crumpled on the floor was just as scared as I was. No matter how the men acted, I guessed that deep down everyone in the room felt the same. I had to show strength too, it didn't matter how I felt. I had to make sure we got to England. I had to do it for Sara. I had to remember that. Then everything would be okay.

The following morning the atmosphere in the apartment was different, despite what we'd seen the day before. All the men and boys huddled together to talk. I sat on the cold, gray concrete opposite Baba, fidgeting with Jiddo's ring, thinking about the plush rugs we'd had back at home. I looked up when I heard a familiar voice.

Aadam, the blue-eyed boy, was telling his story. "I left home five months ago. Mama sent me out to earn money after Baba died. I walked over the Syrian border into Lebanon, and a man there attacked me. He said if I didn't give him all my money he'd kill me." I gulped and looked around the room at the others sitting on mattresses in a circle, all listening as Aadam spoke. "I gave it all to him and tried to run away, but he and his friends recaptured me and forced me to beg for them. If I didn't, they beat me all over."

Goosebumps prickled over my arms as I listened.

"How did you escape from them?" asked one of the men.

"One night, they were all drinking and gambling in a room, making so much noise, I knew it was my chance to get out. I climbed out of the bedroom window, onto a fire escape and down to the courtyard," he said, brushing his nose on his sleeve. "I knocked on the window of the basement and begged the man below to let me in through his apartment and out of his front door."

"So how did you get here?" asked Baba, rubbing his hands together for warmth as he listened.

"I needed money to get across to Turkey, so I begged for a while and then worked in Beirut as a cleaner for about a month. And because they knew I was from Syria, they gave me the worst job . . . cleaning the toilets."

"You can do this one if you like!" one of the men said, laughing. Baba and a few of the others flashed him dirty looks and he stopped. Aadam's cheeks turned flamingo pink, but he ignored the man and continued.

"They were filthy—worse than this one—and I could hear them laughing as they heard me retching. Sometimes I wondered if they made them dirtier on purpose. Anyway, when I had enough money, I jumped on the back of a truck and left."

I turned away, feeling uneasy. *What if I become like him? What if my life becomes like his?*

I fiddled with my shoelaces as a deeper, rougher

voice began to speak in broken English. I looked up. It was a balding man with a goatee.

"I from Afghanistan. Germany take refugees—so I'm go there with wife and daughter." He pointed at his daughter, talking to a woman outside the bathroom. She was dainty and pretty, with long, brown hair that fell down to her elbows. Her nose was slender and her lips were a deep pink against her tanned face.

I blinked. She looked so much like Leila. Beautiful, intelligent Leila. I wondered what she was doing now. Was she at school with Joseph and the others? Was the school even standing? If I'd known I was leaving, I'd have taken a selfie with her and Joseph and the others. I'd never get to tell her that I liked her. I didn't even know if I'd ever see anyone from school again.

I tried to picture Leila at her ice-skating party last year, when Joseph and I had taken my iPad screensaver photo. That was a good day.

Focus on the good days, Sami, I told myself. *You'll be out of here and in England soon.*

Chapter 8

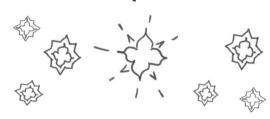

*A*adam *came and sat* next to me that evening. I shifted across my mattress to give him space.

"So, what's your story? You didn't say anything today." He put his arms over his knees and stared at me.

I didn't know what to tell him. Compared to most of these people, we didn't have a story. And I would never have dared to tell it in front of the whole group, anyway.

I decided I'd tell Aadam about the bomb that had gone off in the mall and how it scared my parents enough to leave the country. I talked about the distant airstrikes, the sirens and explosions.

"I used to feel sick when I'd hear planes fly over us," said Aadam, looking at the floor. "You just don't know where they're going to hit. You could be dead in an instant. I remember being out in the market one day and hearing a jet above us. I ducked and then *thwooomp*—the explosion rang through my ears. Clouds of dust rose into the air and spread all over the city, making it difficult to breathe." He stopped and took a deep breath. "I didn't realize at the time that it was my house it hit."

"Sheesh, Aadam . . . that's awful."

There was a long silence. I didn't know how to fill it.

He looked down at the floor for a few seconds then raised his head to look at me, his eyes brighter.

"What's Damascus like? I've always wanted to go there."

I relaxed, relieved he'd changed the subject. "Oh man, it's one of the best places." I looked at him, suddenly homesick. "On Saturdays, I'd meet up with my friend Joseph and go ice-skating at the mall and have pizza, then later I'd meet Mama and Baba for ice cream before going off to the cinema with Joseph and our other friends. I didn't realize how good life was until it all went wrong."

I sighed deeply, thinking about how much we

hadn't done recently. I didn't ever imagine I'd end up being locked up in an apartment in Turkey with total strangers. I glanced at my watch. Joseph would be having his dinner right now.

"I've never been to a mall with an ice rink or cinema. I didn't even know there were ice rinks in Syria. It sounds amazing!" said Aadam.

I felt bad then. I'd been so lucky. "What about football?" I asked. Everyone played football, didn't they? "Do you play?"

Aadam's eyes lit up. "Yeah, of course! Who do you support?"

"Manchester United and Real Madrid obviously! They're the best."

"Me too! *Glory, glory Man United*," he sang, grinning.

"Glory, glory Man United!" I chanted, forgetting where I was. He leaned in toward me and laughed. For the first time in over a week, I was smiling again.

"We really need to up our game though. We're slipping in the table. I'm worried," said Aadam, frowning.

It was the exact same expression Joseph would've made while saying that. I suddenly felt lighter and more relaxed, as if I'd known Aadam for ages. "I know! It's been a while since we were on top—I'm worried too," I said. "They were fifth last week. God knows where they'll be at the end of the season . . ." I drifted off as I realized I had no way of finding out.

"We'll know soon enough," he said with a nod. It was like he'd read my troubled mind. *Joseph and I would hang out with him,* I decided.

Before I could reply, I spotted Baba bringing Sara into the room. He was struggling to hold her as she kicked him and cried. I jumped up, feeling a pang of guilt run through me. "Hang on," I said to Aadam.

"What's wrong?" I asked Baba, walking up to him.

"She's very restless today," said Baba, putting Sara on the floor. "Your mama needed a break. She hasn't slept at all."

"Here, let me take her." I put out my hand to her to see if she'd come, but Sara kept clinging to Baba's leg. "Sara, come on. I'll tell you a story! Come." I crouched on the floor to look her in the eyes and waited.

She peeked around from behind Baba and looked at me. So I covered my face with my hands and then uncovered it. She smiled, so I did it again, which made her giggle a little. I put out my hand again, and she took it. I got up and led her back to my mattress, where Aadam still sat.

"Marhaba, little one," he said, smiling.

Sara recoiled and hid behind me. Aadam and I exchanged a look. "Shhh, it's okay. This is Aadam." I picked her up and sat down with her on my lap. She put her head into my chest, her golden-brown hair covering her face.

"Here. Look: shall we draw?" Aadam held a piece of chipped plaster between his fingers. I raised my eyebrows.

He grinned, pointing to a hole in the wall behind his mattress where bits of plaster had crumbled away, leaving the bricks and mortar exposed. "I got it from here." He'd written his name in Arabic on the wall next to it and drawn a car. It looked like a Ferrari—a pretty good drawing. I took the piece of plaster from him and put it in Sara's hand, then lifted her off my lap and on to my mattress. "Pass me another," I said.

Aadam handed another chunk to me and I got on my knees and faced the wall. Sara watched through the gaps in her hair.

"What shall I draw, Sara?" I asked her.

"My little sister used to have a doll," said Aadam,

moving to his mattress beside mine, his voice slightly trembling. "Like this . . ." He took his piece of plaster and started drawing a floppy rag doll with wiry hair on the wall.

I'd forgotten he had a little sister. He was an older brother too. I thought about how I'd feel if Sara and Mama hadn't made it out of the mall alive, and a thick lump formed in my throat.

"Ah, good idea," I said, still on my knees. "I'll draw Dolly Coco. Remember her, Sara?"

Sara crawled closer to me to watch, her eyes lighting up. I outlined the shape of a doll holding a baby bottle. It wasn't the best drawing I'd done, but I couldn't expect much from a chunk of plaster, and it made me feel good doing something other than lying on my back. I pointed to the piece of plaster in Sara's hand and asked, "You want to color her in?"

She scratched and scribbled around the body. "Not too hard, Sara. It'll come away like over there." I pointed to Aadam's side of the wall. She scribbled a little more, beaming, and then handed me the plaster piece back, smaller than before, the crumbs all over my mattress.

"All done, Thumbelina?" I asked her. She smiled

and nodded. I cuddled her tight, my chin on her head and whispered, "I'm sorry, Sara. I'm so sorry."

We'd just finished eating some stale bread for lunch when we heard a murmur of voices and footsteps overhead. No one had come to the apartment for a few days.

The tall driver and our scrawny one appeared in the doorway, and Baba rushed over to speak to them. I watched them for a few minutes, trying to make out their conversation, which I thought was about boats. Were we leaving? I had to speak to Baba right away.

I leaped up, walked over to Baba, and pulled on his sleeve. "Baba, I need to talk to you."

Baba's eyebrows pulled together. "What is it, Sami? Can't it wait? I'm in the middle of something."

"No." I dragged his arm and pulled him away from our driver.

"Can Aadam come with us please? He's on his own—he has no family."

Baba put his mouth to my ear, so only I could hear him. "No, Sami, he can't. I'd love to help him, but we don't have enough money to take him too, plus it could compromise our safety if we have an extra person to look after. Anyway, we don't know him. Not what he's really like." He tried to turn back to the driver, but I pulled his arm again.

"Baba, how can you *say* that?!" I screeched in a whisper. "He's a kid, his baba is dead, his mama's legs have been bombed to bits, and he's got to get to England to send money back to her. He's *fifteen*. Just two years older than me!"

"Sami, we can't talk about this right now." He tugged his arm away and returned to the driver.

I glared at his back. This wasn't like my baba. He was always trying to help people. So why wasn't he helping Aadam? Had his heart turned to stone somewhere along the journey?

I didn't talk to him for the rest of the day. When he came to offer me fresh bread later that evening, I said I wasn't hungry. I only took some from Mama when she offered me some of hers later.

"What's wrong, Sami?" Aadam asked. "Why are you not talking to your baba?"

"I can't tell you."

"Okay." He looked down and pulled on his sock.

"Look, I want to tell you, but I can't. It's better if I don't. Trust me."

"It's fine, relax. It's not my business anyway."

He was such a good guy and that made me feel even worse. *He shouldn't be going to Europe on his own.*

"He got this far, didn't he?" Mama said softly later on when I took Sara back to her. Now a Hello Kitty was scribbled next to Dolly Coco. Mama stroked my hair and leaned in close to whisper into my ear. "Once we get to England, we can help him. But we need to get there first. We'll be no use to him if we get caught. He can move around quicker without four extra people to worry about."

I closed my eyes and focused on the rhythm of Mama's warm, comforting hands stroking my hair. I guessed she was right, but I didn't want to accept it. How could Aadam's mother have sent him away to another country? How could she be so heartless? Didn't she care about him?

It was late at night a few days later when I saw Aadam at the door asking an old bearded driver to use his phone. The driver shook his head, laughed, and turned back to the man he'd been speaking to.

"Who did you want to call?" I asked him when he got back to his mattress.

"My mama. I need to let her know I'm okay and that it won't be long till I can get some money to her."

"What did the driver say?"

"He said I can't make calls from here, in case they pick up signals. Then he said he'd let me make a call if I give him fifty Turkish lira, but I can't afford to give him any of my boat money. If I spend any more, I'll end up on one of those flimsy dinghies without a captain. I don't have enough for a good boat as it is. My driver said I need at least another thousand dollars to get on a newer one. I need to save for that."

"Oh, Aadam . . . " I wondered how long it'd been since he'd spoken to his mama.

"I'll call once we get to Europe. I've heard there's lots of help for refugees there."

I wish I had money that I could just hand to him, I thought. Baba said he'd gotten us one of the best boats to get to Greece; it wasn't fair that Aadam should get on an old faulty one. It was too dangerous. I turned to Baba who was asleep against the wall, his backpack next to him and his arm through one handle, to make sure no one would steal it. He slept like that every night.

I knew he kept his money in the main compartment, but I couldn't get at it with him holding it like that. I'd have to wait. Baba wouldn't miss fifty lira and Aadam really needed it.

I lay down to sleep instead and my thoughts turned to Leila. I wondered if she was still in Damascus. I imagined her playing with her hair, flicking it over her shoulder the way she always did in class.

I thought about school, and Joseph, and who he was hanging out with now. *Had the bombing affected his family too? Was he okay? Was he ignoring George?* I hoped he was. A pang of guilt twanged in my chest. I left him after I said I wouldn't, ever. I should've told him I was leaving. Sara would get better when we got to England. Then we could return home and I'd go back to school.

Was everyone still going to school?

Were they even alive?

Chapter 9

I woke up realizing I didn't need the money from Baba. I just needed his phone. I flung off my blanket and went to sit next to him. "Baba, do you have your phone?"

"Why do you want to know?" he asked, picking at some peeling skin near his grimy nails.

"I just wanted to look at the photos I took at home. I miss it."

Baba fixed his eyes on mine, then put his arm around me. "Oh, Sami, I know it's been hard for you having to leave everything you know all of a sudden." He squeezed my shoulder. "I'm sorry you weren't given much notice, but we didn't want anyone to know we were leaving. We did it to keep you safe."

Guilt flooded through me. He was being so nice and had no idea what I was planning.

He sighed. "I wasn't going to switch on my phone till we got to England, but you can have a quick look, okay? I just don't want the battery to be used up."

"Thanks, Baba."

"And make sure no one else sees it. The people seem nice here, but they're all desperate. I don't want it to get stolen."

He put his backpack on his lap, unzipped the front compartment and took out his phone. He hunched against the wall, so no one could see him switch it on, entered his password, and handed it to me.

I put it in my jacket pocket quickly. "Can I show Aadam some of the photos?"

"No. You heard what I said."

"Ohh, come on, Baba! He won't do anything."

"Not the ones you took of the house. We don't want anyone to know how we lived. You can show him some photos of days out if you want. But don't be too long."

"Okay." I jumped up and rushed toward where Aadam sat under the tiny, boarded-up window. There was a slight draft coming in and it rustled the top of his hair.

"Here," I whispered, handing him the phone while looking around to make sure no one saw. "Turn around toward me. I'm going to crouch in front of you to cover you while you call your mama. You've got to be quick though, because Baba doesn't know I'm doing this and he can't find out."

"Sami, don't do this for me. You'll get in trouble."

"Listen, just do it. Quickly! Where else are we going to find that fifty lira?" I turned my head to see what Baba was doing. He stood talking to the Iraqi man. "Come on!"

Aadam tapped the number on to the keypad. "Thanks for this, Sami. You're a true friend."

I smiled as he raised the phone to his ear, covering it with his hand. There was a long silence and then, "Hello? Mama?" whispered Aadam, his eyes filling with tears. "Mama?"

I could hear frantic talking down the line.

"I'm okay, Mama, don't worry. I'm safe. I've met good people who are taking care of me . . . It's windy and the water is too choppy for us to cross right now, but I'll be in Europe in a week, God willing, and I'll call you from there. Don't cry, please—I'm okay." He stopped and listened to her speak.

I turned around to check on Baba and smiled at him as he glanced my way and beckoned me to him.

"Aadam, you have to hang up. I'm sorry," I whispered.

"Mama, I have to go. I'm borrowing a phone. I'll call you soon. Pray for me." He tapped the red button and passed the phone back to me. He looked down, clearly trying to fight his tears. A teardrop rolled down his cheek onto the concrete floor. I quickly went into the dial list to delete the outgoing call.

Just as I pressed Delete, I saw Baba's bare feet in the corner of my eye. "Ah, Baba, thanks." I stood up, trying not to shake, and carefully slipped the phone into his hand.

"Did you see the photos, Aadam?" asked Baba. "You look upset . . . Sami, that wasn't the best idea, was it?"

"You're right, Baba. I shouldn't have," I said, my heart pounding. My voice sounded high. Would he notice?

"Okay." He switched the phone off and slipped it into his shirt pocket. He patted me on my arm and then left us to go back to his mattress.

"Oh, man! That was close!" I said, my insides relaxing slightly.

"Yeah," said Aadam, looking down, his cheeks still moist, his brows wrinkled.

I didn't try to talk to him. He looked too upset. Instead, I rested my head back on the wall, running my finger over Jiddo's ring.

I've got to help him, I thought. *I've got to help him get on a better boat.*

I scanned the room, thinking hard. I spotted the stubbly-bearded guy who'd spoken fluent English to the group. He was talking to his driver at the door. I remembered the story he'd told everyone about having to leave a Damascus suburb halfway through his English degree because his street was bombed. He'd worked all the hours he could in Turkey to save money to buy fake papers. He'd saved eleven thousand dollars, which was just enough to get out safely, but then his dad needed emergency surgery back home. He'd sent half to his dad, but he still had enough to pay for a good boat.

I watched the Damascus guy talking and wondered if I could try to reason with Baba again. If Aadam was older, he'd be fine. He could get real work, like this man had. But Aadam hadn't even finished school yet. He was only a kid, like me. If Baba wasn't willing to take Aadam with us, I had to get him the money for a good boat myself. I had to make sure Aadam would be safe. This was an emergency situation—I couldn't let him get on a flimsy old dinghy. He said he only needed a thousand more dollars for a newer boat. And if the Damascus guy could spare almost six thousand to help his dad and still be okay to make it to Europe safely, surely Baba could spare one thousand?

I looked across the room at Baba's backpack. *Baba has enough money. He won't notice if I take just a little bit.*

Chapter 10

*B*aba *had kept hold* of his backpack all day, and I hadn't been able to think of a reason to ask him if I could have it. He put it on his back when he went to the toilet, and even when he washed in the sink in our room. By the evening, I'd decided getting into it while he was asleep was my best chance.

It wasn't hard to stay awake, since it never really went quiet with twenty of us inside what was originally a one-bedroom apartment. I found it hard to fall asleep with just a thin blanket and all the noise.

Eventually the last candle was blown out—the only light came from the moon slithering through the gaps around the boarded-up window, revealing the silhouettes of the men sleeping deeply.

I could hear Sara crying and moaning, having one

of her nightmares in the other room. All was quiet for a few minutes—I guessed Sara had fallen asleep—but then she cried out again. I heard Mama hushing her, then someone else screaming, and all around me, the men tossed and turned and grunted in their sleep. It wasn't only Sara battling nightmares. No one was ever still for long. Even Aadam, stretched out by my feet, groaned and twitched as he dozed. I put my hand on him to reassure him, and he calmed down again.

I don't know if I would *ever* sleep if I'd seen what they had.

I got up slowly as Aadam's body relaxed again and crept around the mattresses toward Baba's. With bare feet, I could walk around the hard concrete floor without making a noise.

I decided that if Baba woke, I'd just say I wanted to talk to him because I couldn't sleep.

I waited until Baba's breathing was really slow. He didn't snore, but his breathing was loud. Sara was quiet at last. I squatted down low next to his arms and saw he had the backpack handle over his shoulder. He'd turned in his sleep to face the wall, so it was behind him. I could get to the main compartment without disturbing him at all. If I was careful. Very careful.

As I moved my hand slowly forward, I held my breath. I tried to unzip the main compartment, millimeter by millimeter. But the zip was stiff and I had to make small jolts to move it along. I stopped and leaned over to see if Baba's eyes were still closed. They were. His breathing was still steady, so I got on my knees to apply more force.

Now I'd created a gap wide enough for my arm to get in. I stopped and looked around the room. My heart was beating so fast I thought it might thump out of my mouth. My fingers found some loose papers and then, stretching further down, a wad of notes tucked right at the bottom. I clutched them and began to draw my arm out slowly.

Baba shot up and gripped my hand, staring at me, his face centimeters from mine. He wasn't blinking. I could see the whites of his eyes. My heart stopped, my stomach in knots. I wanted to throw up.

Baba got on his knees, still clutching my hand.

"What the hell do you think you're doing?!" he growled. Around us some men sat up and one switched on his flashlight. "You bloody thief! I can't believe you'd do this!" He looked me up and down and then added, "I'm ashamed to call you my son."

The words cut into me as if I'd been stabbed through my heart, the pain sharp. The notes fell out of my hand. I pulled my arm away and turned to my mattress, but he got up and came after me.

"Come back here NOW!"

I exploded.

"I wasn't stealing it! I wanted to help Aadam. I wish I wasn't your son! You only think about yourself. I HATE YOU!"

And that's when he slapped me. Right across my face—in front of all the men in the room.

"You've overstepped the line," said Baba through gritted teeth, raising his clenched fists. He lowered them slowly and shook his head as he walked away, back to his side of the room.

My left cheek burned from his slap, but all of me burned with shame. The silence was terrible as everyone looked my way. I couldn't believe my father had hit me, made me look like nothing. He'd made everyone wake up and look at us.

I wanted to run after him, push him to the ground, and whack him back, but Aadam grabbed my wrist and yanked my arm down to the floor. I didn't resist.

"Don't, akhi. You're lucky you still have a father . . .

and one who cares enough to slap you," he whispered.

I looked down at my bare feet. My legs shivered from sitting on the freezing floor. I couldn't look at Aadam or at the men gawping at me.

"Why'd you do it?" he asked, loosening his grip on my arm.

I shuffled backward to my mattress. "I just wanted to help you," I said, sinking into it.

"I'm fine! Look at me—I got this far without you, didn't I?" He went over to his mattress and lay down.

Is he mad at me for wanting to help him? I wanted to scream. I'd tried to steal from *my* baba for *him*, so he wouldn't have to get on a sinking dinghy. Didn't he get why I did it?

If only I could get out of this apartment and run away. But I couldn't. I was stuck. Locked in.

"Just go and say sorry, akhi," said Aadam the next evening, nodding at Baba, who was sitting on his mattress.

"I can't," I said, hanging my head. It felt too hard to make the first move. I'd waited all day for Baba to come to me and say sorry for slapping me in front of everyone. How could he be ashamed of me for trying to help someone?

I don't hate him, I thought. *I hope he knows that deep down.* I shouldn't have said it, but I was upset last night. I was mortified that he'd caught me. *Baba called me a thief. Could I ever make this better?*

"I don't know why I was stupid enough to think he wouldn't notice," I said, still looking down. My stomach grumbled loudly, and I put my arms over it to muffle the sounds. I looked across the room and saw Baba was talking with a Sudanese man. He swiped his hand across his forehead. Baba looked old and tired, not the smart, sophisticated man he had been just a week ago in Damascus.

"Akhi," Aadam said softly. "We don't know how long we're here for—we don't know if we're gonna make it out alive. Trust me, if I could turn back time, I would've made things good with my baba."

I knew he was right. I looked at him and forced a smile, then pushed myself up.

Aadam patted my back in support.

I walked across the room slowly, still unsure whether I wanted to do this. Baba was deep in conversation. "Once we get to England, we have to keep repeating that we weren't safe, over and over again. We must tell the stories we've heard and share them for the whole world to hear, so people will wake up and start helping. . . ."

He trailed off as he spotted me. He muttered something to the Sudanese man that ended their conversation, and the man got up and left. Baba caught my eye and gestured for me to sit with him.

"Sami, come. We need to talk." I sat down on his mattress beside him and stared at the concrete floor beneath us. "Look, son, I'm sorry I hit you yesterday."

He paused. I heard him swallow before he continued. "I shouldn't have reacted like that and I promise it won't happen again. I was just hurt that you could speak to me that way, when you know that I'm doing all of this for you. Everything I've ever done has been for—" His voice began to break; he was trying to fight off tears.

Oh man, I've made my baba cry, I thought. *Now what?*

"I'm really sorry. . . . I—I . . ." I turned to him and met his watery eyes. "I just don't understand why you won't help Aadam when we have so much money. I was going to take a thousand dollars to give to him, so he could get on a better boat. That's all. His smuggler mentioned a newer one that Aadam could take, but he doesn't have enough money."

"Sami, if I had money to spare, I'd give it to Aadam without hesitation. I made a mistake by moving all our savings into Lebanon—I never thought they'd have a financial crisis and I wouldn't be able to get my money out. You think it's easy for me to see a young boy on his own like that? You think I don't want to help him? Do you know nothing about me?"

I gulped. I didn't know what to say.

"Don't you ever, *ever* take anything from me without my permission again."

"I only did it to save Aadam's life—" I protested.

"Sami, please don't start acting up. I can't take it. I know it's hard right now—you haven't eaten properly or showered in a while—but you just have to be a little more patient. We *will* get out of here. We'll give Aadam our details. We'll take his email address and help him as soon as we can. But right now, we aren't in the position to."

I shook my head, refusing to believe it. "What if he dies because he couldn't get on a proper boat? He can't even swim!"

"Sami, please! We could all die on the crossing! You can't think like that. If his death is written, it is written."

My jaw dropped. How could he be so relaxed about this?

I knew I wasn't going to change Baba's mind about Aadam or us taking a boat to Europe. I took a deep breath and sighed, then put my hands on the mattress to stand up.

"Listen, Sami, hold on. I'm sorry. I shouldn't have said that. I know you're worried about the boat journey. I understand. I need to explain something to you before I forget."

I sat back down. He rubbed the back of his neck and continued. "Remember this and you'll be *okay*: if you fall in, make sure you don't take in any water."

I closed my eyes. I didn't want to think about it.

"The cold sea will make you hyperventilate for a moment. Don't panic. Try to get control of your breath. Keep your head above the water. You might accidentally swallow some, but as long as the water doesn't reach your lungs, you'll float and be rescued. You understand?"

I stayed quiet as a shiver went through me. I'd been so scared for Aadam, I'd forgotten about myself. *I can't get on a boat. I can't. I won't.*

Chapter 11

That night, I slept for a few hours and dreamed Joseph and I were playing for Manchester United. Leila was cheering us on from the stand and Ronaldo was our manager, giving us the best strategies to thrash Liverpool, the other team.

It was after I'd scored our second goal that it turned into a nightmare.

As I ran around the pitch celebrating, the sky darkened and a missile landed on the pitch, exploded on impact, and sent everyone flying.

Blood and limbs were scattered everywhere. I ran to Joseph, lying still on the pitch, his eyes closed.

"Joseph, wake up. Come on!" I shouted as I shook him. He was dead. Crying, I got up and ran toward the stalls to find Leila, but the roof of the stadium had crushed everything underneath.

I'd lost them. Both of them. My heart raced as I spun around, looking at the destruction that surrounded me, feeling completely lost and helpless.

I woke up in a sweat.

As my eyes focused, I saw Mama standing above me. "Sami, we need to go."

"Huh? Go?"

"We're leaving Turkey. Our paperwork's ready." She pointed at Baba, who was carefully tucking our two empty luggage bags under the corner of the Iraqi man's mattress, his backpack on his shoulder, Sara clinging to his thigh.

"What about Aadam?" I asked, looking over at him sleeping. He was curled up in a ball, his chin and nose under his blanket.

"Sami, we talked about this," she whispered, bringing her mouth to my ear. "We can't take him, but me and your baba have decided to give him five hundred dollars. That should help him get on to a decent enough boat."

My chest tingled and my body went cold; I couldn't leave again without saying goodbye. First Joseph and now Aadam. I jumped off the mattress and crouched next to Aadam, gently rocking his body to wake him.

He started making the shrill sound that always came with his nightmares.

"Aadam, wake up, please. Please!"

Mama walked away. Aadam opened his eyes and they flicked around, startled.

"What happened? Have we been bombed? Where am I?"

"You're still in the apartment in Turkey. It's Sami. Listen, I'm going." My voice broke, and I couldn't stop myself from crying. "Aadam, I have to go. Mama said we have to leave now to get our paperwork."

Aadam sat up. His eyes welled with tears. I felt like the worst friend.

We hugged each other, his arms wrapped tight around my shoulders. We both wept and I didn't care what anyone thought.

"I'm so sorry. I'm so sorry," was all I could say, because it was all I was feeling.

Aadam pulled away from me and looked into my eyes, his face wet with tears. "Akhi, I'll be fine. Don't you dare worry about me. You stay safe, because we're going to meet again. You're going to help me learn English and we're going to get a ball and we're going to play football. I'll try not to be too harsh on you—I might even let you score." He winked, and another tear rolled down his cheek.

I grinned. "Aadam, bro . . . you're in my heart." I put my hand to my chest. "I really hope I'll see you again. You've got my email address, right?"

He nodded.

"I've memorized yours. As soon as I get to England and can get on the internet, I'll email you. Let me know you're safe as soon as you can?"

"I will, Sami. And when I get a phone, I'll email you the number."

"Deal," I said, and we fist-bumped on it.

"Sami, we need to go." It was Baba, his face tenser than ever. He bent over and brought his face close to Aadam's, lowering his voice. "Aadam, son, listen, if I could take you I would. But I've made arrangements that I can't risk involving you in. Here's five hundred dollars to help you get a better boat. Okay?" Baba looked around before placing his fist on Aadam's palm and releasing cash into it, then he put his hand on Aadam's head.

Aadam covered the cash and slipped his hand into his back pocket. "Uncle, I don't know how to thank you." He jumped up to hug Baba.

"You don't need to. I feel bad enough that I can't do more for you."

"How can you feel bad?" Aadam whispered. "It would've taken me months to make this sort of money, and I had no way of earning it. I wasn't expecting this. Shukran."

"It's fine, son. We need to go now. You take care. You have our email addresses?"

"Yes, I do."

"Let us know when you're in Europe and I'll see what I can do for you." Baba patted Aadam on his back and turned to Mama. I smiled, relieved we'd helped him.

The scrawny driver who had brought us here squinted at us from the doorway, his hands shoved into his denim jacket pockets. Mama rubbed Sara's back as she stared blankly at the floor from over Mama's shoulder.

I hugged Aadam once more and followed Baba. I didn't look back, because if I did I wouldn't be able to leave.

Chapter 12

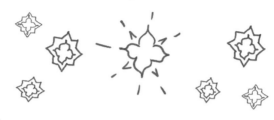

"*You'll be okay.*"

Baba's words spun around my head, muffling the crash of waves surging in front of me in the cold, dark, salty night air. My legs trembled as I stood on the shingle beach, staring at the outline of the small fishing boat floating in the shallow water.

"I can't get in that!" *My life wasn't supposed to turn out like this. This wasn't part of the plan.*

"Sami, there's no time to argue. Just get in!"

I turned round and looked at Baba. "I can't. We'll drown. I can't do it!"

In a split second, I was off my feet. Baba had one arm tight around my back and the other under my knees. I gasped for breath as he squashed my face to his chest, my body thrashing against his as he stepped onto the wooden jetty. I squirmed and yelled but the sound disappeared into the thick fabric of his waterproof jacket, the smell of wax wafting up my nose.

The next moment he tipped me upright again, and something swayed under my feet. The boat. Oh God, not the boat. I kicked but his grip was too strong, burning into my skin as he pushed me down and I crashed painfully onto a hard bench along the edge of the wooden boat. He stood over me with a chilling look in his eyes that made my mouth dry.

Mama and Sara were already on board, so I fixed my gaze on them, the heat rising in my cheeks at the thought of how Baba had just made me look. Sara kneeled on Mama's lap, clinging to her, her thin arms wrapped around Mama's neck.

I wanted to say something to Mama, but kept my mouth shut. *No one's listening to me,* I reminded myself, clenching my jaw. *I have no choice.* If they left me behind, I wouldn't have a clue what to do.

So I sat and stared at the foamy bubbles floating on the surface of the shimmering moonlit sea. It was all I could do. Would we die tonight? It seemed unlikely we'd make it, after everything we'd heard over the last few days. So many people had died in this sea—what chance did we really have? Baba didn't seem to care. I closed my eyes as small raindrops began to moisten my face and started praying that the boat wouldn't capsize.

I thought the last time I got on a boat when I was a kid was bad, but tonight was a thousand times more frightening, and not just because of the dark.

I hated the feeling of floating over deep murky water, not knowing what lurked beneath. I didn't want to drown. I didn't want to be eaten by sharks or whatever swam in these waters. The salty air made me feel queasy, and I wished I was anywhere else but here.

I heard more people approaching from the shore and opened my eyes. They stepped across the small makeshift jetty—made from a stack of wooden pallets—and came on board, making the boat sway. I recognized a couple of men from the apartment in Istanbul, but most of them I'd never seen before. Soon the boat was full of strangers with no interest in making small talk. Everyone was quiet and getting into their places. My heart felt too heavy for my chest. I wondered what Aadam was doing in the apartment all alone and how long he'd have to wait for his boat.

The line of people on the beach was getting shorter. A few men stood on huge boulders, waving their flashlights around. There was another group of people, further along the beach, getting into another dark boat that I couldn't see properly. It looked bigger than ours, but I couldn't be sure. The rocky cliff face bordering the shingle beach made everything look unreal—as if we were on a movie set.

"Move up, quickly!" shouted one of the older men. I blinked away the rain that was falling heavier and shuffled along the bench as gently as possible to avoid the boat rocking more than it already was. I gulped—the rain was going to make the sea even choppier.

"Sami, get on the floor," Baba said when the last two men climbed on board with nowhere to sit. He pointed at a tiny area of floor space in front of him. I held the bench firmly, my fingers gripping the wood underneath me. *Why do I have to move?* I thought. But again, I didn't see the point in saying anything. I took a deep breath and then let go, allowing my body to slide down to the deck of the boat.

Mama's eyes were shut tight; she muttered what seemed to be the Shahada prayer under her breath.

Did she think we were going to die? Was she preparing for it? The hairs on my neck pricked up. Mama was squashed between Baba and a large old woman wearing a striped scarf. Sara's shoes dug into the lady's long skirt, but the old woman had her face in her wrinkly hands and didn't seem to notice.

I sat facing them, a tall, skinny man on my left and a younger one on my right. One of the men in charge gave out orange life jackets. I grabbed one and put it over my head quickly, watching Baba fasten Sara's and Mama's, then copying him and tightening my belt clips.

The men who had been on the boulders watching us waded through the shallow water. One untied the boat and all three pushed us further into sea. An old, bearded man fired up the small engine and water sputtered as the propeller started. My heart raced even faster as the boat began to bob. I felt hot and flustered, yet my skin was prickled with goosebumps.

I searched the floor of the boat, looking for cracks, but it was impossible to with all the shoes and people covering it. Putting my hand beneath me, I touched the dry, smooth planks. There was no water inside. Yet.

I glanced up at the others—some people were praying verses from the Quran, some looked out to sea, and some were scrolling through their phones as if this was just a normal thing to do, the bright light on their faces making them look like ghouls.

A second boat was pushed into the water after ours, and now I could make out that it was a big rubber dinghy packed with people sitting inside and all along its edge. They looked as if they might topple off into the sea with just a small jerk. There was nothing for them to hold onto, and water was already splashing in over the side. I held my knees and looked between them, feeling grateful that at least our boat was wooden and had seats.

"Don't worry, we'll be off this soon." Baba gave me a stiff smile as he leaned over to check my life jacket was fastened properly and tightened the belt as if I was a little kid like Sara.

I looked back at him with blank eyes. What did he mean by "soon"? Hours? Days? What if a storm passed our way? My insides reeled at the thought.

● ● ●

The journey was calm to begin with, but as we got to deeper water, the waves grew. I pushed my fingers into the planks to stay seated as the boat rocked even more. I tried not to think about the bottomless sea right beneath me, only a piece of wood separating me from it, and distracted myself by imagining gentle octopuses, jellyfish, even blue whales that swam in deep water. How could anything live in this harsh environment? It was so bleak and depressing. How did fish spend their whole lives in darkness with no way to leave? Being able to leave somewhere was important. I knew that now.

A wave crashed and my shoulder smashed into the man next to me, pain shooting up my arm. Shrieks rang around me as icy-cold water splashed all over us, drenching my face, and pouring over the side of the boat. I gasped as another strong wave whacked against the side of the boat and sent it tipping. I put my hands out as I slid into Mama's legs, thankful to see she was still in the boat. Mama gripped the wooden bench, her chin on top of Sara's head, trying to stop them both from slipping.

My body trembled and my tummy rolled. The tiny bit of bread I'd eaten on the way to the beach was now sloshing around violently inside me. Sara woke up, looked around, and then closed her eyes again, quickly nestling back into Mama's chest, her fingers digging into Mama's arms. The old lady next to Mama started crying and rocking back and forth.

My body started to shake uncontrollably. *What if this is the beginning of the end?* I panicked. *What if we've made it all this way only to be swallowed by the sea?*

I felt vomit rise in my throat as my stomach churned. If there were any more violent motions, I didn't think I could hold it back. A cold puddle of seawater had formed from the splashes into the boat; my jeans were soaked through to my boxers. I tried to pull my jeans away from my moist skin, pinching the drenched denim as far from me as possible, but they stuck.

I tried to remember what Baba had explained in the apartment. *Don't panic. Just don't inhale the water,* I told myself, clamping my lips together as tightly as possible.

Smaller waves pounded the boat, heaving it upward. With each wave I begged God to get us to safety. *Please Allah, please get us across quickly.*

My prayers were interrupted by screams. I cast my eyes around to see where they were coming from and saw Mama and Baba looking behind them.

The dinghy had capsized. Its passengers were all in the sea, waving at us as they thrashed around in the water, screaming for help. There were so many. There had to be a hundred of them.

"Turn us around! Turn around!" Baba and some of the men yelled at the man in charge.

He shook his head and shouted back in English laced with a thick Turkish accent. "We are too many people. Take no more. No safe. Greek coastguard find them. No worry. They have life jacket. This happens!"

Mama squeezed Baba's knee, giving him a long stare as he tried to get off his seat to stand up. He sat back down and rubbed his hand across his forehead. I looked away as his eyes fell on me.

We could hear children crying, women and men shouting. The sounds hit me in my gut. It was all happening too fast, but at the same time it was in slow motion. I could see shadowy figures holding on to an oval shape, which must have been the upside-down dinghy. I saw arms bobbing up and down in the sea, and then someone's head emerged from the water, gasping for air before submerging again. I closed my eyes, that image locked into my head.

My heart started throbbing painfully. I couldn't do

anything but let the screams ring in my ears. I couldn't watch all those frantic limbs slowly sink beneath the surface of the water. I looked around our boat and saw some frozen expressions, some people wailing with their faces in their hands, their bodies trembling. Their cries began enclosing me and my throat tightened, as if I was being suffocated.

Why was this happening to them—to us? What had we done to deserve it? What if Aadam had to get on a dinghy like that one? What if our captain had brought more people on this one—just a few more . . .

I felt overwhelmed. Exhausted, like a weight was pushing down on me. All I wanted was to get off the boat, but of course I couldn't. It was rolling even more now. All I could do was pray for this nightmare to be over soon.

The air was cold and the clouds seemed close— much closer than normal. As if I could touch them. The hairs on my arms stood up. I wasn't hot anymore, but freezing and shivering. I heard retching and twisted my head to see a bald man violently vomiting into a plastic bag, then quickly looked away.

Feeling helpless, I curled up, put my head into my knees, and clamped my eyes tight. I didn't want to open them. My head buzzed, and all I wanted was to not see or hear or feel any more of this.

I tried to ignore the creaking of the boat and the roar and crash of the waves splashing over us by forcing myself to focus on Joseph. I tried to imagine him walking into school—if it was still standing—playing football, racing around the field, dodging all the defenders, and kicking the ball straight to the back of the net. He'd be shouting, "GOOOOOOAL!!!" and running to bounce his chest off mine to celebrate.

I hoped he knew I had to leave for Sara. That I had no choice.

Chapter 13

*H*ours *later, the eerie* silence on the boat suddenly erupted in rowdy chatter, making me lift my head. Still feeling nauseous, I looked up from my knees at the men cheering above me and stretched upward so I could see what they were pointing at.

A light flashed in the distance, where smaller waves were lashing against something tall and solid—rocks. *LAND! AT LAST!* I wanted to leap up, but my muscles felt weak and instead I almost fell into the legs behind me. *We've made it. We've made it to Greece,* I repeated to myself. Tears seeped out of my eyes, and I gasped, trying to get control of my breath.

The sky was pitch black with a few stars strewn across it. It was still the dead of night. *If I was in Syria, I'd be asleep in my bed,* I thought. The moon cut through the cold, thin mist that veiled us, and I was glad, knowing we couldn't be seen.

Some of the men shouted, "Allah hu Akbar! God is the Greatest!" and jumped over the edge of the boat while the water was still waist-high, splashing through the sea to shore.

Baba sat calmly, so I waited to follow his lead. When the water got shallower, Baba began helping the women and children off. The old lady that had been sitting next to Mama sobbed in relief as she stepped into the waves.

Finally it was our turn, but my knees were locked from being squeezed into one position for so long and my jeans were soaked, making them stiff and heavy.

Mama grabbed Sara, her wet hair hanging down straight beneath her winter hat, and passed her to Baba, who went ahead of us. "Come—hurry, Sami." Mama's lips quivered as she took my numb fingers and helped me to my feet. My knees clicked and I stumbled as I lifted my right leg then the left. I felt dizzy, my eyes blurring for a few seconds before they refocused on Mama's back.

Mama sat on the edge of the boat and slowly slipped her legs into the water. I copied her. The water was icy, but I focused on the shore and keeping a tight hold of Mama's hand. She looked less steady than me, stumbling on a rock and almost falling as we approached the beach, like a baby learning to walk. Her legs wobbled every few steps.

We dashed through the shallow, freezing water and across the pebbly beach, our sodden shoes squelching beneath us. My Air Jordans were ruined. Why hadn't I taken them off on the boat and held them? Baba had asked his friend to get them from abroad for me for my thirteenth birthday, last month. It was stupid to worry about that, I knew, but I had nothing left. Now my only pair of shoes would probably split open.

Baba and Sara neared a truck on the beach. I could hear the men in front of it arguing about something. Next to them, a group of relieved-looking guys from the boat were taking a selfie, probably to prove they'd made it. I gulped as the truck driver stepped away from the group and walked toward us with one hand in his jacket pocket and the other holding a big bright flashlight.

"Women, children, get in! Get in! Quick! Quick!" he shouted at us hoarsely. I looked at Baba, and my stomach lurched, wondering if he'd be left behind.

I could see he was reaching into his backpack for money. It was all he'd done since we left, talk to strange men who asked for money and then asked for even more.

Where would we go now? Would we drive to a hotel or to another apartment? My insides quivered—I needed a bed. Anywhere would do, really.

There were twelve of us, including Mama, Baba, Sara, and me. There were no other children because most families probably didn't have enough money to stay together.

We all huddled quietly into the back of the truck, settling in a small compartment at the front, just behind the wall of the driver's cabin. There were no seats, and the tight space was dark and bare and smelled of dust and rust. The air was stale, like in a cellar that hadn't been unlocked in years.

"You no talk. Be quiet all time, until I let out you. Unless you want be caught. Okay?" the driver said in broken English.

I flinched into Baba and took the deepest breath possible before the driver put back the small metal sheet he'd cut out of the false wall to get us all in. We were now cut off from the outside world.

Everyone was silent. I listened to the driver loading boxes onto the truck, my knuckle in my mouth. He was covering up the compartment wall. It seemed to take ages. I guessed he was filling the truck to make it look as if he was transporting goods.

There was no way of getting out without his help. My breath suddenly became shorter as I panicked at the thought of suffocating to death.

Baba put his hand on my chest. "Deep breaths, Sami. Slow it down."

I focused on Baba's hand and my breaths grew slower. I couldn't see anyone's expressions in the darkness, but I could feel the fear. The atmosphere was tense and silent, not cheerful and chatty, as I had imagined it would be after we'd made it to Europe safely.

I was stupid to think we would be making plans, that people would be smiling in relief. We still had so far to go.

The driver started the engine, and the floor beneath us rumbled. As the truck moved off, the smell of diesel wafted into the compartment, which I found comforting for a moment, a smell I knew. I opened my mouth to breathe and then snapped it shut again.

What if they poisoned us? Was there even enough oxygen in this enclosed space for us all to survive?

I was squished between Baba's legs, even though I wasn't much smaller than him. The man next to us was a lot taller and wider and every time we hit a bump in the road, he fell into Baba and me. It hurt not only my muscles and bones—it hurt deep within, each bump reminding me of what my life had become.

I closed my eyes and tried to think about better times. Again. It was pretty much all I'd done to get me through the long days and miserable nights since we left. I missed Joseph. Even Tete. I missed my life. I missed *home*.

The silence was deafening. I felt as if we'd been swallowed by the darkness that surrounded us. *We're nothing in this black hole*, I thought. *Nobody in Greece even knows we exist. We could die and no one's going to care.*

I hated my brain sometimes. I shook my head to push the thought away. I had to stop thinking like that.

Sara was asleep in Mama's arms. I could hear her inhaling deeply and exhaling with a wheeze. She was good at that—she could fall asleep anywhere. Not me. I had to be in a bed, or at least on a mattress with a thin blanket, like we'd had in Turkey. I thought back to my double bed at home, and my bones ached. I longed to switch off my thoughts and sleep, but I couldn't. I couldn't stop thinking about where we were and how we'd lost everything with barely any warning.

The memory of the shrieks and screams of the people from the capsized dinghy pierced my ears. I put my head between my knees, trying to block it out.

As my eyes welled up, I reached out for Mama's hand on my left. I found it resting on her knee, shaking hard, her legs trembling too. I wanted to ask Mama exactly where we were heading next. I hated not knowing. I hated all the uncertainty. But she was scared too—I had to stay quiet.

I'd learned in geography that it was about five hours on a plane from Syria to England. But how long would it take in a truck? What if it took months? Mama had said we couldn't get caught traveling to England. If we did, we would be forced to stay in the country we were caught in. We'd made it through Syria, Lebanon, and Turkey, and now we *had* to get through Greece to get to England.

It wasn't long before I felt hot even though my

bottom half was clammy. I couldn't take any of my clothes off, not even my woolen hat, because there was no room to move. My damp jeans chafed my inner thighs, but I couldn't pinch them off me.

There was a small vent in the wall in front of us, which allowed in some air from the front of the driver's cabin as he drove. I wondered if he had his window down. It smelled like it hadn't ever been opened. *How many Syrians made this journey before us? How many of them made it to England in one piece?*

After a few hours of driving along bumpy roads, I was desperate to go to the toilet. My stomach ached from holding it in, but I couldn't any longer.

"Baba," I whispered. "I—I need the bottle. . . ." The truck driver had given us empty Coke bottles to pee in, but I'd hoped I wouldn't have to use it. Baba passed it into my right hand. I unscrewed the top and unzipped my jeans.

It was so humiliating doing it in front of everyone, even though no one could see me. I tried, but nothing came out for a few seconds, and then all of a sudden, I missed the bottle. Warm liquid trickled down my hand and onto my jeans. Ugh.

I forced myself to stop, wiped my wet hand on my leg, and tried again. This time I made sure it couldn't go anywhere but in the bottle. The blood in my ears throbbed loudly. I was sure everyone could hear my heart beating.

I finished, screwed the lid firmly back on, and then zipped up my jeans. Everyone would've heard what I was doing, but hopefully they didn't know it was me.

Thank God it wasn't long before the driver stopped the truck. He removed the boxes, then the metal sheet to the compartment, and beckoned us to crawl out. But by then we could hardly move our muscles after being trapped in that little space. Painful cramps threaded through me as I shuffled over to the gap. I thought sitting on that overcrowded boat for a few hours was bad, but, man, this was painful. Once I managed to get out of the small rectangular hole, I stretched out across the truck floor before standing tall. Baba waited behind me patiently, then did exactly the same.

We stretched our legs, ate some bread, and sipped

on some water. Then, while the women and Sara went somewhere to relieve themselves where we couldn't see them, we poured the bottles we'd used in the truck out onto a field at arm's length.

The driver clapped his hands—a signal to climb back into the truck. As we waited in line, I felt like an animal, herded in and out of a cage.

A short old lady stood next to me, and the scent of Vicks VapoRub filled my nostrils, taking me right back to Tete's bedroom, which always smelled of Vicks. Sorrow stabbed at my heart—Tete was a part of us, our life. I remembered the coolness and quietness of Tete's courtyard, sitting there doing my homework while listening to the water trickling down the beautiful tiled fountain. She'd bring me snacks as I worked and kiss me on my forehead, looking at me as if I was the best thing in her life. I should've spent more time with her. I stroked Jiddo's ring. Would I ever see her again?

The driver shouted, "Come! Quick! Must move!"

I pulled in the scent of menthol and eucalyptus as deeply as I could as the old lady hobbled away from me to join the back of the line and took her comforting grandma scent with her.

● ● ●

We'd been traveling in the truck for what felt like two days when it parked in a forest. We all piled out just as the sun was setting and stretched our sore, aching limbs. I looked around the hilly area and at the city lights spread out before us, thousands of houses all built up together. It reminded me of the view of Damascus from Mount Qasioun: sparkling buildings and lit roads snaking their way through the city. I wished I was sitting in a café on the Mount, looking over my home, watching the minarets of the Umayyad Mosque bathed in green light.

"Right, we in Athens," the driver told us. "If someone come you collect, wait here. This agreed pick-up location." His bloodshot eyes with their dark-gray bags were disturbing. Thank God he'd managed to stay awake for so long with hardly any sleep.

I blinked in relief that we wouldn't be getting back in the truck. But what if we were getting picked up by another one? How were we going to get to England from here?

The Vicks VapoRub lady walked away from the group over to a grassy area and dropped onto her knees, weeping as her forehead touched the ground. Some of the men, including the burly one we'd sat beside, walked off into the distance.

"Two days I be driving. I go home to bed," the driver said to Baba with a half-hearted smile. Baba went to talk to him while Mama, Sara, and I stepped forward to gaze at the view.

A cool breeze rustled the leaves around us. The sky bathed the city in shades of orangey-red. Mama took a deep breath, held it for a few seconds then puffed her cheeks out as if she was blowing up a balloon. She tapped my shoulder and said, "Shake your legs, Sami, loosen them up again," as she kicked her right leg and shook her foot forcefully, making her whole leg tremble. Sara pulled on Mama's jacket, her little arms shaking as Mama moved beside her.

"Come on, kick your legs, Thumbelina," I said to Sara, flexing my legs out one after the other.

Sara looked at me and said nothing. Not even a smile. She looked tired. I wondered what on earth she was thinking. Did she even know where we were and why we were doing this? Poor thing.

As we stood there stretching, a tall man in a black leather jacket with short, gray hair approached Baba.

The man studied Baba's face carefully and then broke out into a huge, warm smile. Baba rushed toward him, and the man reached out to hug him.

"Tarek! Let's go!"

"Ah! Daichi! So good to see you, my friend," Baba said in English, wrapping his arms around Daichi tightly. "Have you been waiting long?"

"Only a couple of hours. It's fine. Don't worry!"

"You haven't changed a bit! We should never have left it this long!"

"Ah, you're still a joker! I didn't have this when we were in Paris!" Daichi smiled and pinched some gray hair on his head.

Baba smiled and turned to the driver, shaking his hand, then spun back to us.

"Come on, let's go. Yalla." It was the first time Baba had greeted someone without giving him some money, and that alone made my insides unwind.

We followed Daichi along gravelly paths and tracks for a few minutes until we reached his car, a silver BMW 3 Series Estate. We all piled in, and he took us to a small log cabin in the woods.

Inside, he handed out buckets of water for us to wash ourselves, and a change of clothes. The wind whistled through the cracks around the windows, and crickets and all sorts of strange noisy creatures chittered outside. I couldn't wait to wash, even though the water was cold. In the tiny bathroom, I stripped off my stinking pee-stained clothes, wiped myself down with a wet washcloth, and put on the new pair of jeans and navy V-neck sweater Daichi had given me. When I walked out into the main room, Mama was laying out sleeping bags for us all on the floor. Daichi had gone.

That night, I stretched my body out as much as I could. Even though I didn't have a mattress, it felt good to be able to move freely and lie flat again. I let out a long breath as I closed my eyes. We were closer to England. Everything would be okay again. Soon.

Chapter 14

*T*he *whole log cabin* was lit up with sunlight when I opened my eyes the next morning. It was such a contrast to the cramped darkness of the truck. I blinked to convince myself we were really free.

Sara crouched in a corner, watching a small spider scuttle across the unvarnished wooden floor. She tried to push a piece of ripped-up newspaper underneath it. When it scurried away, she scooped her hands together and raised them into the sunlight, then closed her palms as if she'd caught some and put her hands over the spider, pouring the imaginary light over it. Sara was probably the only girl I'd ever met that wasn't afraid of spiders. It was good to see her playing again.

"We need to get ready, Sami," said Mama, her hand on my shoulder. "We're leaving. Come on. Yalla."

"Where are we going now?" I grumbled. I wanted to stretch out for a few more hours. I couldn't bear the thought of traveling again.

"We'll be leaving for the airport soon. Your baba is outside collecting our British passports. You need to look relaxed now, Sami. Don't be afraid—they need to think you're on vacation and are going back home to England." She stroked my hair and added, "If anyone asks you anything, don't say too much. Just tell them your age, say you go to St. Crispin's Community College in Manchester and are in year eight."

"St. Crispin's Community College in Manchester. Year eight," I repeated, trying to make it stick in my brain.

Mama sat down on the wooden floor next to me, gently straightening out my sleeping bag with her slender fingers.

"Sami, habibi, things will get better now. You'll see. I know this has been so hard on you. I might be busy with Sara, but I want you to know I love you. You've done so well. This is the last step, God willing."

"Are you sure?" I said, resting my head beneath her shoulder and closing my eyes. I listened for her heartbeat, like I did when I was a kid. I'd never do this in front of anyone now, but we were alone so it was okay.

"Yes, this is it. We'll be in England soon."

England, I thought. *We'll be flying to England. Thank God for that!*

I heard a car drive up outside. My stomach rolled. Was it the Greek police coming to arrest us? I jumped up to look out of the window.

Baba was outside with Daichi. A short, bald man jumped out of a small red Fiat. He walked up to Baba, crunching twigs and leaves underneath his boots, and handed him what must've been our passports. Baba inspected each one carefully. After what felt like ages, he put his hand into his back pocket and handed the short guy a thick wad of money. Baba took his backpack off his shoulder and unzipped it to put the passports in, then he reached into the left front pocket of his beige chinos. He got out another smaller wad of dollars and counted out most of the notes and handed them over, leaving what looked like just three or four dollars in his hand. Baba looked tired and worn, his beard the longest and scruffiest I'd seen it. He seemed smaller too, his shoulders hunched and his head lowered.

The bald man got back into his car; the sound of

his engine made birds caw and fly from their branches. Dry brown leaves and twigs flew up in the air as he sped off. Baba and Daichi walked toward the cabin.

I turned round to find that Mama had folded up our sleeping bags in a neat pile and put them on the small table in the corner.

Sara sat at the table, fiddling with her messy golden-brown hair. She still hadn't said a word since the bombing.

"Where's your spider friend gone?" I asked her.

She shrugged her small shoulders and carried on twisting her hair around her fingers. When would she speak? Nothing I did seemed to work. Baba said she'd talk again once she'd got over the shock and we'd got her away from the fighting and to safety. I hoped he was right. I wouldn't forgive myself if she didn't. Everything had to be okay once we got to England.

Baba and Daichi walked into the cabin, Baba's forehead crumpled and Daichi with a broad smile. I guessed he'd arranged for the passports to be made.

"Right, come on, we need to leave quickly," said Baba.

"Don't worry about cleaning up, Zeina," Daichi said to Mama in his strong Greek accent as she swept the cabin floor. "I'll get it all sorted out later on. Let's just get you on that flight, eh?"

Mama smiled as she rested the broom against the cabin wall behind her and turned to the black suitcase Daichi had brought us, lying open on the floor. It was empty—we had hardly anything to fill it. Normally when we traveled, our cases were so full Mama sat on them to help Baba get the zip around.

"We have to look like we're travelers heading back home," said Baba as Mama began piling our dirty clothes into the case, along with extra towels Daichi gave us.

"Here, add these magazines and newspapers so it's heavier," said Baba, passing Mama a pile of papers.

As Baba zipped up the case, Daichi motioned us out. "Come on, we need to get going."

The woods were flooded with sunlight. The sounds of chirping birds filled the air, and I gazed at the green trees and creatures around us as leaves rustled in the gentle wind. A hoopoe sat on the branch of a tall pine tree and watched us get into the car. For weeks all I'd seen were the insides of gray buildings and cars; all I'd felt was darkness and fear. Now it felt as if a heavy cloud had been lifted, as if things might improve. We just had to get through security at the airport and hope no one would stop us getting on the plane.

Daichi drove us in his BMW, chatting to Baba all the way about their time in Paris. He pulled up in a temporary parking spot outside Athens International Airport and helped us all out of the car. He handed Baba the suitcase and gave him a hug. "Good luck, my friend. Call me as soon as you can and let me know you're all okay."

"I will." Baba nodded. "Daichi, I don't know how I'll ever repay you for this. God bless you and your family."

Daichi put his index finger on Baba's lips. "Shhh! You've honored me, Tarek. Don't you ever mention this again."

He opened the driver's door. "Bye, Zeina, kids— you all take care."

"Thank you for everything. Hopefully we'll see you again in better circumstances," Mama said, holding Sara's hand.

Baba smiled and turned. With one arm around me and one pulling the suitcase, we walked toward departures.

● ● ●

Baba frowned at the board as he figured out which desk we had to go to for check-in. I searched the giant screen, found the line that read "Manchester," and saw that it had already started boarding. Baba didn't look too concerned though. He and Daichi must've planned it this way.

Baba walked ahead to the desk and handed in our passports as we gathered behind him. The lady looked through each passport and then at our faces.

I held my breath, scared that even a slight movement might make her suspicious. I could imagine her buzzing her boss over and shouting out, "FAKE!!! ARREST THEM!" but she didn't. She gave all four passports back to Baba.

"Put your suitcase on the weighing belt please," she told him. I wondered if she'd find it strange that we only had one. But she didn't seem surprised. She just wrapped the sticker around the handle, and the conveyor belt took it away.

She handed Baba the boarding passes. "Have a good flight," she said. And that was that. I couldn't believe it. I looked down and followed Baba as he walked away from the desk, anxious that if I lifted my head up and smiled to show my relief, someone might get suspicious and grab us.

We headed toward the boarding gates. At security, Baba took off his watch and put it in the tray, along with his backpack. I took off my Swatch and Jiddo's ring and slowly put them in the tray, then fixed my eyes on my Air Jordans. What if security stopped me?

We all walked through one by one and the scanner didn't beep. Not once. Even though we had no jewelry or any other metal on us, I was still afraid something would make it go off, that we'd get taken away and stopped from getting on the plane. Mama's jewelry used to set the scanners off when we went on vacation—she'd always forget to take it off—but this time she had none. She rubbed her left wrist, where she used to wear her gold bracelets. She'd sold them all to help pay for the journey.

Our FlyHappy Airlines flight was waiting at gate five. We marched after Baba to get there; it had to be taking off pretty soon. As we got to the gate, a family was still boarding, and we gathered behind them. When we reached the front, Baba gave the man our boarding passes and passports. The man paused for a moment and squinted at the papers. I was convinced he'd seen something that wasn't quite right and my heart leaped into my mouth, the air around me closing in.

Have they figured out he isn't from England? I suddenly panicked.

My body tensed. Although Baba's English was perfect, he didn't sound like Harry Potter and he didn't look like an Englishman. The airline man looked at us and then back down, slowly going through each passport one by one, then glancing back at us. *Has he realized they're fake passports?*

My insides rolled. I was sure he was going to report us. Then a female colleague came up to him and whispered something in his ear, making him throw his head back in laughter.

He handed Baba the documents, nodding at a man who joined the line behind us to step forward. I took a deep breath and closed my eyes for a long second before checking out the plane through the huge terminal window as we walked through the gate. It was a Boeing 737, just like the model Joseph had on his windowsill. I'd never been on one before. It was a lot smaller than the plane I'd flown on a few years ago to Dubai. I wanted to run down the corridor and quickly get on the plane, but I stopped myself, kept my arms relaxed by my side, and told myself to walk slowly and confidently, with my head high.

The flight attendant greeted us as we entered the plane. Mama found her seat at the front, Sara beside her, and I followed Baba to our seats a little further on. We were on the same row but either side of the aisle. I didn't mind, as long as I could still see him. I stared ahead to check the police weren't getting on. My body twitched, my right leg trembled uncontrollably. I looked over at Baba, who seemed as panicky as I felt— he circled his thumbs around one another, his lips moving quickly. He was praying.

On my right sat a pot-bellied man, his redheaded wife in the window seat. He shifted a little when I sat down. *I don't smell,* I thought. But then, maybe I did. I hadn't had a hot shower with soap in weeks. I moved toward the edge of my aisle seat and looked across Baba to the window on the opposite side, but I could only see the plane wing.

I clicked my seat belt into place and tilted my head

back on the headrest, closing my eyes, trying not to think about our journey so far—the boat or the truck. I wanted to pretend that sitting on this plane was like every other time I'd sat on one—normal. With our own passports—not illegal.

The smooth tarmac rolled gently beneath us as the plane started taxiing. We were about to take off. We'd made it. *Almost.*

Chapter 15

*M*y *body shook violently,* waking me. I looked around, startled, soon remembering I was on a plane. It was probably just turbulence. My heart calmed again.

Through the window were dense clouds. I checked my watch. 4:03 P.M. We'd been flying for almost four hours already. Familiar plane sounds surrounded me— the beverage cart rattled up the aisle, flight attendants reminded passengers to fasten their seat belts. We were descending!

I looked out the window and saw blankets of green fields. *England.* It was gray outside. The houses and buildings looked tiny, like the ones we played with in Monopoly. The cars on the winding roads were even smaller, their lights glistening white and red.

Everything seemed to be in order and in place.

Every building had a roof, and there were rows of neat streets, bordered by lines of trees. I bet there were no craters in the roads, no abandoned cars. No shattered glass. Nothing like Syria.

My heart ached as I remembered Cham City Center Mall and thought back to what was left of our once beautiful country. Everything in Syria was now ashen and gray, huge patches of broken land where buildings had once stood. Universities, hospitals, office buildings, and now even malls were just rubble, bricks, and dust. Entire villages had been burned, obliterated. People had been forced to leave their homes. Mama and Baba just wanted us to leave before the same thing happened to Damascus. I got it. I understood.

My ears popped as the air pressure changed in the plane. We were about to land. My stomach felt light, my head dizzy.

The plane shuddered and rumbled as the wheels touched down. We had made it.

I couldn't believe it. After so long, we were on British soil. Baba smiled at me and reached to hold my hand, squeezing it. With that touch, I knew that everything was going to be okay.

People unclipped their belts as the plane trundled

across the tarmac toward the white airport building. When it stopped, the passengers ahead of us began filing out, and Baba and I got up and followed when it was our turn. Mama and Sara waited in their seats at the front. Mama stood up as we approached and let out a breath.

The cold, crisp air was sharp on my face as we stepped down the stairs. Mama's blue silk paisley scarf flapped around in the wind. The sky was as gray as the tarmac beneath it and a waft of dampness swam up my nostrils. We walked through the double doors behind the other passengers and into the long, snaking line for passport control. Everyone was mostly quiet, although some children ahead were throwing tantrums and screaming, their parents trying to shush them.

Baba bit his bottom lip as we neared the desk and twirled his thumbs around one another again. The couple in front of us showed their passports to the man behind the desk, who looked at them and then back at the documents. I stared at my feet. I didn't know what my photo or the passports looked like but the staff here would know if they seemed fake. My heart began to thump as I saw Baba's shoes step forward.

I was still looking at the floor when Baba said in English, "We are from Syria. We have come to seek asylum."

Chapter 16

I *glanced up, surprised.* I didn't expect Baba to say anything like that. The passport officer looked more shocked than me. His mouth fell open. I noticed how young he looked in his blue shirt. It could've been his very first day.

"Wait there. I'm just going to get my supervisor." He stood up and ushered over an older man in a blazer buttoned up tight across his belly.

"What's the problem?" he asked gruffly.

"He said they're refugees and have come from Syria."

"Right." The older man paused. "Come with me."

"My family too?" Baba asked in a high-pitched, anxious voice.

"Yes, yes, all of yous," he said, his face growing red.

Mama grabbed my arm and we all followed the man through a set of double doors into a brightly lit corridor. He took us through a side door into a pale-blue room, gesturing angrily to a table with four blue plastic chairs around it. There was a small gray metal filing cabinet in one corner and another two extra chairs against the wall.

"Sit down and someone will come to yous in a minute," said the old man, stony-faced. I was half expecting him to swear at us, but he simply walked back out and shut the door behind him. A second later, I could hear him making a call on his walkie-talkie.

We all stared at the walls in silence. I focused on the clock ahead of me as visions of the sinking dinghy flashed into my mind. *Tick-tock. Tick-tock. Tick-tock.* But the clock couldn't drown out the screams and shrieks of the women and men who had fallen into the sea.

Five minutes later, two police officers walked in dressed in black, their top halves bulky with bright-yellow padded protective vests and pockets for their walkie-talkies and other equipment.

We all shifted in our seats. Why were the police here? Were they going to throw us in jail? I looked at

Baba and Mama and my eyes grew hot with tears. I put my hands to my face to hide them.

"It's all right, son, don't worry," said the male police officer, who had a bushy ginger moustache. "We're not gonna hurt you."

He grabbed a chair from the back wall and smiled. Mama's lips were pale and dry, and Baba's face was so gray he looked like he'd seen a ghost. On Mama's lap, Sara squeezed her eyes tight and curled in on herself. The female officer sat in the spare chair next to Mama and pulled out a notepad. Her hair was tied up in a bun that rested between her hat and the tops of her shoulders.

"Now, we have to do this," continued the male officer. "You're not in *immediate* trouble, don't worry. But we need some details and because you're here illegally we're gonna have to arrest you on immigration offenses." He brought the chair closer to the table and sat down.

Baba opened his mouth to speak but the male police officer put his hand up and added, "An immigration officer will come to see you once we've read you your rights. They'll take you to a safe place to stay and will interview you. If your case is strong enough, you'll be allowed to stay in the UK. Do you understand that?"

"Yes," said Baba quietly, sitting back in his chair. "But I would like to apply for a work visa. I am a doctor in Syria—a surgeon. I want to get a job and provide for my family. Please. I don't want anything from you. I just want us to be safe here. Nothing else. I won't even ask for water."

The police officer looked Baba firmly in his eyes. "I'm going to have to charge you with Entering Without Leave—section 24 of the Immigration Act 1971—but I'll speak to the immigration officer first to see what can be done. All right?" He left the room while the other officer began asking us our names and ages, jotting them down in her notebook.

A couple of minutes later, the male police officer stepped back in the room and sat down, his forehead creased with lines. "Look, I'm gonna have to charge you today . . . but the immigration officer who will take your case will help you prove you're here for work. She can then apply to the Prosecution Service to drop the charges. Okay?" He took off his hat, rubbed the top of his bald head, and put the hat back on. "Do you know anyone here?"

"Yes, we have family in Stockport," replied Baba.

"Okay, well, that's good." His face grew sterner and he continued, "You do not have to say anything, but it may harm your defense if you do not mention, when questioned, something which you later rely on in court. Anything you do say may be given in evidence."

He started to ask Baba details such as our address in Damascus and the route we took to get to England. I didn't want to relive the journey, so I focused on Jiddo's ring, sliding it up and down my finger. Baba's words tuned out as I remembered Jiddo and Tete back in their courtyard.

After the police left, an Indian lady with glasses and bouncy black hair entered. "Good evening. I'm Miss Patel, and I am your assigned immigration officer," she said, putting down her laptop, a file of papers, and a red furry pencil case. She asked the same sort of questions as the policeman and then took photos of us before pulling out a machine for taking all of our fingerprints. When it was my turn, my hands wouldn't stop shaking. I didn't know how hard to press on the machine and why they were taking my prints.

"I'm just going to put your fingerprints through the Eurodac Europe-wide database of fingerprints," she said, attaching a cable to the machine and connecting it to her laptop. "Bear with me." She looked at us and then back at her laptop screen.

"Well, nothing's coming up on the search; this means you haven't registered in another European country and *have* come straight into England to claim asylum," she said, typing something on her keypad. "I'm going to ask some more detailed questions now about your lives in Syria, so we can start making our checks." She asked the name of my school, Baba's work address, where we lived. When Baba explained why we left, she asked what happened in the mall that day.

Baba pulled out his phone from his bag and switched it on—he hadn't used it since I let Aadam call his mama because he couldn't charge it. And now I knew why Baba didn't want to use the battery up. He showed Miss Patel photos of the mall, of the streets around the city. He showed her photos of people he'd treated in the suburbs. I'd never seen these photos before; I didn't even know they existed. He must've saved them in a hidden folder.

As Baba flicked through the photos, tears began to drip down his cheeks. They cut at my heart. Mama put her hand on his arm. Baba was the one we all turned to when things needed fixing, but at that moment I just wished I had a bandage to fix all of the hurt he was feeling.

Miss Patel passed Baba a box of tissues, waiting while he blew his nose. "We'll sort this out. Don't worry, Dr. al-Hafez." It was the first time anyone had called Baba "doctor" since we'd left Syria. "You'll have to go to a detention center," she continued. "I'm going to put your case through a fast-track process, so it'll be dealt with a lot quicker than most. The fact that you have family here to stay with and that you are able to work professionally will help your case."

"What do you mean 'detention'? Are we in trouble?" asked Baba, leaning forward.

"No, it's a center where we hold you while we process your case. Decisions about detained fast-track cases are made quicker. It'll save time in finding accommodation and setting up benefits and we can instead focus on your case and getting you bailed and released to your family friend . . . erm . . . Mr. Muhammad who has agreed to support you." *Detained fast-track cases, benefits* . . . I had no idea what she was talking about. She might as well have been talking in an alien language.

She led us out of the room and took us to another area of the airport, where we were met by black-uniformed security guards with "G4S" embroidered on their sweaters and handcuffs hooked to their belts. I gulped.

"I'll start making calls and compiling your evidence," Miss Patel told us, clasping her files to her chest. "I'll visit you at the detention center later this week, so we can prepare for the substantive interview. And I'll advise Mr. Muhammad to arrange a lawyer for you. These guards will take you to the center." She gave us a quick smile and then walked away.

The guards didn't speak to us. They barely looked at us. We followed them through the airport to an exit door that led to a small parking area.

Mama jumped as the roar of a jet engine made us all look up—a Boeing 747 flew right above our heads. The guards took us to a seven-seater car and slid the door open. We all got in.

"Put your belts on," said the one in the driver's seat.

I looked through the tinted window. It was dark, the streetlights on. My eyes began to close, but before I could even think of sleeping, the car slowed down again at some metal electric gates, set in a towering chain-link fence that was topped with barbed wire.

My stomach lurched. What was this place?

Chapter 17

When the gates had closed behind us, the guards let us out of the car. They led us to a thick blue double door. I wrapped my jacket tightly around me, my whole body shivering. It started to rain; heavy drops fell onto my shoulders, marking the gray pavement and the red bricks of the building.

The sky was a dark navy, dense and low, not a single star to be seen. I don't think we'd even left the airport. A plane took off, launching into the dark, its tiny lights disappearing as quickly as they had appeared.

One of the guards pressed an intercom and said something I couldn't hear. The door buzzed and we followed them in.

The G4S guards left us in a reception area, a small space with eight brown fabric-covered chairs lined up against one wall. Above them were a couple of posters: ASYLUM UK and LEGAL ADVICE. I decided I didn't want to know what they were for. As we all sat down, Baba stood reading them, one hand on his backpack strap.

The receptionist didn't say anything, just made a brief phone call and then stared at her computer screen, completely ignoring us. As if we weren't even in the room. I wanted to ask her if I could use her computer to email Joseph and Aadam, but I didn't dare break the silence.

I wondered if Aadam had made it out yet or whether he was still waiting for his boat. What if the police had caught him? I wished I knew.

My stomach gurgled loudly, making the receptionist glance up. My thoughts turned to food. I couldn't remember when I'd last had a proper meal. My mouth began to water as I thought of Mama's cooking, especially her lamb chops and kibbeh. Would she be able to cook in the detention center? What would it be like here?

Mama had managed to move Sara off her lap and place her on the next chair. She was still sitting without a gap between them, but at least Sara wasn't clinging to her. I didn't know how Mama did it, Sara glued to her day and night.

I remembered how Sara annoyed me before she stopped talking. She was always running into my room and touching my stuff. Once she scribbled all over the beige curtains in my bedroom with her felt-tip pens. I was so angry, but Mama and Baba just laughed and changed them.

Now, I would've given anything to have had that Sara back again.

We used to be a happy family. We went for dinner together, chatted about school and our friends. And now here we were, sitting in a shabby center, not knowing how long we would have to stay, looked down upon by a receptionist.

I guessed, just like this receptionist, I'd never really thought about people who didn't have as much as us. But meeting Aadam and all those people in the apartment in Turkey showed me that you didn't need stuff, you just needed your friends and family. I looked at Mama and Baba. I didn't want to take them for granted ever again.

I knew I had to wait till these detention center people sorted things out, but now we were finally in

Manchester, it felt harder to be patient. I wanted to run out of the door and be free. Play football. Anything but be cooped up again.

I'd counted four planes taking off by the time two new officers walked through a side door, laughing. As soon as they saw us, they straightened their faces.

"Right, can you and your son come with me, please?" said the man to Baba. He sounded like Mufasa in *The Lion King*.

"What about my wife and daughter?" asked Baba, his eyes flicking to Mama and Sara.

"They will go with Amanda to the Women's Detainee Section." He gestured to the guard he'd walked in with.

"No, you can't do that!" Baba put his arm around Mama and Sara, his face growing red. I looked between them, horrified. They couldn't split us up!

"I'm afraid you have no choice. This is how it is here." He took Baba by the arm, about to unchain handcuffs from his belt. Baba unwillingly released Mama and Sara.

"Come on, boy!" the guard yelled, the whites of his eyes popping out. He jolted me out of my chair.

As the man led Baba and me through a painted blue

door, Mama started sobbing, Baba too. I looked back before the door slammed shut and saw her fall back into a chair with her face in her hands. Sara had curled up on her chair, her knees pressed against her face. My heart broke into a hundred pieces. That image would stay with me.

The officer took us to a room and asked us to take our jackets, hats, and shoes off. He said it was "procedure." He searched us—patting our bodies and putting his hands in all of our pockets. Wasn't this how police treated criminals?

He pulled Baba's iPhone out of his backpack. "You're not allowed this during your stay."

"Why not? When will I get it back?" Baba asked, his face beading with sweat.

"When you leave."

"You must look after it. It's expensive and has all my important documents on it."

The officer nodded, zipping it into a plastic bag. "It will be safe. Please sit down."

He sat down on one of the gray plastic chairs and

started to interview Baba, asking the same questions as Miss Patel at the airport.

"I'm a doctor," Baba kept telling him. "I want to work. We have family in Manchester to go to—we don't need to be here."

"We have to do it this way," the officer told Baba firmly. "It's the law. Doesn't matter if you're a doctor, an army general, or a binman. If you enter the country illegally, you have to go through this process."

Over three hours later, we were taken to our room. Our shoes squeaked on the tiles as we walked through a long cream-colored corridor lit by fluorescent lights, passing thick painted-metal doors. We walked up some stairs, and I looked out at an indoor balcony of metal railings, below them a net. It looked like it was there to catch people that fell or even jumped over the railings. Was this place that bad that people would want to do that?

There were no windows. There was a balcony above us lined with more doors—like a hotel, except it was stark and bare. A few clothes lay drying on the metal banisters and railings. Each door had a large number on it.

"This looks like a prison," said Baba.

"Yes, it's run by the prison service," said the officer.

"But we are NOT criminals," said Baba, gritting his teeth.

The officer said nothing and simply opened a door. Inside the green-carpeted room were two single beds with sky-blue sheets and two pillows propped up against the bumpy white wall. There was a small steel toilet with no seat tucked in the corner of the room behind a narrow, cardboard-thin barrier.

A table between the beds was pushed up against a small window with bars on it. I heard the rumble of a jet engine—it seemed more distant from here.

Through the window, I could see the sun was beginning to rise. We'd been up all night again. The bed called to me. I never thought I'd be happy to see a bed in a prison. A PRISON. I couldn't quite get my head around it.

"When will I see my wife?" Baba asked, his voice shaking. "My daughter?"

"You can call them later today."

"Will they have a cell of their own like this? Is it safe in the women's section? Are criminals kept there too?"

"It's like this. Everyone here is an asylum seeker or

an illegal immigrant." And with that the officer walked out of the door and closed it behind him. The hairs on my neck stood up as he turned a key in the lock.

Baba sat on the edge of his bed and put his face in his hands. His beard stuck out at all angles through his fingers. I hadn't ever seen him look this upset. I didn't know what to say to him. I was worried if I said anything he might shout at me. So I stayed quiet.

I walked closer to the window. The view was a brick wall. *How ironic*, I thought. That was exactly how I felt about my life right now.

Chapter 18

*S*houting *outside in the* corridor woke me from another nightmare of people's heads submerging into the sea. I looked at Baba and saw him curled up in a ball on his bed, his forehead creased, his skin dry and flaky. His hair was longer and greasier than I'd ever seen it. I touched mine—it was greasy too. I hadn't seen my reflection in days. I needed a shower. There had to be some here, but there was no way I'd try and find one alone.

The shouting grew more intense—two men's voices, by the sound of it. I rushed to the door but couldn't see anything. The little square window was covered by a sheet of metal on the outside.

I wondered if we were still locked in, but didn't want to check. My heart raced as the shouting got louder and I heard footsteps. The men were coming nearer to our room. My hand hovered over the red switch that had EMERGENCY written above it for a second. I turned to Baba, but he just lay on his bed with his head on his arm, staring at my pillows. He looked beaten, like he had no energy to carry on.

I went and sat on his bed. "Baba, are you okay?"

He didn't answer.

"Shall we call Mama?"

He turned his head slightly to look in my direction and then back to face the wall. He was too upset to talk.

I stood up and took the two steps to my bed. The mattress was soft and bouncy, the opposite of my memory foam one at home. It felt as if it had been used by hundreds of people. But it was a bed—more than I'd had in the past few weeks.

It sounded as if the shouting men had moved away, and the corridors went quiet again. A door slammed shut, and the sound echoed.

I lay on my back and looked at the ceiling. There were twenty-five cracks and marks in it. *Is this what people do in prison?* I wondered. *Just sleep or stare at the walls? Are they never allowed outside?*

If anyone in Syria found out my baba, Dr. Tarek al-Hafez, was in prison in the UK, Tete would have a heart attack. Our family was known for our honor and hard work, as Tete always reminded us, especially during weekend dinners. She'd tell us stories about Jiddo and how he was a doctor, and his father before him too. I was also supposed to study medicine, but that wasn't going to happen now, was it? Didn't matter if I wanted to or not. No one became a doctor in prison.

A knock on the door made me jump. The handle turned and the door slowly opened outward. I wondered when they'd unlocked it.

Baba sat up quickly as a tall, thin, white English guard with gray hair in a neat side-parting walked in. "Afternoon. I hear you speak English. D'you want some lunch? I know you came in early this morning and skipped breakfast, but you might be hungry now?"

My stomach grumbled thinking about the last scrambled eggs and tomatoes Tete had made me for breakfast.

"Um, Sir . . . is my wife okay?" Baba asked, ignoring his question. "I need to check she and my daughter are all right. *Please.*"

The man nodded. "I'll take you to the canteen. Get

yourself some grub, and then I'll show you where the phones are. You don't want to miss your meal—they'll be packing up in half an hour. Has someone shown you where the showers are?"

"No." Baba stood up and I copied him. He picked up his empty-looking backpack and slung it over his shoulder.

"No problem. I'll show you on the way down. Make sure you use them before doors are locked at eight P.M."

We followed the man, his head passing just a few centimeters below the door. I looked up at the big gap between the doorframe and me as I walked out after him.

Outside, some of the doors to rooms were open. A few men stood in the corridor and more downstairs. They all stared as the guard showed us the shower block and then as we came down the steps, probably because we were new. I focused on the floor. I didn't want them to see the panic in my eyes. I caught up with Baba so I could walk beside him. We passed more and more doors that all looked the same. The only thing different in this place were the people.

"Right, here's the canteen," announced the gray-haired guard with a gentle smile. The smell of fried food hit my stomach and it groaned. "Grab a tray and plate. The lady there will serve you what you want. When you're done, just come out of here and turn left, and you'll see a couple of phones. The dial codes are on a sheet. Your wife's in the same building, so you can call the women's section for free."

"Thank you." Baba nodded and grabbed a plastic tray. "Sami, come—let's eat quickly."

I picked up a green tray and walked after him, along the counter. I made sure I didn't look at any of the tables, even as we walked to ours, keeping my head down when everyone stopped and stared at us, my eyes focused on my cold, hardened fries and breaded fish, and some weird brown sauce.

The brown stuff smelled of smoke but tasted sweet and tangy. It was the first cooked meal I'd had since leaving Syria. I chewed each mouthful properly to taste the mushy potato inside the fries and the bland fish wrapped in fine breadcrumbs, combined with the tang from the brown sauce. Baba only ate half his portion before pushing his plate away.

I was still eating when a stocky man in a white T-shirt and baggy jeans pulled out the chair next to mine and banged his tray down. Not daring to look up, I stared down at his pristine white high-tops—the latest Air Jordans—my eyes so wide they hurt. They'd probably come out recently. I felt his eyes on me and then my ruined shoes. I shuffled my feet under my chair.

"Finish quickly, Sami. I need to call your mama," said Baba, watching me.

I gobbled up three more fries, took a long sip of the watery orange juice, and stood up.

"You should look after them better," the man snarled in English, nodding at my battered Air Jordans. This time I glanced at him and noticed he had a gold tooth.

Well, clearly YOU *didn't have to go on a boat and then run through the sea,* I thought, my face feeling warm. But I didn't say anything, I just nodded and tucked my chair back in as we got up to leave.

There were a few men sitting at the other tables eating, the only sound cutlery scraping and falling onto plates. No one was talking. Most of them looked like they hadn't slept in days, unshaven and bloodshot-eyed.

I spotted a couple of younger boys like me. They

didn't look happy either. My heart felt like it'd plunged into my stomach. This was going to be a lot harder than the apartment in Turkey. Everyone had stronger spirits there. We all talked. We had hope. This was like being at a funeral. No—it was worse, because at least at a funeral, people cried and showed their emotions. This place was like a graveyard full of zombies.

I followed Baba out to the phones fixed to a wall in the silent corridor. He used his finger to scan the sheet of paper with the codes on it, then picked up the phone and dialed a number, the curly brown cable dangling over his arm.

"Hello," he said calmly, although his forehead was furrowed. "Can I speak to Mrs. Zeina al-Hafez, please? I am her husband, Dr. Tarek al-Hafez. I am in the men's section. We came last night, and I need to check she's okay." There was a pause. "Yes, but I need to speak to her myself, please. Please." His voice began to sound more desperate. "Okay. Thank you."

He put the phone on his shoulder. "They're going to get her," he told me.

After what seemed like ages, Mama came to the phone. I could hear her crying. Tears fell from Baba's eyes as he spoke to her.

I turned away, my throat burning. I couldn't bear to see Baba looking like this. I spotted a man hiding behind the door to the canteen. My brow tightened. Was he trying to listen in? I tried to ignore Baba's weeping and focus on the man behind the open door. I stood tall. Why was he listening? Was I just being paranoid? Bullies could sense fear—Baba had told me that many times. So I squared up my shoulders and turned back to Baba, who was hunched over and looking completely broken.

He put the phone down, his eyes red-raw. "Come on," he said, putting his arm on my shoulder.

I looked into the canteen as we passed it, but no one was standing there. Maybe I'd imagined it.

Baba didn't say a word until we reached our room. He shut the door behind him quietly, shoved his backpack under his bed, and sat down on it.

"Your mama is okay, don't worry."

"Is Sara okay?" I asked. Guilt seeped into my chest. She must be struggling in a place like this.

"She's being very clingy, but that's understandable." He rubbed his face. "She wet the bed, so your mama had to deal with that. One of the guards wasn't nice about it. I can't believe they've separated us, after everything we've been through." He stood up, glared through the window at the brick wall outside, then started pacing the room.

I lay down and closed my eyes. I *had* to think of better times. I imagined Leila at school, flicking her hair, her hands on her hips, telling Joseph where to go, and him just looking at her goofily because he didn't know why he'd upset her.

I imagined sitting on my bed in my own room, watching the sunset, my body relaxed, without a worry in the world. At home, I hadn't known what worry was, not really.

Chapter 19

I jerked up from my pillow gasping, my throat so tight I could hardly breathe. My face poured with sweat. I'd seen them all drowning. Their boat had capsized just behind ours. Their screams still rang through my ears like I was there. I'd seen that face submerge underwater again.

Then I'd become the submerged person, holding my breath as I frantically kicked up to the surface for air, then something pulled my body backward, sucking it down to the seabed. I hadn't been able to hold my breath any longer, and I opened my mouth, my lungs immediately filling with water, my windpipe bursting with fluid. That was when I'd woken up gasping.

I wondered how much longer I would keep having this nightmare.

Looking to my left, I saw Baba's empty bed. I dashed to the door and gripped the handle. Where was he? Why didn't I hear him go? A thought stopped me from turning it. *What if Baba's been taken away?*

As I was wondering what to do, the door handle turned under my grip. I stepped back, and Baba walked in with wet hair, looking weary.

"Ah, Sami. You were in a deep sleep when I left."

"Where did you go? Are you okay?"

"Yes, yes. I went to have a shower. Go and have one." He dumped a tatty green towel on his bed and slipped out of his scruffy tan leather brogues.

"Is it safe to go alone, though?"

"Yes, it's all refugee men here. Just like in Turkey— don't worry."

I did need a shower but I could wait a while longer. I sat back on my bed. "Baba, how long are we here for? I want to go home."

Baba sighed. "Home? Sami, we have no home now. It's been sold. It might have even been bombed, who knows?" He looked down, shuffling his feet on the green carpet.

"What about Tete? We don't even know if she's okay. When are we going to call her?"

"Soon. We should be seeing a lawyer today," Baba said, looking up and smiling at me encouragingly. "We won't be here too long, because we have Muhammad's house to go to. He's arranging it all. He knows we're here now."

I let out a breath of relief. We had some hope. "Have I met Muhammad before?"

"No. Even I haven't met him," Baba laughed dryly. "His father grew up with your jiddo in Syria. Tete knows the family very well. I spoke to him before we left. He offered to help set us up in the UK once we got here. Anyway, he's Uncle Muhammad to you."

"Oh, right." *It's all going to be okay,* I told myself, relaxing at the thought of freedom. I put my hands over my greasy hair. "I'll go have a shower then."

"Okay. Here, take this." Baba handed me the damp green towel. "It was the last one there."

I stepped out into the cold, dismal corridor, focusing on the socks, underpants, sweaters, and T-shirts drying on the railings. I wondered where they were washed.

All the doors were shut, except one. I peeked in as I walked past and saw it was exactly the same as ours, with a single window looking out to a brick wall and two single beds covered in sky-blue sheets, except these people had a lot of belongings. There were books on their table, clothes and packets of cookies on the floor, and posters covering the walls. It looked like they'd been here a while.

As I approached the door of the shower block, I heard a man shout. I wasn't sure if it came from inside. I took a slow step forward and into the mirrored area. It was empty, but I heard a shuffle and a thud against one of the shower stalls and then a loud groan.

"Don't you talk to me like that again!" someone hissed.

My heart pounding, I ran back into the corridor, wincing as my Jordans squeaked on the floor. Once I was a few doors away, I slowed to a walk, to make it look like it wasn't me who had gone into the showers.

A few seconds later, a stocky man with short, black hair passed me from behind, his shoulders hunched over as he took long strides along the corridor. He turned and glared at me as he walked by, his thick, heavy eyebrows pulled together, his jaw clenched, and his hands in fists. It was the man with the Air Jordans from the canteen.

I slowed down to increase the distance between us.

I didn't want to go back to the showers while he was out in the corridor. Finally, he opened a door about twenty meters ahead, slipped inside, and slammed it shut, the sound echoing against the walls.

I turned and rushed to the shower room. It was quiet and smelled like it had been cleaned recently. I entered the first shower stall, shut the door behind me and hung my towel on the hook.

Ah, a proper shower, I thought with a smile. I'd always taken simple things like that for granted.

I pulled down my jeans, and as I looked at my feet and the cream-colored tiles beneath them, out of the corner of my eye I saw a leg on the floor below the adjoining wall. Someone moaned.

My throat tightened and a cold shiver shot down my spine. I quickly pulled up my jeans, struggling with the zip in my panic.

I stepped out of my stall and walked hesitantly to the one next to it. The door was slightly ajar, and I could see someone slumped against the shower wall holding his bleeding head, wincing.

I scanned the main door to see if anyone was there, then dashed toward it. But then stopped, ran back into a stall, and pressed the red emergency switch. It lit up and buzzed like the ones that call a nurse in a hospital. I prayed no one would see me and that the Air Jordans man wouldn't be coming back. He had to be the one that had attacked the man. My hands trembled. My heart was beating like a drum, blood flooding into my ears. My legs couldn't move fast enough to the corridor outside.

No one was around, so I sprinted to our room, feeling as cold and pale as the walls around me. I entered with my back to Baba, pulling the door in with me and shutting it, my head down. I didn't want him to see my spooked face.

"And then there were two," someone said.

Not Baba.

I turned and saw the Air Jordans man on his knees behind Baba, his muscly arm wrapped around Baba's throat.

Chapter 20

I *couldn't hear anything but* my heartbeat. My limbs buckled, numb with fear, and I fell to the floor. *Get up!* I put my hands on the carpet, slowly pushing myself up to look at Baba's face.

"Ah, welcome back." The Air Jordans man grinned at me like a movie villain, his eyes bloodshot-red, his gold tooth gleaming.

"Sami, don't say a word," said Baba through his teeth.

"No. *You* don't say a word, doctor."

I didn't know what to do. I thought about getting up and running out the door, but I was scared he'd hurt Baba if I did that. He'd do the same if I screamed for help.

I pulled my knees to my chest and covered the fear

on my face with my hands, trying to think. Seconds later came the shouting of men outside, the thumps of people running up the stairs, keys jangling. I froze. Then a siren went off.

"Don't move!" Air Jordans man grimaced. I saw him tense up.

"Call an ambulance!" Someone outside cried.

It was then that I saw the splatter of dried blood on the man's T-shirt. A chill passed through me. My gut told me I had to do something before he hurt us.

"What do you want from us?" I asked him.

"Aha, he speaks. *You* are going to get me out of here."

"How? We're stuck in here ourselves!"

"Yeah, but nobody wants to lose a good *doctor* and his young son," he said, grinning again.

How did he know about Baba?

Baba's call to Mama! It must've been him listening in. I wasn't being paranoid.

He turned his face to Baba's and sneered. "They'll accept my demands to save you. You just keep quiet and do as you're told. Otherwise I'll kill you."

"Please, listen—" I started, my brain struggling to think what to say.

"To you?!" he scoffed. Baba raised his eyebrows at me, and I guessed he was telling me to shut up. But I couldn't do *nothing*. The man pulled his arm tighter around Baba's neck. He had large white scars on both his biceps. I had to tread carefully. I had to make sure he didn't get angrier.

"Is—is it money you need?" I asked, sitting straighter. "I can help you—"

"What do you know, you spoiled little brat? Stop talking!"

My shoulders dropped. I shut my mouth. Anything I said was going to make things worse.

"You are going to help me, you got that right," he said, raising his chin and rolling his eyes at me. "You'll be the reason they negotiate my release from here."

"You don't need to do this," I dared to say. "You can leave us before the guards come looking for you."

"Shut up! *You two* are my ticket out of here. I want the guards to find us in here. I'm going nowhere without you."

"No, listen . . . I know where you can find some money." Maybe he'd leave if I distracted him.

"So go and get it for me, pretty boy."

"I've seen where the guards lock the phones and

cash," I lied. "But I can't do it by myself. I'll stall them all, and you can grab what you want and then make a run for it."

His gold tooth flashed as he pulled his head back and laughed. "You haven't been here long, have you? I can't get out of here like that!"

I wiped the sweat from my forehead, trying to think of another plan.

"Oi," he said, his face straightening. "What's that on your hand? Give it here."

Oh God—Jiddo's ring. I put my left hand under my knee. "Nothing," I said as my insides dipped.

"Take it off. *Now!*"

"I can't," I said, looking down at the carpet.

"You want me to break your finger and get it off for you?"

I kept my eyes down, my heart pulsing in my head.

"I said, hand it here now or your dad gets it."

"It's my grandad's! I—I can't . . ."

"Sami, just give it," said Baba, his voice pinched and desperate.

I looked up; the man's arm had tightened around Baba's throat, and Baba's face was bulging with pressure. My body stiffened.

I slowly started pulling the ring off, my face boiling.

I'd promised Tete that I would keep it safe and pass it on. Her disappointed face flashed in front of my eyes. *All I ever do is let everyone down,* I thought. *Mama, Sara, Joseph, Aadam, and now Tete.*

I slipped it off the top of my finger. "It's not worth anything—it was my grandad's, that's all," I said.

"I'll decide if it's worth anything, you little brat! You seriously want to see your dad gone?"

I sighed and got up to hand it to him. I had no choice. He stretched for it, still on his knees, releasing Baba a little as he tilted forward.

Then, as I shuffled closer on my knees, I saw Tete's face handing me the ring and remembered how I'd promised to look after it and pass it on to the next generation of al-Hafezes. In that split second, I decided I wasn't going to give in.

Air Jordans man leaned further on his knees, unstable on the soft mattress. I reached out to look like I was handing the ring over, locked eyes with Baba, then gripped the man's arm and used all my strength to yank him off the bed, forcing him and Baba to fall to the ground.

As they fell, Baba elbowed the man in the ribs and turned to punch him in the face.

"HELP! HELP! QUICKLY!" I screamed as loud

as I could, hoping the guards down the hall would hear me. Baba wrestled the man on the floor, his face pressed into the carpet. Air Jordans man squirmed and thrashed his legs as Baba sat on top of his back to hold him down.

"HELP! SOMEONE HELP!" I screamed again, throwing the door open and pushing the red emergency switch.

"Get off me, NOW! You're dead. I'm telling you, you're dead!" he screamed, kicking his legs up and down, his pristine Air Jordans getting scuffed on the carpet.

Just as he managed to twist and throw Baba off his back, two guards ran in. They saw him leap onto Baba. I jumped out of their way, my back to the toilet wall, holding my breath as I watched the guards pull the man off.

"DON'T TOUCH ME!" he screeched at them.

Baba got on his knees, rubbing his neck. I exhaled and tried not to think about what Air Jordans man might do to me when he saw me again.

Chapter 21

There was a knock on the door. I leaped up, thinking it was Air Jordans man back to get me, even though the tall, gray-haired guard called David was still sitting on Baba's bed, making sure I was safe while Baba was checked over. David had stayed with me when I was interviewed by the police about what Air Jordans man had done, and he'd told me how his grandad, who was a Jewish refugee, had come to the UK on the Kindertransport. That's why he'd been so kind to me. David stood up to open the door and another guard with short braids walked in.

"All right, son," said the new guard. "I need you to come with me. Your dad's been seen by the medical team. He's fine, but he's gonna meet Immigration and he's worried about ya. He wants you with 'im."

I hurried out of the door behind him, eager to be with Baba again. The police were still around the shower block as the guard took me down the stairs. I took a breath and walked past them toward the room we were interviewed in when we'd first arrived.

The guard opened the door and let me in. Baba sat opposite Miss Patel, the immigration officer, clutching his backpack. He smiled in relief when he saw me.

"Ah, Sami. Come sit."

"Baba, I need to talk to you. It's urgent."

"Just let me finish here." Baba turned back to face Miss Patel and continued answering her questions. I sat down on the chair next to him and listened, fiddling with Jiddo's ring, thankful I still had it.

About twenty minutes later, David, the gray-haired guard knocked on the door. He handed some paperwork to Miss Patel and walked back out without saying a word. I continued to pull Jiddo's ring on and off my finger.

"Oh, good! Here's the written confirmation from Mr. Muhammad, indicating that he's happy to accommodate you." She looked up and smiled. "However, I'm still waiting for the verification of your supporting documents, including your medical qualification certificates. Once you get your leave to remain—that's permission to stay in the UK—you'll need to register with the General Medical Council here before you can apply to work as a surgeon. But in the meantime, I've sent your details to the British Medical Association, who have a refugee doctor initiative, and they will help you find work."

"Thank you. Thank you," said Baba, rocking eagerly back and forth with his hands on his knees.

"I've fast-tracked the application, since you have the ability to support yourself eventually and because of the overwhelming evidence you've provided about the war. I'd like to interview your son now, if you could please leave the room?"

"Um . . . I'm happy to stay?"

"It won't take long. If you could please wait outside, Doctor," she said, resting her hands on the table.

Baba stopped at the door to look back at me before he left the room. I thought I'd better do as I was told so there were no delays and we could get out as soon as possible.

"So, Sami, let's start with which school you went to and what year you were in." She fixed her eyes on me and smiled.

She asked me all the same questions she'd asked Baba when we'd arrived. She wanted to know what happened to Sara and Mama and why we'd left. I answered all of her questions as best as I could.

"Do you have any questions for me, Sami?" she asked after her last question about my life in Syria and the journey here.

"I need to get out of here, Miss," I said, placing my palms on the cold table. "It's not safe." I looked down at my hands, remembering how I'd somehow managed to pull Air Jordans man to the floor. "When can we leave?"

She scribbled something on her notepad, then glanced up at me. "It could be a month, but it could be six months, I can't say for sure. Your case is very strong, so I'm hoping your family will be processed within the next few weeks at most."

"A few more WEEKS? We can't stay here that long! Why can't we go now? What have we done wrong?" I stared straight into her brown eyes. How would she like to be locked up in a prison?

"Nothing—you've done nothing. It's the law here, that's all, because you came in illegally." She closed her notepad. "Thank you, Sami. You can go back to your room." She scraped her chair back and got up, slotting her paperwork into her brown leather satchel.

I was relieved to see Baba sitting outside the room, waiting for me. I didn't want to walk anywhere alone.

"Your mama was interviewed today, and Sara will be assessed by a psychologist soon. It won't be long . . . Miss Patel knows we don't feel safe here."

I stared at Baba as he stood up. "Why did we leave? We were better off in Syria. We had everything we wanted. Yeah, bad stuff started to happen but at least we had money and were all together. I want to go back, Baba."

"Sami, I know. Listen, things will get better. We have to look forward. I'm trying my best here." He focused ahead and tightened his lips. "What did you want to talk to me about back there?"

"Not here." I didn't know who was listening.

As soon as we got to our room and I shut the door behind us, I said to Baba, "The man who held us hostage, will he be coming back?"

"No, thank God, he's been removed from the

center. The police know he didn't just attack us, he attacked a man in the showers too. The idiot dropped his earring in the shower stall and the victim is conscious now and has identified him. Plus the police interviewed us already . . . and it looks as if they've checked our room for evidence while we were out."

I looked at our beds and saw the sheets had all been removed, the beds pulled away from the walls.

"I'm scared, Baba." My voice was so small it was barely a whisper.

Baba put his beloved backpack on the table before turning to me. "Come here, son." He wrapped his arms around my shoulders and hugged me. It was the tightest hug he'd given me in a long time, and I needed it. I felt instantly safer in his arms, just like I had when I was younger.

When Baba finally released me he put his hands on my shoulders and brought his head down to level his eyes with mine. He seemed softer than I'd seen in months, as if something had changed in him.

"I'm so proud of you. You saved my life. . . . You've become quite a man."

It was the first time I'd seen Baba look at me like I wasn't a child. I felt as if I was almost like an equal, like

I had his respect. As he smiled, a tear fell from his eye.

"This has all been too much for you. I know that. It's something that I never thought we'd have to go through . . . " He wiped his eyes with his sleeve. "It's my job to keep you safe and I haven't been able to do that. Everything you've seen: pretend you never saw it, Sami. *Please*. Pretend it was a dream. Do what you have to do, so you don't take this weight with you through life. I can't have that happen to you. This is all killing me inside." More tears rolled down his face and I wished I could stop them. I didn't want my baba to be hurting like this.

He began pacing the floor. "We'll stick together from now on. We'll go to the canteen together, even the showers—the ones downstairs are more visible to the guards than the ones on our floor. We'll use those from now on, okay?"

I nodded, but my mind felt like mush. There was so much to think about, and I didn't want to focus on any of it. It was all a nightmare.

I just wanted to shut my eyes and sleep. Let all of it go away. I didn't want to dream. I wanted nothingness, to see nothing but black. No people, nothing.

I lay on my bare bed. My stomach rumbled but I

didn't want to eat. I didn't want to go to the canteen. I didn't want to see any of the other men in this place. I didn't want to have to shower. Air Jordans man could've hurt me in the showers. *What if he'd attacked me, not the other guy? And what would have happened if I hadn't pulled him off the bed?* I decided there and then that I wasn't going to leave this room again.

My instincts had been right. This wasn't a safe place. I couldn't wait until we got out.

Chapter 22

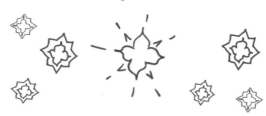

*B*aba insisted I go to the canteen to eat with him and to the showers sometimes, but other than that, I didn't leave our room. The days that passed were by far the most miserable and boring days of my life. We must've been there a week when David, the guard, knocked on our door. I lay still in my bed as he entered and waved around some sheets of paper and a pencil.

"I've got this for you from the office, son, like you asked. Sorry it took a while," he said. "I know you're glum here, and your dad's busy doing the interviews with Immigration and his lawyers, but before I hand these over, you've got to promise me you'll get outta bed and freshen up a bit. It'll do you good."

Finally, I can write to Joseph, I thought. I figured if I couldn't use a computer to email him, I'd write him a letter.

He laid the paper and pencil on our table and gave me a small smile. "I'm glad you asked for paper. Write about whatever worries you—whatever you feel. It'll help, I promise." He patted me on my arm before turning to walk out the room.

"Thanks," I said, smiling back weakly, but I didn't move from my bed.

"Oh, before I forget . . ." He stopped at the door. "I just heard Miss Patel tell your dad his criminal charge of 'Entering Without Leave' is with a government agency who are trying to get it dropped. Isn't that great?" He smiled and walked out saying, "Things'll get better soon, you'll see."

It sounded like people were trying to speed things up and help on the outside. But it still felt like an eternity on the inside.

Even though I had asked for it, for a couple of days the paper just stayed on the table. I kept looking at it, rubbing Jiddo's ring and remembering how I used to write at school and have homework that I hated doing. I wanted to go back to those times. I didn't want to have to write to my best friend from a prison. I didn't have the energy to do anything. But then, one day, when I felt like I might burst with sadness, I picked up the pencil and started writing.

Dear Joseph,

I don't know if it's day or night. I haven't got a clue what the date is, and I just stare at the walls and don't move. I haven't ever felt so empty before. I miss you. I shouldn't have left. I promise you I didn't want to, but I had to for Sara. And now I've got no friends and no mama or sister. I've got no fresh clothes to change into, nothing. I've only got Baba, but he barely speaks, and I don't leave our room unless Baba forces me to go and shower. It doesn't matter that we don't speak. There's nothing to talk about anymore.

Tears blurred my eyes so I stopped. I read it back, scrunched the paper up, and chucked it under Baba's bed.

The next day I started another letter, this time telling Joseph about the boat capsizing and the people fighting in the water to stay afloat. I described the screaming children and the helpless men with their arms up in the air.

I told him about Sara not speaking anymore and how it was my fault and about Mama and Baba crying. I wrote about Air Jordans man holding Baba hostage.

Then I read that one back, crumpled it up, and threw it underneath the bed to join the first letter. I couldn't send either of those to him.

A few days later, I finally wrote a letter that I wanted to keep. In it, I wrote about Damascus, about school and us playing football. I asked Joseph what people were up to back in Syria and what I'd missed since we left.

I wasn't sure how I was going to get the letter to him, but in a way, it didn't matter. Writing about all the things that once made me happy lifted the heavy cloud that had been hanging above me. It transported me back to my bedroom, as if I was writing on my bed again, like when I did my homework.

Once I'd finished, I folded the letter up and put it under my mattress. Then I looked up at the stark cream walls and the shock of where I really was hit me again. But this time, I didn't let it get me down.

You'll be out of here soon and things will be good again,
I told myself. *We'll all be free and together. Come on, Sami,*
you can do this. You've got to do it for Baba, Mama and Sara.

● ● ●

Three or four days must've passed, and I was sitting
on my bed, eating the bowl of Weetabix Baba had
brought me, when David, the guard, walked in.

"Good news, Dr. Tarek, your immigration officer
is here. Pack your stuff! They're moving you on."

"What?" asked Baba, spluttering into his own
cereal. "What do you mean, 'moving us on'?"

"To the address you nominated. You're out of here.
Doesn't happen often! Best of luck to you, mate." He
winked at me and walked out, leaving the door open.

Baba's eyes lit up, a smile that I hadn't seen in a
year spreading across his face. My skin tingled all over.
It couldn't be true, could it?

"Come on, Sami! Yalla! Hurry up! We can go."
Baba jumped off the bed and clanged his bowl on the
table, waving me to stand up. He grabbed his backpack
from under his bed and chucked it over his shoulder,
then neatened his duvet.

I gobbled up my last spoonful and put the bowl on the side table. I stared around, feeling as if everything was in slow motion. Was this a dream? Were we actually leaving this place?

"Why are you looking so lost, Sami? This is really happening! Come on—let's go, before they change their minds!"

We rushed out of our room with our heads high. I tried to hold back my grin, thinking of the men being left behind—unable to leave—thinking back to how we'd walked in when we'd first arrived.

Mama was already at the front reception when we got there. She ran to Baba and me and held us in such a tight group hug, I could hardly breathe. I fought back my tears and held on to her and Baba, who had his lips pressed on Mama's forehead. Sara clung to our legs quietly. When I looked down, I saw her broad smile.

"Let's get out of here," said Baba, ruffling my hair. He gave Mama and Sara a kiss on the cheek before turning to the reception desk to sign some papers.

"Miss Patel will come and go through some more details before you leave," said the blonde receptionist, her brown plastic glasses slipping down her nose.

"Dr. Tarek al-Hafez!" Miss Patel greeted Baba, beaming, her teeth so white they could have been on a toothpaste advert. "Please come over here. I just need to go through some last details with you. I've already done Mrs. al-Hafez's." She took Baba to the office through the reception. I hoped it wouldn't take long. I couldn't wait to leave.

"Sami, habibi—you okay?" Mama looked bony, as if she hadn't eaten since we'd arrived. Her eyes were swollen. She must have cried a lot.

"Yeah, I'm okay. You?"

"I'll be better now I have you both back," she said, her face wrinkling as she smiled. It felt like I hadn't seen her in years. "Sami . . ." She fixed her eyes on mine, and then quickly focused on her shoes. "You're just a child, and you might have felt ignored because we've focused on Sara all this time. . . . I'm sorry. We had to do this, but we didn't know it would be *this* hard, habibi. One day, God willing, we'll forget everything we've been through."

"God willing, Mama," I said, holding back tears. I didn't want her to see how her telling me I was just a child made me feel even more miserable about what we'd been through. I bent down and picked Sara up to change the subject. "Hey, you! What have *you* been up to?" I asked her.

She put her arms around me and snuggled her face into my neck.

"You still not talking to me?" I asked.

She shook her head in my neck.

Oh, Sara! I thought. How could I help her? She was so small and light, it felt as if I had a doll on my shoulder. I never thought I'd be this happy to see her. It was great that she let me pick her up.

Still holding Sara, I sat down next to Mama and took her hand. I hadn't been able to be there for them both—and now I didn't know how to be. I knew I shouldn't show how the past few weeks had affected me, for their sake. We didn't speak but listened as a plane took off from the nearby runway. I looked up, as if I'd be able to see it through the ceiling. *We're almost out of here,* I thought. *Everything will be okay now.*

"Right, Sami and Zeina, can you please come and sign these release forms?" said the receptionist, looking at us from above her glasses.

Mama stood up. I put Sara on the floor and held her hand as we walked to the front desk, my heart thumping. This was it. We would be free again. I was going to walk out onto the streets of Manchester for the first time.

Chapter 23

*A*s *our taxi pulled* up outside Uncle Muhammad's house, he ran outside to greet us in his flip-flops. He'd been expecting us. His wife stood behind him in the white plastic-framed porch door, her face expressionless, like that emoji with a straight line for a mouth.

"Ah, brother, you are here. Come, come in," said Uncle Muhammad, his smile stretching from ear to ear, his plump arms wide open to hug Baba.

We all followed him past an old black Mercedes parked in the driveway and into the tiny porch, taking off our shoes before entering the narrow hallway. I was surprised a house in England could be so small. I thought everything would be grander here. I'd been longing to have my own space since we'd left our duplex apartment and had imagined a spare room all to myself, but I quickly saw it wouldn't be like that at all.

He introduced us to Aunty Fatimah, who gestured us into the compact front room, where the scent of vanilla air freshener filled the air. We sat down on the cream leather sofas, next to a thin, dark-haired teenage boy sat on a reclining chair in the corner, watching TV. All he said was "Salaam," not even looking away from his show. His younger sister, probably about ten or eleven, sat cross-legged on the floor near the fireplace.

"This is Hassan and Iman, our children," Aunty Fatimah said, looking down at the floor. Iman glanced at Sara on Mama's lap and smiled, then got up and left the room.

"Would you like some tea?" Aunty Fatimah asked in English. Weird. Why wasn't she looking at us? Did everyone in England behave like this? And why were her kids at home on a Sunday? Shouldn't they be at school?

Iman returned and handed Sara a brown teddy bear with a red-checked bowtie. Sara grabbed it and hugged it tight without saying a word.

Mama smiled. "Thank you so much, Iman. That's very kind of you."

Baba nodded. "In fact, this is all very kind of you. May God reward you for your help. God willing, we won't be here too long. My immigration officer has already sent off my certificates to be verified. As soon as they're back, I'll be able to apply for work and get a place to live."

I sat squashed at the end of the sofa with my hands over my knees. I didn't know what to do in this strange house. It didn't feel like we were with family friends at all.

"Hassan, why don't you show Sami the bathroom and their bedroom?" said Uncle Muhammad, who then turned to me. "Put your jacket away—maybe play a game or two on the PlayStation?"

"I've packed that away," Hassan snapped. "Had to make space, didn't I?" He stood up and stopped at the door, staring at me for a second before walking out of the room. I guessed that meant I was supposed to follow him.

The upstairs landing was even smaller than the hallway downstairs, with four doors leading off it.

"That's the bathroom," Hassan said, pushing open the first door on the left as we walked past it. He pointed at the room next to the bathroom. "That's my mum and dad's room—don't go in there." He pointed to the furthest door on the right. "And stay out of that one too." He looked at me sideways then stepped through the third door on the landing. "This is my room, but you lot have got it. You better not mess it up."

Inside, there was a double bed in the middle and a single mattress on the floor underneath the window.

"Don't you dare touch my stuff." He walked back out of the room, knocking his shoulder against mine and making me jerk back.

I stood in the middle of the room, unsure what to do or think. I sat on the edge of the double bed. There were two Manchester United posters on the wall opposite. Maybe we'd be able to talk about football, like I'd done with Aadam. But Hassan was clearly annoyed he'd had to give up his room. He wasn't even pretending to hide it. I could tell we weren't going to be friends.

I walked to the window and stood on the mattress to look out. The sky was low and gray. In Damascus it had always felt so high above us. It was a quiet street, lined with many houses—all identical, with one side attached to the house next to it, and the other side to a garage. Everyone had one or two cars parked in their neat, pretty driveways. Some of the cars were still lightly dusted with frost. All of the houses were whole—nothing had been shelled. A plane flew over the rooftops in the distance, pretty low. The airport couldn't have been too far away.

I looked around the room and opened the double wardrobe. Inside were a lot of sweaters and jeans—Hassan's clothes. The red of a Manchester United kit jumped out at me. I rubbed the top between my fingers. If it had been Joseph's, I'd have borrowed it. But Hassan would probably go mad if I did that. Then again, I supposed I would've been the same, if some random family turned up at my house and took over my bedroom. Although that would never have happened in Damascus, because we had a guest bedroom. Here, every room was already being used.

I walked out of the room and into the bathroom. It had a shower, a separate bathtub, a toilet, and a sink. I took my jacket off, draped it over the banister in the hallway, and went back into the bathroom, dropping my jeans and sitting on the toilet seat.

When I'd finished, I looked around. All I could

see to wash with was a plastic measuring jug, like the one Mama had in our kitchen. In Syria and Turkey, there was a water pipe in every toilet. It seemed a bit strange that the UK didn't have those yet. I'd thought the detention center only had toilet paper and nothing to wash with because it was a prison and they wanted to punish us by leaving us dirty.

I reached over to the sink, filled the jug with water and washed myself. I tried to see out to the yard but the window was made of frosted glass.

As I left the bathroom, I bumped into a stony-faced Aunty Fatimah on the landing.

"Don't leave your things lying around. Put your jacket in the bedroom. Hassan's cleared the hooks on the door especially. Then come down to eat." She didn't look at me once, her eyes focused on the stairs—as if I was too disgusting to look at.

Everyone except Hassan was sitting in the small back room—the dining room. The dining table was covered with a white plastic tablecloth, and white plates were set out on red rubber placemats. The walls were covered in extreme flowery peach wallpaper that made my head hurt.

At the end of the table, Uncle Muhammad and Baba were engaged in deep conversation about the war in Syria. Beside Baba sat Mama and then Sara, hugging her new teddy for dear life. I pulled out the chair next to her and asked, "What you gonna call it?"

She looked at me and hugged it even tighter.

"Come on, let's think of a name."

She leaned into Mama, away from me. I sat back in my chair. She still didn't want to talk. Even now that we were all together in England, finally safe. I assumed she'd be okay here. Maybe she just couldn't talk anymore. *What if she's lost her ability to talk forever and it's all my fault?* I thought, hating what I'd done to her.

Aunty Fatimah and Iman came in, carrying dishes full of rice, tabbouleh, kibbeh, baba ghanoush, pita bread, and spinach pastries. The smell of onions, parsley, and ground beef mixed with the smell of cinnamon and cloves wafted up my nose, just like at home. I wondered if I was actually drooling as I pushed my hands under the table to stop myself from grabbing a golden flaky pastry.

As we ate, Baba and Uncle Muhammad were the only ones who talked. Aunty Fatimah sat next to Uncle Muhammad, not looking up once. I noticed Iman glance at me a couple of times, but that was it. I ate the kibbeh and pies with my hands, while she, like Aunty Fatimah, used a fork. Maybe she thought we were uncivilized. I didn't care; I wanted to enjoy my first proper hot meal in months. I wanted to feel and touch every part of it with my fingers and my mouth and remember the meals we used to eat together at home.

After we'd all finished, Mama handed Sara to Baba and helped Aunty Fatimah clear the table. She asked me to go to the front room. I didn't want to go alone, but I felt like a spare part as it was. At least I could stare at the TV.

I walked into the front room, stiffening when I saw Hassan sitting in the same position as before, watching a show called *Coronation Street*. I sat down on the sofa quietly. The people in the show spoke with an unusual English accent. They sounded like some of the guards in the detention center.

I glanced over at Hassan. His eyes were fixed on the TV, his face set in a scowl. *Ask him,* I told myself.

You've got nothing to lose. I bit my lip, took a breath and said, "Hassan—do you have a computer or a laptop?"

"Yeah, why? You want to take that as well d'you?" He didn't tear his eyes from the TV.

"I just wanted to use it to email someone." I had to tell Aadam and Joseph that I was safe. I'd forgotten my letters to Joseph in the detention center—we'd left in such a rush. And I wanted to find out where Aadam was and if he was okay. I had to keep my promise to him. Had he even left Turkey yet?

Now Hassan finally turned to me and glared, raising his eyebrows. "What? You know how to use email?!"

"Doesn't everyone?" I scrunched my face so hard, I almost saw *my* eyebrows.

He didn't reply, just turned away and continued to watch the show, his forehead furrowed. He seemed so angry. I should've just asked his dad, but there never seemed a chance to speak to him. At least he was welcoming and warm—nothing like his son.

The sooner we get out of here the better, I thought to myself, laying my head back on the sofa.

Chapter 24

*T*hat night, *Uncle Muhammad* took us to the mosque for the evening prayer. As we entered the large tiled reception area, he stopped every few seconds to shake hands with people, while Hassan walked off ahead of us.

"I'm a mosque trustee. That's why they all know me," Uncle Muhammad explained to Baba, putting his shoes in the wooden pigeonhole unit. "I'll introduce you to the other doctors here."

The main prayer hall had a domed roof with Quranic Arabic painted around it and a massive chandelier hanging from its center. The rhythmic call to prayer echoed around the building, making me stop and absorb every word. I stood on the green geometrically patterned carpet and took a satisfied breath. A sense of peace settled in my stomach—the first time in months. I felt as if God was welcoming me.

I hadn't expected such a big mosque in England; I thought there would only be huge churches and tiny mosques. But then I remembered the many big, beautiful churches in Syria. When Joseph stayed over at weekends, we'd drop him at his church while we prayed at our mosque next door. *What will be left of them all now?* I wondered.

After the prayer, as we climbed back into the car, Baba looked at me and smiled. "You okay, Sami? We'll call Tete as soon as we get back. It's two hours ahead, so Tete should definitely be home if she's been out."

There would be a lot of tears. I knew it. I wasn't looking forward to speaking to her because she wouldn't be able to speak for crying. But she was my only link to Syria, and maybe she'd know if Joseph was okay. Maybe we could give Uncle Muhammad's number to Tete to pass on to him. *That would be perfect,* I thought as we flitted past rows of red-brick houses, standing firm under the streetlights.

"I'll be at work from tomorrow, Tarek, but please feel welcome and treat the house like your own," Uncle Muhammad said to Baba.

Uhh, like that's going to be possible with Hassan and Aunty Fatimah around, I thought. Had he even noticed how rude they were?

"And don't forget to pop into my friend Siddique's factory around eleven o'clock. I've spoken to him—he's expecting you."

"Oh, good. Shukran," Baba smiled.

A factory? Why would Baba be going to a factory?

"Sami, we also need to get you enrolled into secondary school," Uncle Muhammad continued. "What year are you in?"

"Uh, I-I-I'm in grade eight," I stuttered, stunned by the idea of going to school so soon. I wasn't sure I wanted to go to one in England at all. I wasn't even sure I wanted to live here.

"What is that? Like year nine here?"

"He is thirteen, akhi," said Baba.

"That's year eight then," said Hassan, rolling his eyes.

"Ah, so you are only one year younger than my Hassan. Well, I'm not sure if you will get into his school, but we will certainly try." He held my gaze in the rearview mirror. "Then Hassan can look out for you."

If Uncle Muhammad hadn't still been looking at

me, I would've pulled a face. Hassan didn't seem like the kind of kid who would look out for anyone, let alone me.

When we got back to the house, Uncle Muhammad handed a slim, black cordless phone to Baba. "Take it upstairs and call your mama. Give her my salaams and tell her I'm happy to be helping. We'll sort out a SIM card for your mobile tomorrow, to get it working. I'll ask Hassan to look at some deals tonight. . . . Oh! And"—he rummaged around in his tweed blazer pockets—"here's the card for that psychologist my friend used for his son—she's the best. Ask the doctor to do an urgent referral to her waiting list when you go to register at the practice."

"Thank you, akhi. Bless you."

I went up to our bedroom while Baba continued talking to Uncle Muhammad. Mama was sitting on a prayer mat, wearing a brown scarf I hadn't seen before. Aunty Fatimah must have given it to her. The next thing I noticed was that the mattress on the floor now had a pink Cinderella duvet and pillow.

"Is that for Sara? Where am I sleeping?" I asked Mama.

"No, that's your bed. Sara will sleep with us in this

one," she said, pointing to the double bed, where Sara was asleep between the two pillows.

Great. I thought. *If it wasn't humiliating enough to have to take Hassan's room, now I have to sleep in his sister's bedding.*

I took off my jacket and hung it on the door hook.

"Go and have a shower. There's a towel for you on the bed."

I grabbed it and started walking to the door.

"Take those pajamas with you too. Fatimah kindly gave you Hassan's old ones."

I felt my face burn. I didn't want to wear that nasty vomit's hand-me-downs. I wanted to chuck them in the garbage. But of course I had no choice. I couldn't complain. I had to take everything given to me gratefully.

I remembered packing my old clothes in a garbage bag for Baba to drop to a charity for poor children in Darayya. I was fine with someone else wearing my clothes, but now *I* was that someone else and that stung my insides.

Standing in Hassan's room and having to wear *his* things seemed like the biggest insult so far. Was it just me who was struggling? Mama and Baba were grateful and seemed a lot happier than they had been since we left Syria; even Sara was smiling again. Living in England just wasn't what I had expected it to be. We had no space and still had no lives of our own.

I clutched Hassan's old pajamas and the gray towel and went into the bathroom.

I stayed in the hot shower long after I needed to. There, I could imagine I was in my own shower at home. The steam transported me to Syria as water trickled down my head and over my face. Finally, I felt clean. I closed my eyes and imagined I was showering to get ready to go to the mall with Joseph.

A loud banging broke my thoughts.

Flustered, I turned the shower off and listened. Someone pounded on the door again.

"Sami, get out!" Hassan yelled. "I need to use the bathroom!"

My skin went clammy; the water trickling down my body felt cold. I climbed out and grabbed the towel.

"Give me a minute, please," I said, quickly rubbing myself dry.

"HURRY UP!" he shouted furiously.

I got dressed, grabbed my dirty clothes, and

opened the door. Hassan stood right outside it.

"You're such an idiot," he said, pushing past me into the bathroom.

"I was taking a *shower*," I said, looking back at him as I walked out. I never liked fighting but right then, I wished I could thump him and walk out of his stupid house.

Baba was on the bed, the phone to his ear. His eyes were red and full of tears. Mama looked as if she'd been crying too. She sat up in bed next to Sara, who was still asleep, her mouth wide.

"Ah, Sami, come. You need to speak to Tete. She was asking for you," whispered Mama. She ushered me to sit on the bed near her feet. I dumped my dirty clothes on the floor and sat down.

Baba finished his conversation and handed the phone to me. I put it slowly to my ear.

"As-salaamu alaikum, Tete—" I began but all I could hear was crying and sniffling and fast words that I couldn't quite make out.

"There's no point living now, habibi. . . . I miss you. . . . I have nothing left. I am all alone," she cried.

"Tete, we'll see you soon, don't cry—please." Her words made me feel hollow.

"I'll see you in heaven now, habibi. Heaven is our next meeting place . . ." She started sobbing loudly but then it was abruptly replaced with a long buzz on the line.

"Tete? Tete? Hello? Tete?" I took the phone from my ear, looked at it and then pressed it to my ear again. I sighed. She must've cut it off accidentally. I handed the phone to Baba, wishing we'd brought Tete with us. She was alone in Syria now, with no one to look after her. If she died, no one would find her for days. We wouldn't even be at her funeral. *I wish I'd told her that I loved her before we left. If only I could go back home. I should be there for her. I don't belong here anyway.*

Chapter 25

The next morning I'd been awake for about an hour. Everyone had gone downstairs, but I hadn't gotten out of bed because I couldn't face Aunty Fatimah and Hassan—when Hassan actually barged into the room. He looked around, grimacing, and opened his wardrobe doors.

I stayed still, unsure whether he'd seen I was awake.

"Stupid foreign idiots," he muttered under his breath. "Dunno why Dad had to say they could stay here. Bloody goody-two-shoes. Never thinks about us."

I closed my eyes tight. I definitely didn't want him to realize that I'd heard him.

He slammed the wardrobe doors shut and stomped out of the room, leaving the bedroom door wide open.

I wished Mama and Baba had heard him. They had no idea what he was like. They kept thanking him for giving up his room, which made me want to throw up.

I thought about what I was going to do that day. I needed to email Aadam and Joseph, but there was no point in asking Hassan again and his dad would be at work by now. I'd have to try Aunty Fatimah.

I got up off the mattress and stretched my arms, reminding me that I was wearing that vomit's clothes. I got out of them and threw them on the pink duvet, noticing a neat pile of freshly folded clothes on Hassan's tidy desk.

I drew the curtains to get more light into the room and saw a gray top that looked like mine. I pulled it out of the carefully arranged pile to check the label—it was. As I drew it over my waist, Mama walked in.

"Ah, Sami, you're awake. I washed our clothes last night—they're on the desk."

"Yeah, I know, I just found them. Thanks."

Mama looked at me as if she wanted to say something, opening her mouth to speak. Then she hesitated and walked back out of the room.

"Mama!" I called after her. "Shall I come down? Where's Sara and Baba?"

"Your baba's gone to meet the lawyer." She reappeared at the door. "He's trying to sort out the paperwork to get those police charges dropped. Then he's going to the factory to sort out his work."

Work in a factory? I thought. *A doctor, in a factory?* Tete would be horrified.

"I think he's going to try to sort out your school too," Mama continued.

"Oh, Mamaaaa . . ." I hunched my shoulders.

"You've missed far more than we would've liked, Sami. I think you'll agree it's time to get back into your studies."

"But . . . I—" I didn't want to go to school. Especially not here.

"But nothing, Sami. Come down and I'll make you some breakfast. Hurry up, because I need you to sit with Sara. Fatimah is taking me to a house to arrange some work after dropping Iman off." She walked out of the room quickly, before I could reply.

Work? Where was she going to work? In a house? I pulled on my jeans and followed Mama.

Downstairs, Sara was snuggled with Iman on the sofa, watching a TV show called *Balamory*.

Mama came in and handed me a bowl of cornflakes

and sat down on the sofa next to Sara, who had her eyes glued to the TV and didn't even notice. I crunched them loudly—I could finally eat without worrying about being attacked by weird men. I couldn't believe what I'd been through. It now felt as if Air Jordans guy had been in a nightmare—as if the attack hadn't really happened.

I knew we were a lot better off than when we were in the detention center. I told myself to remember that the next time Hassan said something nasty to me.

Aunty Fatimah walked into the room wearing a long, beige coat and matching scarf. "Sami, can you bring your bowl into the kitchen when you're done?" she said.

"Okay, Aunty."

Mama looked down, shifting her feet.

I finished off my cereal, slurped the leftover milk, and took the bowl to the kitchen. Aunty Fatimah sat at the breakfast bar, the washing machine rumbling quietly in the background.

"Sami, can I have a word?" She got up, took the bowl from me, and put it in the dishwasher.

My hands felt clammy, as if I'd been sent to the principal for being disruptive in class.

She walked back, towering over me, and looked me in the eyes. "This is my house and there are some rules you need to stick to," she said, her eyes narrowing.

I took a step back.

"*You* are not allowed to enter my room or Iman's. You understand?"

"Yes, Hassan told me yesterday—" I started. I wondered if Hassan had lied about me going into her room.

"You are to tidy up after yourself, including in the bathroom. I don't want to be wiping up after you." She leaned further in to my face. "Don't pester Hassan. He's a good boy, studying for his exams—he doesn't need distracting. Just know, I'm watching your every move."

Her fancy long coat and mean face reminded me of Cruella de Vil in *101 Dalmatians*. Ugh. Why was she being like this?

But I had her attention—I had to make the most of it. "Can I use your laptop please, Aunty? I need to send one email. I'll be very quick."

Her eyes narrowed more. "Have you heard a word of what I've just said?"

"Yes. It's just—"

"Well, what do you have to say about it?"

"Yes, I'll do all of that. I promise."

She sighed loudly.

"Can I please send one email? It's urgent."

"Who do you need to send it to? And why?"

"To my friend. I just need to let him know I'm okay. That I made it to Manchester. I promised I would."

"You can ask Hassan when he gets in from school."

There was no way Hassan would let me use his laptop. I thought quickly. "Um . . . Aunty, can't I just get it done now? You said I shouldn't distract him."

"Parasites," she muttered, walking out of the kitchen.

My mouth dropped open, stunned. Had she really just said that? I exhaled a long breath. Now I knew where Hassan got his attitude.

I wasn't expecting her to return, so I gasped when she stormed back in and thumped something silver down on the black granite breakfast bar. "Here. Just this once. Don't ask me again." She opened the lid of the MacBook and entered a password. "What account have you got?" she snapped.

"Gmail," I said quietly.

She got the website up and slid the laptop along

the counter to me. I typed in my login details and looked at her sideways, hoping she'd leave.

"Oh, I'm not leaving you with it, if that's what you're expecting!" She folded her arms and stood over me.

I didn't want to check my inbox with her looking, so I quickly pressed Compose at the top of the page and started typing.

I began writing to Aadam, trying to ignore Aunty's eyes piercing into the screen. She sat back on the bar stool, folded her arms, and scoffed when she saw me type:

How are you? Hope you made it to England safely.
Email me as soon as you get this. I need to know
you're safe. I'm hoping you'll come to Manchester. I'm
in an area called Stockport. I don't have a number yet,
but when I do, I'll email it to you. Sami ☺

As soon as I pressed Send, Aunty Fatimah snatched the laptop away and slammed it shut. I turned to her, my mouth hanging open.

"You've sent your email. Now *leave*," she said, baring her teeth.

I didn't dare ask her to let me email Joseph too, so I rushed out of the kitchen and closed the door behind me.

Chapter 26

Later that Monday, after Hassan got back from school, the phone rang as we sat watching a quiz show in the living room. Sara was drawing on an Etch a Sketch with Iman, the two of them nestled close together. Sara seemed to like her a lot and Iman was really good with her.

Hassan picked up the phone. He stared at the TV, his brow furrowed.

"Yeah, I'm going in a bit. . . . But Dad! I can't take him to football! He can't just join the team!" He paused then tutted and clenched his jaw. "All right! He can watch. But *that's* it—he ain't playing."

Hassan continued to listen for a few seconds then put the phone down.

I didn't want to play football with him and I

didn't want to watch, but I couldn't be rude to Uncle Muhammad. I knew he was just being kind.

As soon as we'd left the front drive, Hassan said, "I ain't goin' nowhere with you, parasite," and walked off ahead of me. "You better be at the top of the street in an hour!" he shouted back.

I stopped and shook my head. He was the nastiest kid I'd ever met. We wouldn't dare treat a guest like this in Syria. All I wanted right then was to be with Joseph, around my people. I left him when I said I wouldn't. I said I'd always stick up for him. I *had* to go back home. Where I was needed. Where I belonged. I didn't want to be in horrid England anymore.

I waited for Hassan to get to the end of the street and then walked in the opposite direction, toward the main road, soon reaching a small park with a play area. I pushed open the gate and sat on the swings. The younger kids around me kept looking over as if I was a loser. Which I was, I supposed. I'd lost everything. I had no friends, no house, no bedroom, nothing.

I sat with my hands in my pockets on the park swing, barely swaying, just staring up at the sky above. The sun was setting and the sky flamed in pinks, oranges, and yellow. Every ten minutes a plane flew through its colors.

A couple of older-looking boys strode into the park. I didn't want any trouble so I got off the swing and walked to the exit, my head hung low, my hands shoved even deeper in my jacket pockets.

I almost walked past the library on the main road but stopped when I realized they might have computers. I wouldn't have to ask anyone again and I could email Joseph in peace. I walked in through the automatic barrier and stopped in front of the blonde-haired lady sitting behind a computer. The smell of books hugged me in the quiet, calm library. A few people inside browsed books and read at tables.

"Uh . . . hi . . . can I use a computer, please?" I asked in my best English accent.

"Have you booked?" she asked, standing up to face me and straightening her bright-purple cardigan.

"Uh . . . no . . ." I didn't know I had to book an appointment or even how to.

"If you give me your library card, I'll book you in for a slot. Because we're quiet, you can use one now."

"I don't have a library card," I said, rubbing Jiddo's ring.

"Do you want to set one up?" she asked, sighing. "I'll need proof of your address. Have you got anything with you?"

I shook my head briefly. There was no way I could get proof of where we lived. I panicked, turned around, and walked back through the barrier, pulling it inward so I could leave.

I ran out of the building and back along the road. Traffic shot past me. Where would I go now? I couldn't use the computers without a proper home—and I couldn't go back to the house because I was meant to be with Hassan at football.

I walked past a convenience store, and a football magazine in the window caught my eye. I wished I could just walk in and buy it like I used to in Damascus, but I had no money. I felt empty inside. The shop assistant frowned at me through the window. I couldn't remember anyone smiling at me here, apart from Uncle Muhammad. It was so different from Syria, where everyone was so welcoming. This place was nothing like I thought it would be. Everything sucked here. Life was much better back home. I gulped some air and continued to walk down the road.

I sat on a plastic bench at a bus stop and looked at the giant oak tree that stood tall next to it, its thick roots pushing through the cracked pavement below.

An old man sitting next to me was reading a newspaper, waiting for his bus. He looked as if he knew what he was doing, where he was going. Everyone else in England did. Except me.

Sitting watching the cars and trucks whoosh past, I thought about how much I wanted to go back to Syria. I *needed* to go back to Tete and Joseph. Manchester wasn't the place for me, I knew it already. *Damascus must be safe again,* I thought. *The government must've fought off the rebels by now.* Joseph always said they'd never let the rebels take over Damascus.

There was a construction site across the road surrounded by steel fencing. It looked as if a building had been demolished between two others, leaving a wide gap ready to be filled. Men in yellow hard hats worked on the ground, with one on a digger, piling earth on a mound in the corner. Another poured powder into the cement mixer, while another builder had begun to lay big gray bricks to form the foundation of the building.

I thought back to the demolished places in Syria.

This is what I can do when I get back, I thought. *I can help rebuild it!* Baba would be disappointed if I didn't become a doctor, but I could be a builder or an engineer instead, and that was important too. I'd known deep down that I didn't want to become a doctor, but I never dared to tell Baba. Going to the hospital to see Mama and Sara had confirmed that it wasn't for me. I had to be mature like Baba wanted me to be—and make my own decisions. I could help rebuild Syria so that everyone who wanted to could go home again. I felt lighter just thinking about it.

A bus screeched and stopped at the sidewalk. The old man put his newspaper on the bench and got on the bus. With no one else around, I picked it up. I wanted to see if I could still read English. As soon as I started reading, a part of me wished I couldn't.

The headline on the front page read:

BRITAIN TO BAN MIGRANTS

I gulped and quickly turned the page to look for the sports section. I didn't want to read a sentence of that article. But midway through the paper, I came across another headline that made me stop.

STOWAWAY SURVIVES 11-HOUR JOURNEY FROM SOUTH AFRICA

As I read the description of the man who'd stowed away in the hold of a plane, my mouth fell open. I could do this. I could get away from Hassan and miserable England and go back home. I wouldn't need to ask Baba to give me any money or stress him out anymore. The airport was really close—all I needed to do was figure out how to get on a plane without being caught.

The article explained that one man had fallen and died as the plane landed, because he'd hidden in the wheel arches of the plane. But the other had survived because he'd been in the luggage hold. So all I needed to do was get to the airport and watch how they loaded the luggage to see how I could get inside. I didn't know how to get to the airport, but I'd work it out. I had to. I had to get back to Syria. Mama and Baba could fix Sara over here. And I could be there for Tete and Joseph. Tete couldn't die all alone. She sounded so scared on the phone.

I looked at my Swatch—over an hour had passed. I put the newspaper down and walked back to the end of the road to meet Hassan. He was already there waiting.

"Idiot," he sneered before jogging off toward his house. I walked behind him, dragging my legs wearily.

When I walked into the house, I found Baba, grinning from ear to ear, in the hallway.

"Here's your new uniform." He waved a gray sweater and a white shirt around. "You start on Wednesday at Hassan's school. I just got the call!"

I walked up the stairs, my head down. I could feel Baba's smile fade as he stepped up behind me.

"Sami, what is this? You know how much this uniform cost? I'm going to have to do overtime at the factory for three days to pay for it."

"I didn't ask you to."

"Stop that, now!" he shouted as we walked into the bedroom. He sighed and sat down next to me on the double bed. "You think I wanted to take you out of your old school?" he asked, folding up the uniform on his lap.

"No . . ."

"Do you know how it feels to work in a factory, lifting boxes in and out of trucks all day, when all you ever held before was a pen or scalpel? You have *no* idea."

Baba looked exhausted, his body thin.

I dipped my chin into my chest and slumped. "I know . . . I didn't mean it like that. I'm just . . . upset. I really hate it here," I admitted, staring at my nails. They needed cutting.

"I know you do. It's not easy for us either, believe me . . . but we have no choice right now." He got up to walk to the window. "I'm grateful that we aren't out on the streets or in a refugee camp."

I glanced at the uniform and a thought struck me. "They'll have computers in school, won't they?"

Baba shook his head. "What is it with you and computers? You're going to learn, not mess about."

"I want to email Joseph," I explained. "But Aunty Fatimah doesn't like me using her laptop."

"Oh, why didn't you say? You can use my phone. Muhammad gave me the wi-fi code. Here." He took the phone out of his pocket.

Why hadn't I thought of that? Baba didn't have a SIM to make calls, but I'd completely forgotten he could still use it with wi-fi. If I was going to be an engineer, I'd have to smarten up.

He typed in his password, opened up a browser window, and handed me the phone. He left his hand on mine for a few seconds. "It will get better, son, I promise," he said with a smile.

I smiled back. It was a moment we hadn't had for so long.

Baba eased himself off the bed as I logged into my email. I scanned my inbox and counted three unread emails from Joseph.

I bounced on the bed like a little kid. "He's emailed me! He's emailed, Baba!"

Baba nodded. "I'll leave you to read them. Put it on to charge when you're done and don't you dare go on any other websites. Okay?"

"Yesss, Baba," I said without looking up.

He closed the bedroom door as I scrolled down to find the first email Joseph had sent.

SAMI WHERE ARE YOU?!!

WHEN YOU COMING BACK TO SCHOOL? WHY AREN'T YOU ANSWERING YOUR PHONE? YOUR MAMA STILL GOT THE IPAD? YOU MUST BE SOOO BORED.

That boy always pressed caps lock on his keyboard. Always. I checked the date—it had been sent a day after we left Syria.

I skipped to the next email from him:

OKAY. I KNOW YOU LEFT IN A RUSH. YOUR TETE TOLD
MAMA THE OTHER DAY. SHE SAID YOUR BABA DIDN'T
WANT ANYONE TO KNOW SO YOU COULD GET OUT
QUICKLY AND SAFELY.
MY BABA IS THINKING TO DO THE SAME. I HEARD HIM
AND MAMA TALKING ABOUT IT. I'M SCARED. HOW ARE
YOU MAN?
I HOPE YOU CHECK YOUR EMAILS SOON AND REPLY
BACK.

A stab of guilt went through me, but the next
email made me feel *much* worse.

SAMI, WHY AREN'T YOU WRITING BACK??????

ARE YOU OKAY?! PLEASE REPLY!

WE'RE ALWAYS HEARING EXPLOSIONS AND GUNFIRE
NOW. I THINK BABA WILL DEFINITELY MAKE US LEAVE
SOON. WHERE ARE YOU?!!

WE MET YOUR TETE AS SHE WAS COMING OUT OF
THE MOSQUE ON OUR WAY TO CHURCH. SHE SAID
SHE DIDN'T KNOW WHERE YOU ARE AND SHE HASN'T

HEARD FROM YOU. SHE WAS CRYING A LOT. SHE
LOOKED SO SAD. I'M REALLY WORRIED, SAMI.

I MISS YOU MAN. WE SHOULD BE DOING THIS
TOGETHER. PLEASE PLEASE WRITE BACK. TELL ME
YOU'RE ALIVE. PLEASE.

JOSEPH ☹

My eyes welled up and my heart ached. He'd had
to go through all of that, not knowing if I was even
okay, yet he still kept trying to contact me. I *had* to see
him.

I started to type, telling him everything we'd been
through, how hard it'd been, and how much I missed
him. I said sorry for not emailing before and explained
the reasons why, but I felt so guilty. I told him that I'd
thought of us playing football together when things
had been really bad and that I couldn't wait to see his
chubby face again.

I pressed Send, then checked the date of his last
email—almost two months ago. Why hadn't he
written again? Had he left? Or given up on me? I hoped
more than anything that he was okay.

I scrolled all the way through my inbox again but there was no email from Aadam. Had he made it out of Turkey safely? Had he got my first email? I emailed him again to give him our full address in Stockport and to let him know I was thinking of him.

As I pressed Send the door flung open and Hassan barged into the room. "Get off my bed," he sneered as he opened his wardrobe door and began rifling through it. I wasn't going to let him talk to me like I was a piece of dirt. I'd had enough.

"Make me," I replied, logging out of my email account and sliding Baba's phone into my jeans pocket.

"Don't make me laugh. I'd have you on the floor in a second."

"Try it then." I stood up.

Hassan closed the wardrobe door and strode over to me, squaring up his shoulders and bringing his face close to mine. "GO BACK TO WHERE YOU CAME FROM!"

I recoiled as his spit spluttered into my face. He pushed his fist into my left shoulder and I fell to the bed, then he turned around and walked out, slamming the door behind him.

I lay on the bed and thought of my plan. I had to

get away from here. From him. *I am going back to where I came from,* I thought, *don't you worry.* I wanted to get as far away from him as I possibly could.

Chapter 27

A gigantic wave came crashing over us, forcing Sara from Mama's lap. She went flying over the edge of the boat and I leaped up, pushing Mama and the old lady apart to dive in after her. I struggled to move in the freezing cold water. I couldn't see anything at first, let alone Sara. I searched the water around me as I heard Mama wailing and Baba shouting.

Sara's face appeared beneath the surface right in front of me. She kicked and waved her arms, gasping for air. I grabbed her head and pulled her toward me, looking around frantically for our boat.

I could just make it out in the distance. Putting my left arm over Sara's chest, trying to keep her afloat, I swam back to the boat. I was swimming forever, but finally I saw Baba hanging over the edge, shouting,

"SAMI! OVER HERE! SWIM, SON, SWIM!"

Flicking my wet hair from my face, I made my way to his voice. As we approached, Baba grabbed Sara and pulled her into the boat. A man beside him helped me climb back in and soon I stood dripping all over Mama.

Baba gave Sara the kiss of life on the floor of the boat. Mama rubbed my legs to warm me up, but I couldn't stop shivering. I couldn't believe I'd just done that. I'd jumped into the one thing I hated most in the entire world. As Sara began breathing, Baba grabbed me by the shoulders and said, "Sami, you've made me a very proud man today. Thank you."

A loud bang woke me up. I looked around, listening for the sound again. At least the nightmare was getting better. At least we'd all survived. There was nothing but silence now. Maybe Hassan had left for school. I slid out from under my duvet and headed downstairs, my stomach grumbling.

As I walked down the last two steps, I heard an odd sound—someone crying. I stood still in the hallway to listen to where it was coming from.

The TV blared in the front room, the extractor fan whirred in the kitchen. The smell of rice cooking swam up my nostrils. Was the crying coming from the dining room? Was it Sara? Even though she still wasn't talking, she'd been so much happier recently, so what had happened?

I opened the door and froze. Mama sat at the dining table, sobbing. She looked down at her hands, laid out in front of her. I stepped forward and saw they were raw and red with deep cuts all over her fingers. The cuts on her middle finger were bleeding.

"Mama, what's wrong? What's happened?"

She jolted round, clearly startled to see me.

"I'm okay, Sami," she said as she wiped away her tears and pushed back the wooden chair to stand up.

I put my hand on her arm. "Mama, please. Tell me."

"I don't have anything to say, Sami."

"Why are your hands so sore? What happened to them?"

"Oh, it's from the cleaning I've been doing. A couple of the ladies told me to use bleach and strong chemicals without wearing gloves. They were so horrible . . ." She sniffed.

Mama had been cleaning? Then it hit me—of course she couldn't work at a school yet, just like Baba couldn't work as a doctor. I didn't know what to say, so I just put my arms around her shoulders and put my head to hers.

She put her hand on mine. I winced—it felt as rough as sandpaper.

"Have you shown Baba? He'll know how to fix them."

"I've not had a chance to talk to him since he left to see the lawyer yesterday morning. Anyway, he's so exhausted—I don't want to trouble him."

I thought of Baba having to work at the factory. "When will he be able to work as a doctor again? Do you know?"

Mama sighed. "It can take a long time for the government to check the paperwork. They can't just let anyone into their hospitals. Plus, he'll have to apply to register himself first and go through a long interview process." She slid my arms off her shoulders and got up.

I stepped back and let her leave the room, but seeing her wet, pink face made me want to scream. *How much longer are we going to be punished like this?* I wondered. *How much longer can we live like this?*

We'd lost everything we owned, and now my

parents were losing their self-respect. I couldn't see Mama cry like this anymore. I sprinted upstairs to grab my jacket from the bedroom door.

"I'm just going for a quick walk!" I shouted and left the house before Mama could stop me.

I walked to the shops that I'd passed on the main road when I was supposed to be watching Hassan play football. I passed the pharmacy and the butcher then stopped outside the convenience store's glass doors, pulling up my shoulders before stepping in. The shopkeeper glanced up from behind his newspaper, he eyed me head to toe, then went back to it. His white hair was gelled to the side, a contrast against his brown skin and almost purple lips.

I slowly walked up to the cluttered front counter, rubbing my finger over Jiddo's ring, and took a deep breath. "Hello, Sir, um . . ."

He eyed me again. "Can I help you, young man?" he said in an Indian accent.

"Um . . . Do you have any jobs I can do for you today?"

He smiled. "What are you looking for, hmm?"

"I don't know really. I just need something to earn some money to help my parents."

He looked concerned. "What's wrong with them?"

"Um, nothing really. They just need help with money right now."

"Look, I don't have anything at the moment. I've already got a paperboy."

"A paperboy? What does he do?"

He laughed. "Deliver the newspapers, of course!"

"Oh." I felt stupid.

"Leave me your telephone number and I'll contact you if anything small comes up, yah?"

"I don't have a telephone number."

"You don't have a house phone?"

"Um, yes . . . but I don't know it." And Aunty Fatimah definitely wouldn't be happy to give it to me.

"Tut, kids these days! If you don't know your own number, what good will you be at working, eh?" He snickered, shook his head, and started reading again.

I stood there for a few seconds, unsure what to say next. Finally, I managed, "Thank you for your time."

"Okay, boy. Bye."

I let my shoulders slump as I walked slowly back to the house, passing house after house with their pristine driveways, some with lawns, some with paving and some with black tar. *This place is destroying us.* I told myself. *How am I going to convince Baba to go back to Damascus? He'll never listen. But maybe if I go back first and am there with Tete, I could persuade them all to come back.*

As I walked up the drive, Sara waved at me. She had her nose pressed against the front room window— it looked so out of shape, I couldn't help but laugh. Mama rushed to the front door, flinging it open.

"Where did you go, Sami? You can't just walk out like that!"

"I just needed a walk. Don't worry about it—"

"Don't you talk to me like that!"

I ignored her and headed for the stairs. I couldn't tell her I went looking for a job to help her. She'd feel even worse.

"Sami, get back down here now! You've got to behave more maturely. What's wrong with you? You haven't even gotten properly dressed. Get in there and look after Sara!"

I was trying to be mature, just as I'd tried to be ever since leaving Syria, to make up for what I'd done, but it wasn't enough. *Nothing I do is enough. What's the point of me being here? I'll be more useful at home with Tete.*

I paused on the stairs, closed my eyes for a long second, and sighed deeply. "I'll just go and hang up my jacket," I said.

Chapter 28

*H*assan *was told to* take me out to play football again that evening. As we walked out the front door, passing his dad's Mercedes, he glanced back at me, his dark brown eyes narrowed.

"I want my room back. You better get out my house soon. Otherwise I'm gonna make your life hell at school."

I held back a step and let him walk away. I couldn't stand him, but there was nothing I could do while living in his house. Aunty Fatimah already thought I was a savage who'd lead her golden boy astray; I didn't want to do anything to prove her right. So I followed him halfway up the road, watched him turn the corner, then turned back around and headed toward the house. A plane flew overhead; I looked up as it rose steadily into the clouds.

Aunty Fatimah's tall, lanky body appeared in the porch window. "Why are you back? Where's Hassan? Is he okay?" she asked, in a panic.

"Yeah, he's fine, I just don't feel well enough to go to football today, so I came back."

She rolled her eyes and let me through the door.

I watched Baba playing "Teacher Teacher" with Sara on the beige carpet in the front room. Mama was out cleaning, no one else was there. After about ten minutes of watching Sara running around collecting papers and giving silent instructions with her hands, I spoke.

"Baba, can we go out?" I wondered if I could persuade him to go to the airport. I needed to check out the planes and work out how to get on one.

He looked me over. "I thought you weren't well?"

"I'm feeling better now."

"Hmmm . . ." He raised his eyebrows and carried on playing with Sara for a minute then added, "Do you know what? Let's go. We haven't done anything together for months."

"Years, more like!" I joked.

He gave me a look and stood up. "Come on, Sara—Baba will take you to the shops. You need some fresh air. Let's get you some treats." In that moment, he seemed so much more relaxed—like he used to be before the war.

"Can't we go to the airport?" I asked, keeping my face straight, trying not to look like I cared.

"The airport? What do you want to go there for? That place will bring back bad memories." He shuddered. "I'm surprised you said that. We only just left it!"

"The planes. We could watch them—it'll be fun."

Baba shook his head. "No, it wouldn't be good for Sara to go back there. Let's go get some chocolate. That'll be fun and a lot cheaper."

I followed him into the hallway, unable to think of another reason for him to take us. Chocolate was better than being stuck in this house, I decided as I chucked my jacket back on.

It was a cold day. The sun was setting in the fiery red sky. Traffic on the main road had come to a standstill, and people sat inside cafes, talking and drinking coffee.

Baba held Sara's hand, put his right arm around me, and smiled. He walked with his head high, asking us questions and pointing out different shops and buildings. Sara loved the pigeons, so we stopped to watch them on the sidewalk for a few minutes.

I smiled at Sara and at Baba. I realized we were *all* actually smiling for once. *They'll be fine without me here,* I decided. *Look at them.* Sara still wasn't talking but wasn't stuck to Mama as much and the spark had returned to her eyes. Her voice would come back too, as soon as Baba got her to that famous psychologist. I needed to go back for Tete. And to make sure Joseph was okay.

We passed the construction site I'd seen before. I thought about becoming an engineer again—Joseph too. He was great at science; we could both become engineers and help rebuild Syria once things calmed down.

It would all work out. Mama and Baba could come back in a few months, once Sara had recovered properly. I could help Tete while they fixed Sara. We'd all be doing something useful. My stomach fluttered thinking about it.

"Right, let's go and get a treat," said Baba, as he stepped into the same convenience store I'd been to that very morning. My chest tightened. I kept my head down, hoping the shopkeeper wouldn't see me with Baba and say something about me wanting a job. When I peeked behind the counter, I saw a woman with a small red dot on her forehead.

"Choose one thing you'd like, then!" said Baba, grinning as he counted the coins from his pocket. I picked up a KitKat, and Sara chose a colorful box of Nerds, some candy I'd never seen before. Holding the bright-red wrapper in my hands made me realize I hadn't had a KitKat in ages. I couldn't even remember how it tasted. I couldn't wait to smell the creamy milky chocolate.

We walked back, munching on our treats. I imagined my stomach grinning at tasting the sweet, crisp wafer after so long. But the happy moment evaporated as soon as we stepped onto Hassan's road, my stomach rocking. I didn't want to go back to that house. I *had* to think of a way to get to the airport and leave.

That night, after dinner, Baba let me check my emails on his phone, but there was nothing from Joseph or Aadam. It was my turn to worry about them.

I was about to return Baba's phone when I heard a commotion downstairs. Baba and Uncle were shouting, then I heard someone run up the stairs.

Baba burst into the room. "Sami! The criminal charges have been dropped!" He wore the biggest grin I'd seen on his face in a long time, his eyes swimming with relief.

"Huh?"

"I just opened this from Miss Patel—Muhammad forgot to give me it earlier!" he said, waving a letter around. "Her application to the Prosecution Service was successful! They accepted all our evidence—the government's agreed to drop the charges because our lives were in danger and we had no choice but to leave Syria."

"That's great!" I remembered David, the guard, telling me Miss Patel was trying to get the charges dropped.

"And because we've got somewhere to stay, Miss Patel's trying to get them to grant us refugee status quickly. Then I can start looking for work. Proper work . . . Oh, Sami!" He hugged me tight, grabbing my head and holding it to his shoulders. "Things will get better—we will be happy here," Baba added.

You will, I thought. *But I'm going back. I have to.*

Chapter 29

Wednesday came too fast. I woke up to Baba shaking my shoulder and whispering loudly, as if he were an actor on stage.

"Sami, come on. You've got school today. Wake up!"

I batted him away. "Ugh. I don't need to go school."

"Don't be stupid. Get up."

I groaned, lifted the pink duvet off my warm body, and put my feet on the floor. Sara was still asleep in bed, snoring as if she'd not slept for years, her hair spread wildly across the pillow.

"Sami! We haven't got long. Your uniform's on the bed. Get dressed and come downstairs. I've asked the boss for two hours off work to take you in. Come on! We have a meeting with the headteacher before the other children arrive."

I showered, dressed, and trudged downstairs, almost zombie-like. I wasn't used to waking up early anymore and having nightmare-filled sleep was tiring. But I was going to go to school for one reason alone—the computers. I could find out how to get to the airport and the flight times to Syria without anyone else knowing.

In the kitchen Mama handed me a black blazer with a yellow logo embroidered on it. "Here—it's one of Hassan's—he left it out for you."

"I don't need it—this sweater's fine." I pushed the blazer back to her. The kettle boiled, a burst of steam erupting from its spout.

"Sami, you have to wear a jacket—it's part of the uniform policy. Just put it on. And you're not wearing those dirty Nikes either. There's a pair of Hassan's school shoes in the porch for you to wear. You've got to look the part."

I hung my shoulders and frowned. I didn't want any more of that vomit Hassan's hand-me-downs, but I had no choice, so I took the blazer and put it on the breakfast bar, next to my bowl full of Crunchy Nut Cornflakes.

"Eat quickly!" Baba said as I poured milk over the

crisp flakes. "It'll take us twenty minutes to walk there and they're expecting us before eight." He glanced at the wall clock.

I took a deep breath and hunched over my cereal, trying to focus on the sweet peanut smell and not where we were going.

"You'll be fine. Don't worry," said Mama, stroking my back before handing Baba a mug of tea and leaving the kitchen.

Yeah, I'll be fine, I thought. *As always. No choice but to be fine.* I picked up the bowl to drink the leftover milk.

"Right, let's go. Get that on, Sami." Baba pointed at the blazer, hovering over me. "I've got to be at work before ten."

I tutted, grabbed the blazer, slid my arms into it, and followed Baba out of the kitchen door.

We walked in silence down the road, my hands in my pockets, while Baba tried to call Uncle Bashir, but his mobile wasn't connecting. "He must've changed it," he said, looking at me. But I only had school on my mind.

I wanted to tell Baba that I didn't want to go to Hassan's school, but I couldn't find the strength to say it to him. If Hassan was so nasty at home, he'd be ten times worse at school.

Baba was so happy I'd gotten into a school so quickly. He could tick me off his "settling into the UK list" now. *But I'm never going to settle here,* I thought. *Damascus is where I belong.*

We walked alongside the school grounds, eventually approaching the tall, black school gates with the huge yellow-brick building beyond. How many kids went here? It had to be thousands. It was a lot bigger than my school back home. I felt goosebumps cover my arms and folded them as we entered the main gate.

"It's pretty big, isn't it?" said Baba. "You'll be fine, Sami, you'll see."

"You don't know that for sure."

"Just walk with your head up high. You've got nothing to be ashamed of. You belong here as much as anyone else. You've memorized my new number, right?"

"Yeah."

"Okay, good. Remember, your baba's a doctor and I'll be serving these families soon." He patted my back and added, "Don't tell anyone I'm working in the factory."

"Why not?" I asked. Was he embarrassed?

"Because we're not allowed to be working here yet. Mama too—so don't mention her cleaning. It's just to help us get by until I can work legally. No one should find out—otherwise we'll get into trouble, okay?"

"Uhh . . . okay." I tipped my head to look at him. *At least he'll have one less person to feed when I'm gone.*

I looked down as we walked through the automatic double doors. It was warm inside, the heat rushing over us as we entered the reception area.

"Hello," said Baba, through a glass screen. "We are here to see Mrs. Greenwood."

"Oh, yes, are you Mr. al-Hafez?"

"Yes, I'm Dr. al-Hafez."

"Please take a seat and I'll get her for you."

There wasn't much to look at in the reception area, but in the larger hallway beyond it, I could see a giant painting and a trophy cabinet. I felt hot, so took off the blazer, folding it over my arm.

"Ah, hello! Mr. al-Hafez—Sami," said a redheaded woman in a skirt suit as she walked through the double doors. "I'm Mrs. Greenwood."

"Good morning," said Baba, getting up and firmly shaking her hand. I stared at the brown carpeted tiles. I didn't know what to do.

Mrs. Greenwood turned. "Just come through here."

We followed her through the doors into a pale-blue corridor with artwork displayed on the walls, then entered a large office with a big desk under a window. There were trophies and photos in a glass cabinet and rows of books on shelves. The room smelled of black coffee.

"Please take a seat." Mrs. Greenwood pointed to the black leather chairs opposite her desk, which was covered in sticky notes, pens, and pads of paper.

"Right, let's go through some basic details first." Her voice was hoarse. I wondered if she smoked. Lots of Tete's friends smoked shisha and they all had similar-sounding voices.

She asked Baba to check a pre-filled form. Over his shoulder, I saw it listed my name, address, date of birth, subjects I'd studied in Syria, medical history, and emergency details.

"So, what's your favorite subject, Sami?" the headteacher asked.

"Uh . . . science, Ma'am," I replied as a bird chirped outside.

"Oh, you don't have to call me Ma'am—we're not that posh over here! Mrs. Greenwood will do." She laughed and reclined in her high-backed chair, and I relaxed a little.

Maybe it'll be okay. I'll get through today, I told myself.

"Once your dad's checked the form and we've had a short chat, I'll show you around the school."

"Okay . . ."

"You'll be in year eight, Sami. It's an important year." She looked over at Baba and then back at me. "Now, I know you went to an English school and you were studying the baccalaureate?" She raised her eyebrows. "Well, it's a little different here. We'll do some assessments of your work so we can put you in the right groups in a week or so. . . . Don't worry, you'll have lots of support if you need it. Just ask if you're not sure about anything. We're here to help you."

I looked at the blazer on my lap and circled my thumbnail with my index finger, over and over again. What assessments would I have to do? I didn't even want to be here!

"Have you got your school blazer with you, Sami?" Mrs. Greenwood asked, glancing at Baba signing a form. "You need to wear it."

"Um, yeah . . ." I said, raising my hands to show it to her. "I was feeling hot."

"That's okay." She smiled. "Make sure you put it back on once the bell rings."

Baba handed back the form with the black pen. "Sami's a bright boy—he was doing very well in Syria. He wants to follow the sciences." He picked up his backpack off the floor and started unzipping it. "Here are his certificates of achievement," Baba said, pulling out pieces of paper.

So THAT'S *what he had in there!* I couldn't believe Baba had brought them all the way from Syria. I was glad there was finally some proof that I wasn't always a loser. Phew.

"Well, we have a triple science option here if he wants to go for that. But we will have to assess him ourselves first, Mr. al-Hafez." She leafed through the form slowly. "So you have a younger daughter who should be in primary reception?"

"Yes. We're waiting for her to be assessed by a psychologist before she is given a school place. She's stopped talking, you see." Baba pushed his hair off his forehead.

"Oh . . . I'm sorry to hear that." Mrs. Greenwood put the form down and rested her hands in her lap, looking at us.

"She was present when a bomb went off in a mall," Baba explained, "and she hasn't spoken since. . . . But we are seeing progress—she is clinging less to her mother recently and she is playing more independently."

"Well, that's good. Was Sami there when the bomb exploded?"

"No, he was at school, thank God. He didn't see a thing . . . though he has seen destruction in Syria." Baba leaned forward with his hands on his legs. "He witnessed a bad incident at the detention center here in Manchester, but he's dealing with it well." He looked at me and smiled. I was still circling my thumbnail with my finger. I couldn't stop.

"Have you made any friends since you got here, Sami?" Mrs. Greenwood asked.

"No," I said, hoping Baba wouldn't mention Hassan. He wasn't my friend.

"Well, that'll be one of the things that'll help most in getting you settled into school." Mrs. Greenwood smiled. "Someone you can talk to and turn to when you need help. The first week is always the hardest, but everything will seem simpler after that. It's a big school, and we usually give our new students who come from primary school two weeks to fully settle in and get used to the buildings, the timetable, the people, and so on. So don't be too harsh on yourself, especially as you are joining mid-year. . . ." She pushed her chair back. "Right, let's show you around, shall we?"

She put the form in her filing tray and stood up, straightening her skirt. We followed her as she turned left out of the office.

◉ ◉ ◉

The school was empty, which I was glad about. I didn't want it to be full of kids. She showed us the humanities rooms and then took us up a staircase to the music room and the English and maths departments.

The staff room was upstairs and next to it, a library. *Computers?* I wondered. I couldn't wait to go and use them. We then entered a newer building that housed all of the science labs, similar to what we'd had in Syria but with more stools around the longer benches and more gas valves.

She took us down some stairs into a bright area bordered by windows and showed us more classrooms and then the dinner hall, which stank of boiled vegetables. Next to that were the changing rooms and the sports hall. I was surprised there wasn't a swimming pool or a proper basketball court like we'd had in Damascus. I had assumed every school had those, especially in England.

Then she took us outside and showed us the outdoor classrooms that looked like they were made out of thick cardboard. *How come schools in England can't afford proper buildings?* I wondered.

Some children were beginning to arrive through the gates, some in groups of just girls, some just boys, and some a mix of both. It looked like an international school, with kids from all sorts of races and backgrounds. They laughed and shouted but looked over at me as they talked. I must've stood out because I was with the headteacher. I wanted to lock myself into an empty classroom and hide.

"Right, that's the school done," Mrs. Greenwood announced. "Let me take you to your form room and introduce you to your form tutor." She led us back up the light and airy stairs near the science labs and past an IT room, full of computers. *Brilliant,* I thought. *I can use these if the library doesn't have any.*

Mrs. Greenwood turned into another classroom. A tall, plump man with glasses stood at his desk at the front. His greasy brown hair was parted to the side.

"Ah, Mr. Williams, this is Sami al-Hafez. He starts today," said Mrs. Greenwood.

"Good morning, Sami! Do you want to take a seat somewhere?" Mr. Williams shook Baba's hand, and as I looked around the empty room, my head started to pulse. "We'll do our best to help Sami settle in, Mr. al-Hafez. Please feel free to call me if you'd like to meet up to discuss his progress—or anything else."

"Oh good . . . Yes, I will do. Thank you." Baba's eyes shone back at Mr. Williams.

"Right, the bell is about to go. Shall I show you out, Mr. al-Hafez?" Mrs. Greenwood walked to the door.

"Um . . . okay." Baba's brow wrinkled. "Sami, I will see you later. Walk back with Hassan. School finishes at 3:15 P.M.?" he asked, looking at Mrs. Greenwood.

Hassan? I scoffed in my head. *Unlikely. I'll just have to find my own way back.*

"Yes, that's right," Mrs. Greenwood said, opening the door. "We'll leave you in Mr. Williams's capable hands, Sami. He'll talk you through your timetable, give you a map, and introduce you to your teaching assistant. Bye for now."

Baba pursed his lips together, gave me the tiniest of smiles, and followed Mrs. Greenwood out of the door.

I sat on one of the plastic chairs and looked at the brown table, chipped at the corners. *God help me,* I thought to myself as the school bell rang loudly. I unfolded the blazer from my hand and slipped it back on.

Chapter 30

I kept my head down through form registration, only saying, "Here, Sir," like everyone else, when Mr. Williams said my name. No one bothered speaking to me, so I didn't know what any of the kids looked like—but the first face I did see in the corridor after registration was Hassan's. My mouth went dry, thinking he'd say something nasty, but thankfully he just ignored me and carried on talking with his friends. I had to avoid him somehow. It was bad enough seeing him at his house.

As I walked away from Hassan, a group of kids started pointing and burst out laughing. "You're in the wrong school, mate," yelled one. "You need to be at St. Wilfred's!" He bent over laughing as he pointed at the yellow logo on my blazer.

My stomach dropped to my feet. I looked at the logo on my chest and realized that Hassan had given me a blazer from his previous school, the nasty rat. His dad had mentioned he'd moved to this school in year eight. Everyone here wore black blazers with a *silver* logo.

I tore it off and shoved it in my backpack, my cheeks on fire.

I turned up late for history after losing sight of the teaching assistant who told me to follow her and not being able to figure out the map Mr. Williams had given me. Some of the boys at the back jeered when I walked in. They knew I was the new kid and everyone had seen me in that dumb blazer. I kept my head low and sat down at the front, where the teacher told me to—that suited me fine. Just like in Syria, that was where the nerdy and shy kids sat quietly, with their books already open.

Listening to the teacher talk about British history made me wish that I'd visited all the famous historic sites in Syria before we'd left. I should've spent more time in the Old City, exploring the markets and the Silk Road with Tete. When I got back, I'd make sure I took her there. We'd do exactly what she wanted to do. I wouldn't rush her through Souk al-Hamidiyeh, and I'd let her buy as many spices and olive soaps as she wanted. No moaning. Not anymore.

At break, I eventually managed to use the map to get to the library, but all the computers were being used.

"What you doing, new boy?" hissed a pupil as I walked out. "We heard the teachers talking about you. Go back to your terrorist country!" His friends all exploded with laughter. I walked past them quickly, my eyes fixed on the corridor ahead, pretending I hadn't heard. A backpack slammed to the floor beside me—it had missed, but only just.

The bell rang at the end of French, and everyone rushed out of class, running toward the lunch hall. But I was going back to the library.

Just my luck, all the computers were being used again, so this time I sat on one of the gray plastic chairs and waited, opening a book someone had left on the table in front of me to make it look like I was busy reading.

Mr. Williams walked in. He glanced at me and then leaned over the counter to ask the librarian something.

"You okay there, Sami?" he asked as he passed me again. "You should go outside and get some fresh air while you can."

"It's too cold outside, Sir." I wasn't lying, it was—especially without a blazer to wear.

"Cold? It's not cold!" he said as he walked out of the door.

A girl got up from a computer and tucked her chair in. I half-jogged over to grab her spot and immediately Googled "Manchester Airport flight times." I typed in "Damascus" in the Flight Departures search, but there was nothing. I looked through the list to find other cities, but nowhere in Syria was listed. I should have guessed. If there was a direct flight from Syria, Baba would've got us on one. I typed in "Beirut" because we'd flown from there to Turkey, but that wasn't there either. I just about stopped myself from slamming my hands on to the keyboard. *I have to get out of here. Why aren't there any flights?* I thought.

I'd have to go to Turkey. That was where we'd flown

to before getting into Europe. I went back to Google and searched for a map of Turkey. I memorized the five major cities, went back to the Manchester Airport website, and typed them in.

Finally! There was a flight from Terminal 1 to Antalya in the evening. The flight took four hours and forty minutes. *I can survive that in a luggage hold,* I told myself. I had to.

The bell rang, but I hadn't researched how to get to the airport yet. I should've checked that first. As much as I didn't want to, I'd have to come back to school tomorrow to find that out before I could get away.

"Sami, can you stay back for a quick word?" Mr. Williams asked at the end of afternoon registration. "I've asked Ali to help you settle in. He transferred here and knows what it's like to join mid-year. I've just spoken to him and he'll be sitting with you during registration from tomorrow morning. Okay?"

"I'm fine, sir." I didn't want to be singled out. It'd only give the kids another reason to pick on me.

"Yes, you are, but he's a good kid and you'll like

him. Give him a chance. Go on, off you go, you'll be late for science."

But I didn't want to make any friends. I didn't want to talk to anyone. I was fine by myself. No one cared that I was there, and I didn't care about them. It was easier this way. Then I wouldn't have any friends to lose when I left.

Not like last time.

Chapter 31

"Sami!" Mama shouted as I opened the porch door the next morning. "Here. You forgot your history trip money." She handed me the yellow signed slip and a ten-pound note. "Make sure you hand it in today—it says the payment deadline's tomorrow."

"Oh, yeah! Thanks, Mama," I said, crumpling both up and putting them in my pocket. Finally, a lucky break. Next week's War Museum trip meant I now had money to get to the airport, without even having to lie to get it. I felt bad for taking the money Mama had worked hard for, but this was best in the long run, I knew it.

Sara shuffled sleepily down the stairs, watching me and carrying a picture book.

"Oh, and don't worry about your blazer." Mama

briefly glanced at Sara, then whispered, "Your baba will call your headteacher and explain it'll take a while to buy the proper one."

"I can't believe Hassan did that to me. I hate him," I said, pulling on my shoes, my face feeling redder.

She cleared her throat and turned round to see if anyone had heard as I opened the front door.

When I got to my form room, a thin boy with curly, jet-black hair shaved around the sides called over to me, "Sami, sit here. I'm Ali."

I slid into the chair next to him. He didn't say anything else, so I didn't either. I didn't look at him, just down at the graffiti on the table.

Mr. Williams came in wearing a bright-pink shirt that popped open at his belly button. "Ah, I see you've met. Good." He sat down at the front with a smile, looking smug.

Ali didn't say a word throughout registration, but as we stood up to go to first lesson he said, "Follow me to English. We're in the same class."

We walked down the corridor, Ali slightly ahead,

as if he was trying to look like he wasn't with me.

When we got to English, he traipsed to the back of the class to sit with his friends, while I stayed at the front, where I belonged, and sat down. Near the exit.

The way the teachers taught was different in each class. Yesterday, the history teacher was relaxed and joked around with the class about the trip next week, but the biology teacher was really strict and organized, like in my old school. He had our work ready and we all just had to sit down and get on with it. I preferred that lesson, where no questions were asked—we didn't have to put our hands up and the teacher didn't pick on you.

In our English lesson, Mrs. Palfrey said we had to read *Animal Farm*. She asked who wanted to read aloud and two hands went up, both of them girls. But she asked Tom at the back to read first. When he'd finished, Mrs. Palfrey turned to me. "Sami, would you like to read next?" I felt my cheeks turn red and I looked down.

"Yeah, let's hear the foreign boy read," shouted a boy from the back of the room. "He can be the pig! Oink!" He snorted into laughter.

"Nathan!" Mrs. Palfrey said, her face growing

salmon pink. "You'll stay back at the end of lesson. I don't want to hear another word from you until then!" She turned to me again. "Sami?"

"Yeah, I'll read," I said. My heart began to beat as if it was going to run away from me.

I heard some gasps. They all thought I couldn't speak English. Well, I'd show them.

"Okay, Sami, you want to start at chapter two?"

"Okay . . ."

I took a deep breath and began. I read a whole paragraph, changing my voice when there were speech marks and trying to remember everything Miss Majida had taught us back in Damascus. She used to be an actress, so she always wanted us to read animatedly, but we didn't mind because we all wanted to show off our English skills and accents, imitating the English that she'd shown us on the TV. In England, no one seemed to want to read out loud in class. It was weird.

"Well done, Sami. That was great," said Mrs. Palfrey, looking at me through her oval glasses as she swept her straw-colored hair from her forehead. I could feel the arteries in my neck pulsating like they were going to explode, and my hands shook. I couldn't believe I'd done that.

Other kids read after me, and I began to relax. But I kept my eyes on the book, not daring to turn around to see who was in the class. I didn't want to know.

The bell rang. As I picked up my book to put it in my bag, Ali stopped at my table.

"You from America or something?"

"No."

"How come you got an American accent then?"

"I don't know." I didn't think I sounded American. Did I?

"Where you from then?"

I stood up and walked out of the room. I didn't want to answer his question—he'd only say something nasty.

"Oi, what's up?" Ali stepped beside me.

"Nothing. I just don't wanna talk about it."

He didn't say anything, but to my surprise, stayed with me and we walked to maths. We had a Mrs. Justin in this class. She reminded me of Aunty Noor, Uncle Bashir's wife, with her short, spiky blonde hair, business-like suit, and high heels. Aunty Noor taught at the university in Damascus and was a Christian. She used to take us to church at Christmas time when we were younger, before they moved to Aleppo.

I wondered how she was coping. She loved shopping and going for fancy lunches with her family. Tete had always frowned when we ate out and she saw the bill. She said we wasted too much money.

If I couldn't cope without a clean toilet in Turkey, Aunty Noor would be freaking out if she was in a camp somewhere. I could just imagine her face. Her nose would wrinkle when she saw anything dirty and her house was always spotlessly clean. She'd even spray air freshener in the bathroom immediately after someone walked out of it. What if they were already in the UK and we didn't even know and that's why Uncle Bashir had changed his number?

"So, where you from then?" Ali interrupted my thoughts, pulling out the chair next to me and sitting down.

"I thought you sat at the back. What about your friends? Won't they laugh at you for sitting with the new boy?" I said, looking down at the blue cover of my maths book.

"Nah, don't worry 'bout them. They're okay. I've told them I'm sitting with you."

I raised my eyebrows and turned to him. He smiled and then looked through his book. *He seems genuine,* I thought, and before I could change my mind, I said, "From Damascus. Syria."

"Whoa! No way!" His eyes sparkled and his grin stretched from ear to ear. "You seen any gun battles?"

I didn't know what to say. He clearly didn't understand what guns could do. Maybe he didn't watch the news.

"Right, everyone!" shouted Mrs. Justin, rubbing her hands together with a grin. "Today we are going to do some trigonometry!"

Everyone groaned out loud.

Ali looked at me and smirked. I smiled back and looked down.

I'd just washed my hands after I'd been to the toilet and was flicking them over the sink when I felt something hard hit me on my back.

I ducked, covering my head with my arms, then slowly turned. No one else was in the gray-tiled bathroom; water pipes gurgled in the wall.

Reaching round to touch my shoulder blade, I found egg slime dripping off my sweater onto the floor, broken eggshells splatted across the tiles. A sudden coldness hit my core. *Who did that?* I grabbed at the paper towel dispenser and began wiping the slime from my back.

An ugly laughter filled the toilets. I froze, mid-wipe. Nathan burst out of one of the stalls, his chest thrust out, his legs wide as he walked. He leered his way over to me and shouted, "All right, terrorist?" right in my ear. I pushed past him, but he yanked me by my shirt collar and pushed me onto a hand dryer.

"I know what you are. My dad's told me all about you and how evil you people are." He showed all his teeth as he spoke, his eyes cold and small.

"I dunno what you're talking about," I said, trying to kick him off me. His face was in mine, his hands fisted as he held my collar. I could feel my body tensing. *Punch him. Punch him, Sami. Do it.* I clenched my fists and growled.

The door flung open and Ali appeared. He stopped for a second, taking in the scene, and then shouted, "Oi! What the hell you doing, you turd?!" He pulled Nathan from behind, by his blazer, and threw him to the floor, just missing the sinks. I tried to catch my breath and loosened my collar.

Ali put his shoe on Nathan's stomach. "Don't touch him again," he said. "Otherwise, trust me, you're dead."

Ali nodded at the door, indicating I should get out. I looked at both of them, my hands trembling, let out a big breath, and then ran out of the toilets as fast as I could, not looking back, my body stiff and my knees buckling. I wanted to run out of school and get on the first plane to Syria. But I couldn't. I still didn't know how to get to the airport. I'd have to wait till lunchtime to go to the library. As usual, I had to just get through whatever was thrown at me. Even eggs. But I wouldn't have to for much longer.

◦ ◦ ◦

Skipping lunch yesterday hadn't been a good idea. I was starving by the time I got home, and if I was going to get on a plane today, I had to make sure I ate.

So I went to the lunch hall first, planning to eat quickly, then head to the library. As I sat down with my food, Ali came over to me. I glanced up at him and moved my tray to make space for him at the empty table. "Thanks . . . you know . . . for earlier," I said as I scooped some hot fries and beans into my mouth. The hall was buzzing with noise—cutlery clanking, kids talking loudly, trays slamming, and chairs scraping. I wasn't sure he'd heard me.

"S'right. He's a total idiot," he said, sitting down. "His dad's a right racist—used to give Aaron Lawrence a hard time when he lived near them."

I looked at him but carried on eating, saying nothing.

"Have you seen his house?" Ali asked, cutting through his cheese and onion pasty.

"Nah . . ."

"They're Britain First supporters. Got a massive flag hanging in front."

My face must've been blank. I didn't know why that was a bad thing.

"You know—the kind that don't like brown people or just anyone from abroad."

"Oh." I took a sip of my water. That explained a lot.

"So, what's Syria like then? Must've been well scary. You miss it?"

I nodded. The urge to tell someone about where I'd come from pushed the words from my throat.

"It's not all like what you see on the news, you know," I said, looking at him then back at my plate. "We're not dangerous or evil. We're educated, we go to schools, universities. We've got libraries and bookshops"—I noticed the serving counter—"coffee shops, restaurants, cinemas. We had lives, just the same as everyone in Manchester. Proper lives. These people who don't want us here . . . they should know that we don't want to be here either." I met Ali's eyes. "I'm going back," I told him, pushing my plate away and sitting back in my chair.

Ali was smiling at me, which was odd. "Come play football with us after," Ali said, nudging my arm with his elbow. "I'm just gonna go and see the boys." He picked up his tray and headed to his mates. I watched him walk away to the popular table. *That was me, once upon a time.*

After I'd eaten, I went outside to let Ali know I couldn't play because I had to send an email. I couldn't ignore him. I owed him that much.

Outside, everyone seemed to be laughing and

shouting, enjoying themselves—everyone except me. A gust of wind blew over me as I walked across the playground and a gold chocolate wrapper fluttered into my chest. *Even the wind thinks I'm only worth trash,* I thought.

"Come on! We're a player down," Ali called over, running up to me.

I traipsed behind him with my hands in my pockets, along the painted court markings on the tarmac and onto the field, wondering if I should join him. The grass was tinged with yellow and had patches of mud where it no longer grew. It needed sun but the sky was cloudy, a really pale gray, fading to white in the distance.

I watched Ali run back into the game and kick the ball toward the other side of the makeshift pitch, the goal marked by two piles of coats.

I stood on the sidelines for a few seconds, then turned to walk away. I didn't have the heart to play football or to explain myself to Ali. I didn't want to pretend I was okay, that I was a part of all of this. What was the point? I didn't belong—there was no point faking it.

"Hey!" Ali tapped me on my shoulder and walked

breathlessly with me back onto the tarmac. "What's up with you? Don't you play?"

"Do you know which bus goes to the airport?" I said, looking down. *Don't connect with him,* I told myself.

"Think it goes from Stockport bus station—that's where we got it once. Why? Where you off to?"

I shrugged.

"You're well weird," he said and ran off back toward the field.

Yeah, too weird for your perfect country. I thought. I looked up at the sky and asked God to make the next three hours fly by so I could get out of here.

But before lunchtime finished, I had work to do. I strode to the library, where one computer was free. I sat down and Googled "buses to Manchester Airport." Ali was right—there was a direct bus from Stockport bus station, the 199, which only took about twenty minutes to get there. I felt the ten-pound note in my pocket. I'd be out of here soon. I did a mental checklist—I already knew which flight to take from my previous search and the terminal it flew from, and now I knew which bus to take there, but I still needed to check out how the luggage was loaded before I got on the plane. I Googled how to find the best airside viewing platform at the airport and came across some aircraft-spotting blogs that gave a list of the best ones. Luckily, the best views were from Terminal 1. *It's time to leave,* I thought, as I sat back in the chair and sighed.

● ● ●

As soon as the last bell rang, I was out of school like a shot and ran to the bus stop. It was already packed with kids swearing, shouting, and pushing each other. I kept my head down and waited for the bus that went to Stockport bus station, taking deep breaths to try and control my breathing. *Just get to Terminal 1 and find the plane to Antalya,* I told myself.

Once I got to Turkey, I'd have to travel along the coast until I somehow got to the Syrian border. After that, I had no idea how I'd get to Damascus, but at least I'd be back in Syria. I'd figure it out.

I felt a tap on my shoulder and swung round. It was Ali. "What you doing here? I thought you lived that way . . . near me?" He pointed in the other direction.

"Um . . . yeah, I do. I just . . . um . . ."

"Come with us." He tilted his head toward his

friend Mark, who was kicking the wall behind. "We'll grab a burger and then play some footy, yeah?"

I shuffled my feet. How could I get out of this? Why was Ali even here?

Ali looked straight at me. "What Nathan said and did is just bull. Don't worry 'bout him. I can handle him. You got me now." He held out his fist for me to bump.

A bus had hissed to a halt, but I'd missed the sign to see where it was stopping. All the rowdy kids started pushing onto it.

I didn't know what to say. I fist-bumped Ali back slowly. *Is this a sign from God that I shouldn't leave today?* I thought. *Maybe the flight's been canceled? Maybe I should wait until tomorrow, to check the flight's on time before I leave?* At least the weekend in England started on Saturday and not a Friday, like in Syria.

"Come on!" Ali shouted, gripping my arm and dragging me out of the crowd.

Chapter 32

"Oi, Sami!" Ali shouted from the hall door at lunchtime the next day. "Come here!"

I walked toward him, putting my tray away as I went.

"Come play football with me and Mark."

"Um . . ."

"Come on, man!"

"We're a player down," said Mark.

"Yeah, you'd be helping us out," said Ali.

"I . . . I—"

"Come on, Sami! You smashed the ball into the net yesterday! We need you!" Ali shoved a fist in my shoulder.

"All right," I said, shuffling my feet, remembering how good it felt to kick a ball about in the park after school. I followed them outside. I'd already checked the flight schedule at break. It was on time and leaving at 6:40 P.M. I had plenty of time to get there after school.

Being on a pitch again made me feel alive. I was quick to dodge the other players and dribble the ball to Ali, Mark, and their team. I didn't score this time, but I think the others could see I had skills and wasn't a total loser.

● ● ●

The seconds ticked by so slowly through the afternoon. When the school bell finally rang, I jumped out of my chair, slung my backpack over my shoulder, and dashed to get out of the door.

Ali ran to catch me in the corridor. "Man, I'm glad it's Friday," he said, zipping up his backpack. "Where you off now? Home?"

"Yeah . . ." For a moment, I thought about telling him where I was going, but I couldn't risk it. I didn't know him, not really.

"Come with me and Mark for a quick kick-about. We're going to the park again. Then you can come

just like Joseph and I used to. It was weird sitting in Ali's living room, as if I was back at home on a normal day with Joseph. I lost myself, not thinking about anything other than the game and beating Ali.

After we'd played four games, Ali started flicking through the movie channels. "So, did your house get bombed?" he asked. "What was it like living there?"

I don't really know why, but everything began pouring out. Maybe it was because it felt easy to talk to Ali, because I felt I could trust him, especially after he'd saved me from Nathan the day before. Or just because I really needed to talk about it to someone—I guessed if I was with Joseph, I'd be telling him.

He listened to me, not saying a word until I'd finished. "Yeah, I saw it on the news. Not everyone that leaves is poor . . . and they miss their lives back home 'cause they were better off there. That happened to my cousins from Pakistan too. I get it."

I closed my eyes for a short second and sighed deeply. *Finally, someone who understands we didn't want to leave.*

"Oh, and that crudhead Hassan needs a punch in the face," he added. "Don't let him bring you down— I've never liked him."

I smiled. Ali was a good guy. He would've been a good friend, if I was staying. "So where's your dad? At work?" I asked, feeling more relaxed than I had in months.

"Oh, you'll never see him. My parents are divorced," he said, sitting back into the sofa.

"Oh, right . . ."

"I don't know much about him. He got remarried and had more children," Ali said casually, flicking the channels again. "Haven't seen him for years." He stared at the remote control.

I didn't know what to say. We both had lives that weren't perfect.

● ● ●

"Come round tomorrow?" asked Ali as I was opening his front door to leave.

"Tomorrow?" I stopped. "But it's Saturday."

"Yeaaaah, and?" He laughed. "We'll just hang out. What you gonna do all day, anyway? Look at Hassan's screwed-up face?"

"True . . ." He was right. I'd have to wait till Monday to leave for the airport now and I'd much rather spend the weekend with Ali than be in that house. "Mum and Dad are working anyway. So yeah, all right!" I smiled. "I'm sure they'll say yes."

Ali and I were in the middle of a frantic *FIFA* match early Saturday evening when his mum walked into the living room and switched on the light. "Sami, it's five to six. You better get back. Your dad said six o'clock, didn't he?"

"Oh, yeah," I replied, pulling up one side of my mouth to show my disappointment. I yanked my jacket from the back of the sofa and put it on.

"Ali, can you please go and pick up some milk for me?" Ali's mum fumbled in her purse and handed him some coins.

"Yeah, go on then," he said to his mum, getting up and following me out of the room. "I'll walk you home." He nodded to me.

I didn't speak as we began to walk back. I was dreading the evening meal because I'd have to look at Hassan's irritating face across the table. Ali and I'd had such a good day just chilling, I didn't want to ruin it. Hassan made my skin crawl.

I looked up at the dark sky to get him out of my mind. The stars were dotted everywhere, like freckles on a face.

"You're quiet," Ali said, hunching into his hood to keep warm.

"I don't wanna go back," I admitted. He knew why.

"You wanna get a burger?" Ali asked.

I smiled. It was exactly what Joseph would have suggested. But it wasn't that easy anymore. "I can't. I haven't got any money." I couldn't waste the ten-pound note on a burger.

"I'll pay. It's only 99p," he said.

"Really? Thanks, Ali!"

"Hang on, what about your dad? You wanna tell him first?" asked Ali.

"We won't be long," I said. "He'll be fine. Let's do it." I put my hands in my pockets and smiled.

Chapter 33

The air was cold and fresh. I blew circles of mist from my mouth as we walked. On the main road, lots of gray pigeons had gathered by a set of bins where children were throwing bread to them from a shop doorway. Buses roared and beeped in the background. More pigeons flew down and watched curiously, before creeping forward slowly to grab a tiny grain of bread.

We passed a homeless man sitting on the cold pavement, huddled in a dark doorway. He was in combat uniform with a sign that said HOMELESS AND HUNGRY. PLEASE DONATE.

I felt the folded ten-pound note in my pocket, almost pulling it out, but I couldn't. I needed it. I looked at the man and mouthed, "Sorry."

I stepped into the warmth of the fast-food shop behind Ali. I felt free and alive, being outside and away from Hassan's house. There were a few people munching at the tables and three people lined up ahead of us. Behind the counter, burgers sizzled and the smell of cooked French fries rose into the air. The cash register slammed open with a ping. The man at the front gave his ticket and walked away with his paper bag of food.

The voice I heard next was so familiar, it seemed like I was imagining it.

"Yes . . . ketchup and vinegar," the guy at the counter said to the cashier who was handing him a receipt.

It can't be, can it? I strained my neck forward. This guy looked dirty and older, but I could only see the back of him. I coughed loudly and then swallowed. Ali turned to me, and so did the guy at the front. I froze. I'd never forget those blue eyes.

"Aadam?" My voice was high, unbelieving.

His eyes grew wide and his mouth fell open. Then he burst into a smile. "Sami!" He coughed.

I rushed forward and we wrapped our arms around each other and hugged tightly.

"What? How . . . ? I can't believe this!" My face ached from grinning. "Come with me, come!" As Ali and the other customers stared, I grabbed Aadam's arm and led him to the door to take him outside, away from all of the attention. "I'll be right back," I said to Ali, who looked baffled.

On the sidewalk, I looked at Aadam properly under the streetlight. He had been through a difficult time—his clothes were dirty and worn and looked like the same ones that we'd left him in months ago. His dark blond hair had grown and clumped together, and he had light stubble around his cheeks. But his blue eyes were the same.

"You okay?" I asked him, holding the tops of his arms.

"I can't believe it's you, Sami," he said slowly. His voice seemed deeper. Coarser. "I just got handed a flyer for some hot food. I was hoping I'd find you here. I came after I read your last email, but I forgot the exact address—I never thought this would actually happen." He pulled his sleeves over his grimy, rough hands.

"I know—me too! I didn't think you'd got my email! You never replied!" I raised my eyebrows. "Where have you been staying?"

"Just around Manchester."

"On the streets?"

"Yeah . . ." He looked down at his battered Adidas.

I couldn't believe he'd made it all this way with no one to help him, and he'd spent God knows how long living on the cold streets, while we had warm beds. I made a snap decision. "You'll come back with me tonight."

"You have a house?"

"Yes. Well, no . . ." I slowed down, remembering where we were staying. I tried not to think about how Aunty Fatimah or Hassan would react when I turned up with Aadam. "Um . . . just don't worry about it. Okay? I'm here now and I won't take no for an answer," I said, holding my head higher to show I could take care of him. "Let's get that burger first though, yeah?" I said, leading him back into the takeaway.

Ali was now second from the front. "Ali, this is Aadam," I said as we came alongside him. "We met in Turkey. Remember I told you?"

"Oh, yeah . . . Salaam, bro," Ali said to Aadam.

"Let me get you some food. You must be hungry. Grab a table." I pointed to an empty one. I'd worry about the money later.

"I've already ordered using the voucher," said Aadam. He held up his receipt.

"I'm, err, gonna head back, yeah?" said Ali, leaving the line just as it was his turn. "I'm not hungry anyways, and you two have got a lot to catch up on."

"You don't have to. Stay, man," I said as Aadam sat down at one of the plastic tables and moved some unused ketchup sachets to the side.

"I'm supposed to be getting Mum some milk, remember?" Ali leaned in close to my face and whispered, "What you gonna do with Aadam?"

"I'm taking him back home."

"You mad? Aunty's gonna kill you!" Ali backed away from me.

"Well, I can't leave him here, can I?" I whispered. "Look at him."

"Yeah, I know, but I don't envy being you tonight, mate."

"I know." I gulped.

Ali nodded. "All right, man. Good luck. I'm off. I'll catch you tomorrow—Mark's coming over as well, yeah?" He gave me a fist bump and walked out as I lined up to order myself a 99p chicken burger.

● ● ●

I let Aadam sit and eat his food in silence, taking bite after bite without stopping, long after I'd finished my burger. It seemed he hadn't eaten in a while. He closed his eyes with each mouthful, chewing each piece carefully.

When he finally finished, I slid our food wrappers into the bin and paused as I turned back to him. Aadam wasn't the same as before. He had hardly spoken and just stared into space. I felt bad to think it, but he smelled. I wondered how long it'd been since he'd washed. We'd soon fix that.

I knew Aunty Fatimah would probably kill me, but I couldn't leave him again. "Shall we go?" I asked him, biting my lip.

Chapter 34

We walked in silence back to the house, Aadam with his head lowered and shoulders hunched. Maybe he was exhausted and had no energy to speak, or maybe he'd been through something awful and was traumatized like Sara. I couldn't work it out.

To break the silence, I asked, "So, where have you been? How did you get to Manchester?"

"Sami . . ." He sighed. "Where shall I start?" His body sagged, as if he was haunted by memories.

"I made it to France, to the Jungle," he began. "That was just a muddy place, in freezing cold weather. No house, just a flimsy tent. Much worse than Turkey." He glanced at me before continuing. "I met some men there and we tried to jump onto a moving truck going back to England."

"What? How?!" My mouth hung open.

"The first two times were a disaster. I got caught on the motorway bridge and sent back to the Jungle. The third time, I fell off the top of the moving truck."

"Aadam!"

"I know. I hurt my leg really badly and couldn't walk. I had to stay in the Jungle for ages after that—but I was desperate to get to Manchester to find you."

I sighed and looked at my ruined Air Jordans. Just months ago, my life was all about the latest shoes and my iPad—now I was just grateful for Aadam and my family being alive.

"On my fourth try, I managed to stay on and I climbed into the container on the back of the truck when it stopped. It was the hardest thing not knowing if I'd make it. But I did. I ended up in Liverpool."

"Liverpool?" I asked, surprised. "You walked *forty* miles to get here?"

"No. I slept on the streets for a few nights before I spotted a truck with Manchester United flags in its window, parked overnight. I figured it would bring me here. I watched and waited until morning, then I clung underneath the truck until it left."

"No way!" It sounded so dangerous. I couldn't understand how he hung on.

"I felt lost after getting to Manchester—it's so big," he said, looking down. "I slept on the streets again, begging. I finally got enough money to use an internet café to check my emails and saw your last one, but my time ran out before I could finish my reply, so I just made my way here." He hung his head low.

"Aadam . . . I'm so glad you found me, man. Everything will be fine now," I said, trying to make him feel better.

We were almost at the house. I counted the cracks along the dimly lit paving slabs. My mouth got dryer as we neared the driveway. I took a deep breath and rang the doorbell, wondering whose horrible face I'd see first.

Luckily it was Mama who answered the door. Her forehead furrowed when she opened it. "Where have you been, Sami? You've been gone—" Her face cleared quickly and she gasped as she covered her mouth. "Aadam?"

"I found him on the main road." I lowered my voice and came close to her ear. "He's been homeless for ages, Mama."

"Um . . . I'll just get your baba." Mama rushed back into the house.

We took off our shoes and entered the hallway. It smelled like they'd had lamb for dinner.

Baba opened the front room door slightly and slipped into the hallway, quickly shutting the door behind him.

"Look who it is!" I said, trying to get a positive reaction.

He looked at both of us, his eyebrows almost hitting his hairline, then his mouth broke into a forced smile. "Aadam," he said, stepping forward. "You made it! Allah hu Akbar! Allah is truly the Greatest!"

Aadam stood still and smiled, his hands in his pockets.

"Baba," I said, widening my eyes and directing them to the front room. *Let us in then!*

Baba looked Aadam up and down and rubbed his beard. "You look like you need a good night's sleep." He reached for one of the banister spindles, let go of it, and then held it again. He couldn't stand still.

"Is Uncle Muhammad here?" I asked, trying to step forward, but Baba moved in front of me.

"No—he's out," said Baba.

I leaned into Baba and whispered in his ear. "We can't let him go this time."

Aadam still stood by the front door, his eyes on his holey gray socks. Baba's forehead was creased. I hadn't seen him look like that since the detention center. My stomach dipped.

Mama came back out into the hallway, leaned on the radiator, and cleared her throat. "Sami, Aadam . . . we're just going to speak to Fatimah and let her know before we take you in. This isn't our house, you see." Her voice shook as she looked at Aadam. "Just stay here, okay? Don't go up yet." She glanced at Baba, who was twiddling his fingers around one another. He rubbed his cheek and turned toward the front room.

"Umm, Fatimah, can we talk, please?" he said, opening the door. There was a long silence before Aunty Fatimah emerged through the door. Her mouth crumpled as soon as she saw Aadam.

I looked down immediately, away from her evil glare.

Baba opened the dining room door and ushered her in, Mama followed behind them.

"Who is that?!" she shouted as Mama shut the door.

I went and sat on the first step of the stairs, my

heart racing, while Aadam hovered in front of me, shuffling his feet.

I heard Baba mumbling something for about half a minute before Aunty Fatimah said, "NO! Absolutely NOT!"

Baba tried to say some more, but she cut him off.

"We've had enough! My kids have lost their space, you've already taken over the house. I'm not taking in another. Enough is enough. I want you all out. ALL OF YOU!"

Hassan rushed out of the front room and into the dining room, briefly glancing at Aadam on the way.

"What's going on? Is he hurting you?" I heard Hassan ask Aunty Fatimah.

"No. Out. Hassan. Get out!"

Hassan emerged again, his face full of confusion and fury.

"Who the hell is this?" he said, walking toward Aadam, his chest pushed out and legs wide.

"I . . . errr . . ." Aadam stepped back into the wall.

Hassan turned to look down at me. My heart shot into my throat. "This—this—" I started, then straightened my shoulders and proudly said, "is Aadam. My friend."

"You can't bring your dirty mates here. Who do you think you are? Get him out of here. NOW." He sucked his teeth and walked into the front room, slamming the door.

I could hear Baba saying something else, then Mama ran out of the dining room crying and rushed past me up the stairs.

Baba came out quickly after her and began stamping upstairs. "Come on, Sami, we're leaving. Get Sara and bring her upstairs."

We were leaving? I looked at Aadam. "You wait here. Please don't move, okay?"

"Sami, I've got to go. Look what I've done."

"No. You promise me. Don't move." I squeezed his arm and ran into the front room. "Hey, Sara, come here," I said.

Hassan gave me a dirty look and then went back to staring at the TV. Iman smiled nervously and I smiled back, then took Sara's hand and led her out of the room.

"Come upstairs," I said to Aadam, walking past him.

Aadam didn't move.

"Just come on," I whispered desperately.

In the bedroom, Baba was on the phone to some-one, while Mama put things into a plastic bag.

"Take Sara to the bathroom," she said, tears streaming down her face.

I did as Mama said while Aadam waited in the upstairs hallway, looking uncomfortable and self-conscious, staring down at his feet. I felt sorry for him but had no time to make him feel better right then.

We're leaving. We're leaving! I felt proud of Baba for sticking up for us and tried not to think about where we'd go. Anywhere would be better than here.

I sent Sara to Mama and quickly used the bath-room myself, not knowing when we'd have the chance to use a nice clean one again.

When I returned to the bedroom, two plastic bags were at Baba's feet, Sara was wearing her jacket and hat, and Mama was stripping the beds.

"Just leave it, Zeina. We don't have time. I don't want to be here when Muhammad gets back. He'll just make us stay, and I don't want to look at that woman's face again."

"No. I'm leaving it clean. So all she has to do is wash them. They can have their room back!" shrieked Mama, her face wet.

I looked around to see if we'd left anything. "Have you got my stuff?" I asked Baba.

"It's all in your school bag," he snapped, pointing at my backpack leaning against the wall near the door.

I opened it to check everything was inside. It was bursting, but I managed to close the zip and put it on my back.

I took Sara's hand gently. "Don't worry, Sara, it's okay. Mama just doesn't wanna make the beds, that's all. That's why she's crying. It's 'cause she's tired."

I took her outside and found Aadam leaning over the banister. "She's fuming . . ."

I rolled my eyes. "Is she still going on?"

"Yeah, she's in the kitchen banging pots and swearing."

"You wanna go to the bathroom before we leave?"

"I'm okay. I just went at the takeaway—remember what it's like? We learn to hold it in."

"Yeah, I remember." I sighed as I took Sara down the stairs.

We pulled our shoes on and waited in the tiny porch, my head pulsing, scared that Aunty Fatimah would come out and attack us with a knife from the kitchen or something.

Baba came down with the two plastic bags, Mama behind, wiping her face with her sleeve.

Baba pushed into us in the tight porch, but Mama walked toward the kitchen. "What are you doing, Zeina?" asked Baba.

She ignored him and opened the door.

"Thank you for everything, Fatimah—we can't thank you enough. May God bless you with more than you have." She burst into more tears as she shut the door, then walked into the front room. "Hassan and Iman, thank you for everything. We're leaving. Please say a big thanks to your baba too when he gets home. You can have your rooms back now. You've been very patient and kind. Bless you."

Mama stepped back into the hallway with Iman running after her. "I'm sorry! I didn't know you were leaving today."

"Neither did we, habibti," said Baba. "Thank you for everything." He opened the door to let us out.

"Bye, Iman. Take care," I said as I followed him out, my heart sinking to my shoes. *What have I done?* I thought. *Where will we go now?*

Mama gave Iman a kiss on the cheek and closed the door, leaving her standing in the hallway.

Chapter 35

*B*aba *began making calls* as we headed to the bus stop to get to Manchester city center. Once we got on the bus, his knee jerked constantly. I hadn't seen him look this tense since the detention center. Finally, he put his phone back in his pocket and rubbed his chin.

"Miss Patel has found us a hostel for the night," he explained to Mama, who was holding Sara. "She made an emergency referral. We'll have somewhere to sleep." It should have been good news—but the look on Baba's face didn't give that impression. It couldn't be as bad as the detention center, could it? My stomach was in knots.

It was ironic that we'd gone from helping Aadam, someone who was homeless, to becoming homeless ourselves in just one evening.

"I can't believe we left," I said to him.

"Yeah, and it's all my fault."

Someone started coughing loudly at the back of the bus.

"Don't be silly! I'm glad to be out of that hellhole."
At least I don't have to see Hassan anymore.

"Sami, you haven't seen a hellhole if you thought that house was one."

"You know what I mean." I looked down at my lap, embarrassed.

"Trust me, I don't. I'd have done anything to stay in a house like that. Do you even realize where we're going?"

"Some hostel, Baba said."

"And you think that's good?" His eyes narrowed. "Homeless hostels are dangerous, full of drunks and drug addicts. You don't get it, do you?"

"Really?" I sank in my seat, finally understanding why Baba looked so tense. "I just thought they were like hotels for the homeless."

Aadam rolled his eyes and turned to look out of the window.

"Did you stay in a hostel, then?" I asked Aadam, trying to somehow clear the air.

He nodded, his head facing the window. "I followed some homeless people and found where they went for food and to sleep. I got into a shelter for a couple of nights but was mostly turned away because no one had referred me. Anyway, some people in the hostels were really cruel."

"What did they do?" I asked, then wished I hadn't. Maybe Aadam didn't want to talk about it.

"I got beaten up in the last shelter by a drunk man who called me an 'invading terrorist trying to take over his country.' That's when I decided I was better off on the streets." He shifted his body toward the window. I think he was telling me he was done talking.

I understood why he was annoyed with me. I'd had it so easy compared to him.

Mama and Baba leaned into each other and talked quietly, looking like they were discussing something important. I strained to hear them. "I don't know how we'll get to work on time tomorrow," Baba said to Mama.

"Let's not worry about that right now, Tarek. Let's just get through tonight." Mama sniffed and hugged Sara tighter.

It turned out we had to get a second bus toward Salford from the city center, so we walked a little to find the next bus stop. Once we'd found the right bus, we sat in silence for the whole journey.

The hostel was in an old warehouse in a big brick building on a back street. When we got to its glass door, Baba stopped outside, his breath forming clouds in the cold air.

"Right, a few rules . . . No one—and I mean no one, that includes you, Aadam—is to leave the room we are given. If you desperately need to go to the bathroom, I'll go with you." He looked at all of our faces, one by one. "Let's all just get inside and try to sleep."

"Sleep?" Mama asked bitingly.

Baba ignored her and carried on. "Don't talk to anyone. Just look down and make no eye contact if someone strange tries to approach you."

My stomach rolled. He was scaring me. He hadn't behaved like this in Turkey or when we'd first got to England. I wondered if he'd dealt with people from hostels in Syria and that was why he was so worried about us staying in one. *What have I done?* I thought. *I'm such an idiot.*

The first thing that hit me as we walked in was the smell, like a dirty toilet with bleach mixed in. I closed my mouth and pinched my nose, trying not to heave. Mama covered her mouth too.

We walked up a small ramp covered in blue-squared linoleum flooring toward a reception window. A small woman with short, brown hair that was shaved on one side and longer on the other greeted us. She asked Baba some questions, handed him five small tickets, then escorted us to a large room that was set up like a café. It smelled of cigarette smoke and vegetable soup.

There were foldaway tables surrounded by plastic chairs, with lots of men and women in hoodies eating quietly. A few were talking in whispers.

Everyone in the room froze, their eyes fixed on us as we walked through to the serving window. I wanted to run, but I couldn't. There was nowhere for me to run to.

I chose a tuna mayo sandwich and a carton of apple juice, even though I wasn't that hungry after my 99p burger. We sat down at an empty table and ate quickly and quietly.

A thin man with a receding hairline wearing a turtleneck approached us. "Hi, I'm Mike," he said, pulling up a plastic chair. "I understand you're here for the night, but could be here for a few days?"

"Yes," said Baba.

"Did Sheila give you the rules?"

"Umm . . . no."

He handed Baba a sheet of paper and a medical evaluation form. "But you've been given the bed tickets?"

"Yes."

"Now, I'm sure you lovely people won't cause any problems, but we have to tell everyone this. If you stay out of trouble, then we can extend your stay. Breakfast is at 6:30 A.M. and dinner is at 5:30 P.M. Most people leave the shelter in the day to look for work. We can help you with that too, if you need it."

"Okay. Thank you," Baba said, looking down at his unfinished sandwich. Mama just sniffed.

"Okay, well, please fill in these forms and hand them to Sheila. Then you'll be shown to the dormitories."

"Dormitories?" asked Baba.

"Yes, they're separate for men and women, but we'll keep your beds near your children, don't worry."

Baba's face dropped and Mama's chin started quivering.

"It's just for during the night—we can't have men and women on the same floor. You can see each other again in the morning." He smiled, pulled his chair back and walked out of the dining hall. I sank in my chair and hung my head low.

After we'd eaten, we watched Baba fill out the forms. He rubbed Mama's shoulder and told her, "Don't worry. Miss Patel will phone me on Monday to discuss our immigration status. God willing, we won't be here long."

We took the forms back to the reception area, and Sheila led us all up the stairs. The first floor contained rows and rows of bunk beds, all covered with bedding, some with black bags and clothes on them.

"Those beds are for our long-term residents," said Sheila, smiling and heading up a further set of stairs that took us to the second floor, which smelled of strong disinfectant.

"This is where you three will be sleeping," she said, pointing to me, Baba, and Aadam. "Give your tickets to Graham, and he'll show you to your mattresses and hand you a clean sheet and a towel." The room was filled with thin mattresses covered in black plastic leatherette.

Mama gave Baba a tight hug and began sobbing. "I can't believe we're being split up again," she cried. I dipped my chin to my chest, unable to look at them.

"It's okay. It's nice up there," said Sheila. I looked up to see her taking Sara's hand. "Women with young children have separate rooms." Sara looked at Mama and tried to pull her hand away. Mama held on to Sara's other hand and nodded to her to follow Sheila.

A bald man with a gray goatee and glasses came through the wooden door as Mama and Sara left. "Hello! I'm Graham. Here's a towel for each of you. You'll need to take a shower and then I'll show you to your beds."

"But we're clean. We've come from a house," I said. I didn't want to shower here.

"Sorry, young man, but it's our policy. You can't sleep here without a shower." He pursed his lips and put his hands behind his back.

"You've got to do it," said Aadam quietly, his eyes fixed to the floor.

"If you have any money, take it with you and guard it," said Graham, leading us to the shower room.

There were about ten showerheads in the beige-and-brown-tiled room. We slowly took off our clothes. I thought I could get away with not showering, just pretending I had.

"Baba, do we have to?" I said, staring at the black bucket with bars of soap in the middle of the room.

"Sami, just have a quick shower, but don't touch the soap," Baba said crankily, frowning as he put his iPhone and wallet into his socks, which he shoved in his shoes.

I showered for about ten seconds before jumping away and drying myself with the small brown towel Graham had given me. We got dressed and met him outside the shower room.

"Right, you'll need to go downstairs now and give these tickets to Mike in the cafeteria—he'll give you your mattresses and sheets."

"I thought we were going to sleep on this floor?" asked Baba, his mouth hung open.

"Yes, you were supposed to, but we don't have space up here to place three mattresses together. If you don't want to be split up, then it would be best to sleep downstairs."

We trudged down the stairs, back to the cafeteria. The stench in the hallway hit me again. Either someone had soiled themselves or they had the worst farts in the world.

Mike stood at the door. He asked Baba for our tickets and handed each of us a thin black plastic mattress and a fitted sheet. All of the tables and chairs had been cleared away and there were already about thirty men lying on the floor. We dragged our mattresses over to a space big enough for the three of us, under the window. I could feel a draft coming through it, but at least we were together.

Baba put his mattress next to the man closest to us, who was snoring loudly. Then he wrapped his sheet around both his mattress and his backpack and put his head on it, all without looking at us.

Aadam and I glanced at each other, took our bags and did the same. I knew right then that I wouldn't be able to sleep. It wasn't just the noise and the smell that would bother me, it was the lack of sheet or anything over my body.

I sat on my mattress and looked over at Aadam. He smiled weakly and lay his head down on his plastic bag.

What had I done? My family was homeless again . . . and it was all my fault.

Chapter 36

I *must've fallen asleep eventually,* because I woke up the next day to the sound of the kitchen staff singing and talking loudly, pots clanging. A few minutes later, Graham came charging in to wake us all up and collect our mattresses and sheets. Some of the men helped him sweep up and set up the room for eating, while everyone else rushed upstairs to use the bathrooms before the rest of the shelter awoke.

Mama came rushing into the cafeteria with Sara in her arms, and guilt tingled right through me. Baba jumped out of his chair and ran to hug them both, taking Sara from Mama, who had a pink, blotchy face.

We all left after having some toast and tea, catching two buses to get back to Stockport. As we got off on the main road near Ali's house, Baba turned to Mama and said, "Right, Zeina, meet me at the factory after you finish. You sure they'll be okay with you cleaning with Sara around?"

"What choice do I have?" said Mama, her eyes stony.

"I'll look after her," I chipped in quickly. "Me and Aadam can." But Mama shook her head and walked off, struggling to carry Sara in her arms.

Baba turned to Aadam. "You can come with me and load boxes in the warehouse. I could do with the help for tonight's shipment. The boss'll be fine."

Aadam straightened his shoulders. "Yes, Uncle. Of course."

"What about me?" I asked.

Baba waved a hand. "You can go to Ali's house," he said. "You should know your way. Be back here at six." With that, he strode off.

Aadam tapped my shoulder. "See you later," he said before jogging to catch up with Baba.

I felt a quiver in my stomach and the hairs on my neck stood up. *Baba's just tired.* I told myself. *Don't think about it—he'll forgive you.*

"You're early! Thought you were Mark," said Ali, opening his front door.

I didn't say anything, trying to keep my eyes open after having only one or two hours' sleep.

"What's up with you? You look mashed!"

"Nothing," I said quickly, while slipping my shoes off in the hallway.

"What d'you mean 'nothing'? You look sick, and I don't mean in a good way."

"Just didn't get much sleep." I stood tall and tried to widen my eyes.

"Your clothes are looking rough too. Didn't Aunty let you iron them or something?" He walked off into the front room.

"I told you what she's like," I said, following him in.

"Ohhh . . . 'cause you took Aadam home? What happened? Tell me!" He sat down and turned to me.

I didn't say a word. I couldn't tell him what I'd done to my family.

"Sami, don't be thick—just tell me."

"She . . ." I began.

"She what?!"

"She . . ."

"Listen, if you don't tell me, I'll just ask Hassan

at school tomorrow." Ali dropped his PlayStation controller on his lap.

"She kicked us out."

"WHAT? No way!"

"Seriously."

"So where you staying?"

"Near central . . ."

"Manchester?" He picked up his controller again, his gaze on me.

"Yeah, they gave us temporary accommodation."

"Oh, right . . ."

"My dad's been acting weird. Hasn't spoken to me since."

"He must be stressed, man!"

"Yeah . . . he's meeting up with the immigration lady and his lawyer again."

"Wow. That must be hard."

"Yup . . ."

Someone rang the doorbell. A few seconds later, Mark walked in, and to my relief we didn't talk about it anymore.

We met at six P.M. as planned. Baba didn't talk to me on the double bus journey back. Aadam slept, his head banging on the back of the seat. I tried to sleep too, but I couldn't.

When we got to the hostel, we'd been upgraded to the second floor, but it was just the same as in the café really—the same mattresses, the same terrible smell.

As I pulled the sheet around the thin mattress, Baba got up and walked out into the corridor. I raised my head—he was speaking to Mama, who passed him Sara. He hadn't even looked at me all day. But he was carrying her in his arms like she was a toddler.

I could see tears rolling down Mama's face as she spoke to Baba, his body hunched over. She looked withered, like a bag of bones. Carrying Sara around everywhere didn't help. Sara's eyes were wide and she was shivering, like she was frightened.

I jumped off my mattress to try to help. "Here, let me take Sara, Baba. You need a break," I said, putting my hands out to take her.

"A break?" He scowled. "Hmmmph," he added, blowing air out of his nose. "Get out of here—I think you've done enough!"

I dropped my arms and stepped back. My chin started wobbling.

"Don't," Mama said to Baba, putting a hand on his arm.

"No, he's got to understand. If he just thought things through. . . . He's caused us so much stress!" Baba said, shaking his head at me, his face red with anger, his eyes bulging. "We were safe, and now, because of his immaturity, we're out on the streets. I can't look at him!"

I turned away to my mattress, my chest tight, a pain at the back of my throat. Baba was right. It was my fault. ALL OF IT.

If I hadn't forced Mama to go to the mall to get my football boots, we'd never have had to leave our house. We'd never have lost everything. Then, after all the traveling and being locked up in the detention center, when we were finally safe, like an idiot, I made my family homeless again. All I'd done was cause them grief and ruin their lives. Mama and Baba lost their well-paid jobs and were having to work illegally. They were better off without me. I couldn't bring them any more pain.

Aadam tried to say something to me, but I was in

a daze. I sank on to my mattress, put my head on my backpack, and stared into space. When he nudged me, I blurted out the first thing that came into my head.

"I'm sorry, Aadam. For everything. I hope things work out for you." Then I turned my body away from him and closed my eyes.

Chapter 37

When we got off the second bus the next morning near Ali's house, Mama walked off with Sara, while Baba paced around the bus stop, talking animatedly on his phone. I didn't say goodbye, just pulled up my hood and put my head down. I hadn't said a word all morning.

"You okay?" Aadam asked me as I headed toward Ali's.

Emotions burned hot inside me. I wasn't okay, no. And my parents hadn't even noticed—they hadn't looked at me since last night.

I turned abruptly and hugged Aadam tight. "Take care of them, bro," I said, then spun round without looking at him and ran off down the road.

As I approached Ali's house, he ran out to join

me, and we began walking to school. I felt sick, my stomach twitching, thinking about what I was about to do.

"Got dumb physics today," said Ali. "Haven't done my homework—have you?" It was just a normal day for him.

"Um, no. I forgot," I said, my hands in my pocket, my head still down. *Why doesn't he get that I don't want to talk?* I thought.

He took his earphones out of his jacket pocket. "You want one?" he asked, holding out an ear bud.

"Nah, I'm all right."

He put them in and we walked the rest of the way in silence.

As we got through the main gates, among the throng of school kids, I stopped. "Ali!" I shouted. He turned round and took his ear buds out of his ears. "Listen . . . umm . . just . . thanks for everything, yeah?"

"What's up with you?" He frowned, then laughed awkwardly. "You look like you ain't slept a wink. You okay?"

"Yeah, no . . . I'm fine. You're a really good mate, yeah?"

"What you getting soppy for? Come on," he said, lightly punching my arm. Mark walked toward us as the bell rang, and Ali joined him on the path to the school. I stopped and watched them approach the doors. My heart was beating hard, my mouth dry. I turned back to the gate and ran. I ran as fast as I'd ever run, and I didn't look back. I had to do this. I had no choice. It was best for everyone.

The bus came just as I got to the stop. All of the school kids and people on their way to work had gone. I followed an old lady on, shielding my eyes from the morning sun and trying not to breathe in the lingering smell of deodorant and stinky armpits. I dropped my coins into the money collector, pulled my ticket, grabbed my change, and sat near the front, closing my eyes. *I should've just left the first time,* I told myself. *If Ali hadn't stopped me, I would've been back in Syria by now. Sara would still be playing happily with Iman, and Mama and Baba wouldn't be homeless. But I can do something about it now.*

Ping. The bell chimed. Over and over again. The

bus kept stopping and letting people on and off—
mostly old people, alone with shopping trolleys. *Tete
would never get on a bus alone,* I thought. I couldn't
stop rocking as the bus continued on its journey.
You've got to do this, I told myself again and again. *It's
for the best.*

After about ten stops, we reached Stockport bus
station. It looked tiny against the tall red-brick viaduct
standing behind it, like something I'd seen in a black-
and-white photo in a history book. A red-and-white
train hurtled over the arches, like a toy train on a
playset. I stood up to follow the other passengers
off the bus, but my legs wobbled, and I grabbed the
handrail.

"Where do I get the bus to the airport, please?" I
asked the bus driver.

He pointed to a tunnel of bus shelters straight
ahead. I stepped off and walked along reading the bus-
stop signs until I saw one further down with people
holding suitcases and large bags. That had to be it.
Yes—I checked the sign. The 199 stopped here.

There were only a few people at the stop, and I
knew I must have looked odd standing there in my
uniform with only my school backpack. I hadn't

thought that through. But no one said anything, just stared at their phones.

The airport bus came within five minutes. It was red and shiny-new; the air from the brakes whooshed as it stopped. The doors slid open and let off a man in a thin flowery shirt heaving a big black suitcase.

I stepped into line and listened carefully to what the others said to buy their ticket.

"Single to Manchester Airport, please," said the curly-haired woman in front of me.

I asked for the same and tried to look like I knew what I was doing. My heart was beating double-time. What if she said no kids were allowed?

"Is that a half?" asked the bus driver.

"Umm . . . yes, please." I had no idea what that meant, but it sounded better than a whole.

"I need to see your igo card." She pursed her lips.

What was that? "Um . . ." I twisted Jiddo's ring. "I don't have one." She was going to kick me off.

"Well, you'll have to pay in full then."

"Okay." I quickly handed her my coins, took the change and ticket, and walked up the wide aisle dividing the two sides of the bus.

The bus didn't stop at all. Jackets rustled, shoes

scuffled, but no one spoke. A gust of cold air came through a slightly opened window. I wanted to close it but couldn't risk drawing any attention to myself.

How am I going to find the right plane? I worried. *What if I get caught? I can't get caught. Breathe, Sami. Deep breaths. Everything will be fine once you're in the luggage hold. Focus, just, focus.*

When the bus finally got to the airport, I let out a long breath and stepped off. I needed to get to Terminal 1 and figure out how to get in a luggage hold.

I walked through the automated glass doors into a large open area. Ahead were the check-in counters, with snaking lines full of excited people chatting. The smell of fresh coffee wafted up my nose. I made it to the monitors that displayed the flight times. I could feel the pulse in my neck throbbing.

AYT 18.40   ON TIME   CHECK IN CLOSED

I had hours to work things out.

I'd seen on an aircraft-spotting blog that the best airside viewing platforms were near Penny's Café. I walked through the airport trying to avoid the rushing travelers with their trolleys, past the baggage drop-off areas, toilets, and cash-exchange desks. Where was the food court? There!

Up ahead was the café. As I got closer, I could see planes being loaded just the other side of the café's large window. I couldn't have asked for a better view.

I had to have a reason to sit inside the café, so I lined up at the counter and bought a small hot chocolate with the change from the bus. I took it to an empty bar stool, which looked out at the runway, and leaned my arms on the high table, almost collapsing with relief. I'd made it. I was going to do this. Mama, Baba, Sara, and Aadam would be much happier without me and my stupid decisions ruining their lives. I was on my way back to Syria, where I belonged. With Tete and Joseph. *Home*. I'd call Mama and Baba once I got to Antalya and let them know I was okay. I stopped and held my rolling stomach before sipping my drink, then got comfortable to watch the crew unpack the luggage carts.

Every so often I looked around at the people in the café, drinking, checking their tickets, and making phone calls. No one seemed to care that I was sitting alone, looking at the planes.

Outside the window, I watched a luggage cart drive up to a Jet Easy plane. I leaned over the high-top table to see if I could spot a DreamAir plane. They had only one flight later that day—the one going directly to Antalya. A baggage handler jumped off the cart and started chucking suitcases into an open plane compartment, while the driver walked round the truck to pass them to him, one by one.

Oh, man. I'd have to get into the Antalya plane's hold when it was ready to be loaded, but *before* the baggage handler arrived. I bit my lip. This wasn't going to be easy. *What if I fall out and die? Don't think about it*, I told myself. *You can do this.*

A thirst came over me as if I hadn't drunk anything all day. I downed the last of my hot chocolate and quietly slid off the barstool. I needed to find the doors that led out to the runway. My eyes darted all over the place as I searched the nearby area. I couldn't keep them focused on one thing. Past the café was a sushi bar and then nothing. It was quieter at this end of the airport. The stores stopped and the white walls of a corridor reappeared, narrowing to a set of double doors, STAFF ONLY printed above them. I blew out a set of short breaths to compose myself.

I walked through the doors and along a corridor. Finally, I came to a single door with a push bar to exit the terminal. I stared at the metal bar. *Will the alarm go off if I open it?*

THUMP, THUMP, THUMP. I could hear every beat of my heart.

I took a deep breath and raised my hands to press the handle.

"SAMI!" someone screamed.

Chapter 38

I *gasped and jumped back,* my heart nearly shooting out of my mouth. I turned and gaped at Ali.

"What the hell are you doing?!" he shouted, holding his palms out. Aadam came running up behind him, out of breath.

My jaw stiffened. I must've turned beetroot-red. I couldn't speak. *What are they doing here?!*

Ali walked over calmly and I backed away from the door.

"What you doing, Sami? Come on, let's go home," he said.

"I . . . how . . . how did you know I-I-I was here?" I stuttered. My face tingled and my neck and ears felt unbearably hot.

Aadam inched forward now. "You were being

weird this morning. I knew you were upset about something, so I told your baba I had to do an errand and followed you to school. I saw you run away, so I shouted to Ali."

Ugh, I was so gripped by my own feelings, I didn't even think about anyone watching what I was doing. How stupid. But I wasn't going to let them stop me. "It's none of your business, Aadam, or you, Ali. Just leave me alone!" I walked back to the door, but Ali blocked it.

"Mate, if you're gonna get on a plane like that and risk your life, I'm making it my business." Ali raised his hands in the air and pushed out his chest. "Things ain't that bad, man, come on."

"I'm not risking my life! What do you know?" I said, throwing my fist at him. I needed him to move away from the door. "How'd you even know I was going to get on a plane?"

Ali grabbed me, somehow twisting my body around and put me in a headlock. I struggled, but my neck was stuck tight. "That day when Nathan attacked you, you were acting well weird at lunch. I knew you were upset, so I came to find you and saw you in the library. I saw what you were Googling and you'd asked me about the airport bus, so I put it all together. Didn't you wonder why I came and got you at the bus stop that day?"

I had no idea he'd come to the library. *Oof.* I'd been oblivious to the world. "You haven't got a clue, Ali! Your life's okay. Your mum loves you loads," I said through gritted teeth, squirming to back out of his hold. "Get off me!"

His grip tightened for a few seconds and then relaxed. "I do have a clue, actually," he said and released me. I stood up, rubbing my neck.

"What you talking about?" He'd got my attention. I looked at him carefully—his face had dropped, his shoulders were slumped, and his arms hung down by his sides.

"Look, man, let's get out of here, and I'll tell you in the car."

"Car?"

"Oh, yeah." He pushed his hair back into place. "I got my sister to drive us here. She owed me one anyway for covering for her last week."

"What? Who else knows?"

"No one." Ali put his hand on my shoulder. "Trust me. I told Williams that you had an asthma attack and I had to help your dad find the hospital. And my sis doesn't know." He gripped my jacket and started pulling me to the double doors. "I told her you had my phone and I had to get it back. I even called her from a phone box, man."

Man, he's smart, I thought, twisting out of his grasp and squaring up to him, my fists ready to push him aside. My ears throbbed, my body prickled. I wasn't going to let him get in my way. I had to get on a plane today. No more delays.

"Sami, wait!" Aadam's voice stopped me. "Look, it's not so bad here that you need to get on a plane and go away. Why are you doing this? What about your mama and bab—"

"They hate me for what I've done to them!" I shouted, shoving past Ali.

"Oi!" Ali jumped in front of me. "Listen, yeah . . . I ain't told no one this, but I'm gonna tell you just once. When my dad left us, my life took a serious dive. He didn't wanna know us. Everything fell apart. My mum blamed us kids." His eyes were fixed to the ground, but he stood firmly in front of me. "I packed my bags to run away from everything, as well. Sami, I get it."

Aadam stepped forward and held my face, his hands on each cheek. "Sami, they love you. Why can't you see that?" He lowered his head to look directly into my eyes.

"None of this is your fault, man," Ali chipped in. "Yeah, your baba's been stressed and not himself. But things are gonna get better."

"Yeah, right. They're only getting worse. We're homeless." I peeled Aadam's hands off my cheeks and walked away.

"Sami!" Aadam grabbed my shoulders. "Why are you saying this? You've got it." He stared at me, his eyes sharp. "You've been given leave to remain in the UK!"

I looked at him blankly. What was he going on about?

"They accepted your asylum application—you're now officially refugees in the UK, all of you! Your Uncle Muhammad got the letter this morning and called your baba when we got off the bus. Didn't you hear him?" he said, searching my eyes with his.

"What?" I gasped.

"*Yes!* It means you'll have your own house soon." He glanced over at Ali, then turned back to me.

"Are you lying?" I asked.

"No! I swear! I can't believe you didn't hear him!

I thought you were just being quiet because of your argument last night. Call your baba—ask him yourself," said Aadam, finally letting go of me. "Come on, man, you're my brother. You can't leave." His voice broke. "I've got no one but you."

I felt tears build up under my eyelids and tried to force them back.

Ali stepped forward. "Look at what you've got, Sami. A mum, dad, sister, and TWO brothers, man." He grinned and put out a fist. "You don't need to do this. *We* need you right here in Manchester. I mean, who else am I gonna thrash at football?"

I couldn't help but smile. I didn't know what to say. I fist-bumped him back. *Maybe I should just stay.*

"Here," said Ali, handing me his phone. "Call your dad. You don't have to tell him we're here—just tell him you're calling him during break. Go on!"

I took the phone slowly.

"Just dial it, man!" said Ali. "Ask him about that 'leave to remain' thing. Go on."

I began pressing the digits slowly, trying to remember the number Baba had made me memorize.

I held the phone to my ear. It rang for a few seconds.

"Hello?" said Baba, although he sounded different,

lighter, like he was the day we took Sara to the shops to buy treats.

"Baba . . ."

"Sami?"

"I'm calling on Ali's phone . . . I just wanted to ask you—"

"Sami? What's happened? You okay?"

"Yes, fine—it's just break." I looked at Aadam and Ali's nosy faces close to mine.

"Oh, okay. I'm glad you called. I didn't get a chance to talk to you before you left the bus. But you heard what happened, right?"

"Umm, I think so."

"We got it! We got it today! God is so great! I can find work. . . . Your baba will work as a doctor again and get us a house. Our own house again!"

"Baba, I'm so sorry . . . for everything."

He didn't respond for a long second.

"Listen, Sami. What happened is not your fault. I was just tired and upset last night. I didn't mean it. I shouldn't have lashed out at you."

"I'm really sorry. You were right—it *is* all my fault. I just don't think." I turned away from Ali and Aadam, so they couldn't see my tears.

"No. No, Sami. Stop. What you did was exactly what I would've done. You helped your friend in need, and of course, you wouldn't have known what was going to happen at the house. Whatever has happened to us is because it was written this way. It's fate."

Tears rolled down my cheeks, but my insides felt light, my shoulders less tense.

"Sami? You okay?"

"Yeah . . ."

"I love you. I'm really proud of who you're becoming." His voice cracked a little. "Listen, I must go—the boss is coming. I'll talk to you properly tonight, okay?"

"Okay."

I hung up and handed the phone back to Ali.

Aadam put his arm over my shoulder, and Ali copied on the other side. We pushed through the double doors and joined the travelers flowing through the busy airport. I noticed Aadam had a bounce in his step I hadn't seen before.

As we headed toward one of the short stay car parks, the sun filtered through some clouds, and I lifted my face to it. A sense of calm floated over me, and I finally felt some hope.

I looked at Aadam and then at Ali and smiled as my stomach fluttered. I'd lost everything, but I'd also found something—and it was priceless. Two awesome friends who genuinely cared about me.

Maybe living in England wouldn't be so bad after all.

Epilogue

MY GRIN WAS SO BIG, my face hurt. I pressed the mic button on Baba's phone and started talking.

"Josephhhh! Man, I can't tell you how good it was to hear your voice. Thanks for sending me a million WhatsApp voice messages! It just took me fifteen minutes to listen to them all." I laughed into the phone.

"That kid in your new school sounds just like Hassan—what you said to him was hilarious though! I bet he won't try it again. It'll get better—I know it. Just hang in there. It took ages for things to improve for me, but they finally are. I can't believe it's been three months already since we got to officially stay here! And at least you've got Karim—he sounds like a good mate.

"I loved the pics of your new apartment! That view is awesome. Qatar looks like a cool place, man! Not like here—the weather's awful. Wish I could come see you. It's a shame you haven't heard from Leila or anyone else. I wonder where George is at? Do you think he left too? Mama said to say hello to your mama and baba. She said she'll set up a Skype chat soon. I can't wait to see all your faces!

"Okay, so now to answer your looooooong list of questions! I'm gonna be here all day!

"So the house is now FINALLY clean and decorated. Boy, was it disgusting. It's a weird neighborhood—most of the men and women are dressed like they're going for a run, but they never do. No one really goes to work. They sneer at Mama in her hijab, but she just ignores them.

"At least getting to school's a lot easier than from the hostel, and we've finally got our own space to do what we want. But when we first got inside, it stank! Like someone had died in it. It was moldy and musty, and Mama ran around the house pinching her nose and opening all of the windows. We helped Baba rip up all of the old patterned carpets and chucked them outside. And after we washed down the floorboards the house suddenly smelled normal, but it took a few days for Mama to get the bathroom to look clean. All you could hear was her retching upstairs. *Bleurgh.* I know you don't like it, but you don't know how lucky you are to have moved to a nice apartment, trust me . . .

"Mama's started baking cakes and, man, do I love that smell! Being together again in our own space is the best thing. I'm so glad you weren't split from anyone, Joseph. It was awful in the detention center. You're so lucky your uncle helped your dad get a new job straightaway too. I heard Baba telling Mama we only came to England 'cause he knew Uncle Muhammad here and couldn't think of anywhere else where we'd have support. Can you imagine if we had family in Qatar? We'd still be at school together! Or even better, imagine if the war hadn't come to Damascus. We'd still be there. And nothing would've changed. I miss you, man."

I sighed and pressed Send before recording my next voice message.

"Aadam's loosened up loads—like he's always been part of the family. We share the second largest room in the house—it's like having an older brother. Mama and Baba have put in an official refugee application so he can stay legally as one of their dependents. Baba sends Aadam on errands and he always gets things spot-on and I don't even mind. I'm a bit like you now. I'm not the oldest. I can finally get away with lazing around. Ha!

"We're still sleeping on the floor, in the sleeping bags that Ali's mum gave us. But it's better than that stinky hostel, so I don't care. We've been to so many charity shops to buy a sofa, it's unreal. I'm just grateful for having our own house, even if we're surrounded by neighbors who hate us.

"Anyway, the good news is, Baba's now a refugee member of the British Medical Association, and he's applied to top up his qualifications. He can't be a surgeon here straightaway like your dad in Qatar can, so he's got a job working shifts in the emergency department. He doesn't stop, when he's not at the hospital, he's working on the house and he's always got a smile on his face— it's like he's a different person now he's been given a chance to start life over again. And so even though I miss home so bad and want life to be as easy as it was back in Syria, it's harder to look back when Mama and Baba are making the most of what we have here.

"Mama's cut down on the number of houses she cleans and spends more time with Sara. And Sara's starting school after the summer holidays—she's doing so much better, and even though she's still not speaking, she hums when she's playing. She's going to start seeing a therapist. Man, I hope she talks soon. I don't think I'll ever stop feeling bad about what happened."

I stopped to take a breath.

"She's still sleeping with Mama and Baba, but they're trying to get her into her own room—the smallest one. We managed to get some red paint and mixed it with the white we had leftover after painting the floorboards so we could paint her bedroom pink—it's a vomit-inducing milkshake-pink. *Bleurgh*.

"What else? . . . Um . . . winter's finally over, and the spring's brought *some* sunshine, at last. Ali, Aadam, Mark, and me play football in the park every evening, away from all the racists in my area. Aadam's way better than the rest of us and he knows it. I'm gonna send you a video after this message—he's the kind of player we needed on our team back home. You'll love how fast he is with a ball. I miss you lots, akhi."

"SAMI!" Baba called from downstairs. "Come down for dinner!"

Oh no. I have to answer Joseph's questions before I forget them!

"Okay, so this is my last message. School's getting a lot easier—I mainly hang out with Ali and Mark. I hardly ever see Hassan, and when I do we both look down and pretend we haven't noticed each other. He's still an idiot, though. Mama and Baba went back to their house with gifts to thank them for having us, but I didn't go. Mama invited them over to ours for tea, but only Uncle Muhammad came.

"I don't know if you guys heard—Tete's gone. I still can't believe it, man. We spoke to her every day after our wi-fi was set up. She'd said things were getting worse in Syria, that even more people we knew had been killed and it was good we left when we did. She sounded weak and ill, Joseph, but she refused to come here. She wouldn't even let Baba try to ask the government to let him visit her—said she wouldn't meet him because it was too dangerous. I was mad for weeks after she died, because I was supposed to go back. I wanted to be there for her, man. I only started feeling better after Mama said she was surrounded by her friends praying for her when she died—she wasn't alone. And the last thing she said to Mama was she was glad we were safe and that she wouldn't have to spend her time in heaven worrying about us getting bombed. I suppose that's true, but I still can't imagine Damascus without Tete in it."

I took a breath.

"Tete gave our number to Uncle Bashir a while back and he called us from Germany. He and Aunty Noor are now settled and working in Nuremburg. Baba said they should join us here, but they don't want to. Uncle Bashir said he's tired and just wants to enjoy the peace and calm while he can. How's your tete? Is she still in Damascus? I hope she's okay, man.

"Nightmares—yeah, I'm still having them, but each

time I wake, I try to distract myself by thinking about that time we took all those *dumb* selfies and then you accidentally sent them to the class group chat." I snorted thinking about them. "Are you laughing too . . . ?

"It's weird how life works out. If you'd asked me a year ago where we'd be living, I would've said Damascus. I never thought we'd leave! I know you didn't either. I loved our life, our house—even our school! I never for a minute thought I'd lose it all. We just never thought it would affect us, right? But I've realized how sheltered we were. Our dads saw the worst of it in the hospitals and made sure we were safe. We were lucky to get away unhurt, man. So lucky. I finally appreciate everything Baba did for us, now more than ever. Can you believe I'm saying that?

"Listen, I'm gonna have to go. The phone battery's low, and I have to go down for dinner. What are you doing? You got your new PlayStation yet?

"I'll send you more voice messages later. Be ready for a list of my questions that will be waaaaaaaaay longer than yours! Can you hear me grinning?

"Message me soon, akhi! Love you, bro!"

 Glossary

Akhi: my brother

Alhamdulillah: praise be to God (Allah)

Allah hu Akbar: God is (the) Greatest

As-salaamu alaikum: peace be upon you (a Muslim greeting)

Habibi: my love / my darling (male)

Habibti: my love / my darling (female)

Tete: Grandma (pronounced Tey-tey)

Jiddo: Grandad

Kibbeh: a deep fried croquette made of bulgur wheat and filled with minced meat

Maqluba: a traditional Syrian dish made of meat, rice, and fried vegetables, cooked in a pot, which is served upside down

Marhaba: hello / welcome

Sambousek: a triangle shaped savory pastry filled with meat, usually served as a starter

Shahada: the statement of belief in God and His prophet Muhammad, which makes you a Muslim and is preferably said before dying

Shisha: a pipe for burning tobacco, which passes through water before it is breathed in

Shukran: thank you

Ulad masooleen: children of government officials

Walaikum as-salaam: peace be upon you too (in response to the Muslim greeting As-salaamu alaikum)

Yalla: hurry up or come on

Author's Note

THE CIVIL WAR IN SYRIA began in March 2011, when schoolboys in the southern city of Daraa wrote graffiti on a school wall asking for a change in the political regime. By 2015, when I first began writing *Boy, Everywhere*, millions of Syrians had been forced to leave their homes and seek refuge elsewhere in Syria or in other countries. Around the world, people watched countless news pieces describing the crisis, the influx of refugees, and the rising hatred toward them. Our constantly informed world shared their plight, but people soon became desensitized to their story.

Boy, Everywhere was inspired by a news interview that showed refugees in muddy camps wearing Nike trainers, holding smartphones, and talking about what they'd left behind. Looking around my comfortable living room, I realized that it could easily have been me. Due to media coverage at the time, many people assumed refugees were poor, uneducated, and wanted to come to Europe because they'd have a better life. But the more Syrian people I met and the more research I did, the more I realized that if it weren't for the war, most Syrians would never have left. It became clear their lives were very similar to ours in the West, and a civil war could easily bring the same fate upon any of us.

For years we've only seen grey rubble and debris on the news, or refugees on boats — it's easy to forget that Syria is one of the oldest civilized countries in the world. It has embraced, harbored, and protected thousands of refugees from other countries—most recently those fleeing from the Iraq war. But when the time came for Syrians to seek refuge, the world struggled to help. And that pained me. Because of my own family's story of cross-cultural relocation and immigration, I know what it's like to leave everything behind and start again, and so I have long had an affinity toward Syrians. I had been supporting refugees by setting up various fundraising campaigns to provide food and aid for many years, but I knew this wasn't enough. I wanted to do something long-lasting by sharing their incredible achievements, culture, and backgrounds. Through *Boy, Everywhere* I wanted to focus not only on the arduous journey a refugee takes to get to safety, but also what and who they leave behind and how difficult it is to start again. I wanted the focus to be on who they were and are, their identities as Syrians, not just the temporary political status attributed to them in their new country.

The Syrians I've met in the UK and in Damascus want the world to know what they have been through. They want people to know that they had good lives and were forced to leave. They want the world to know this wasn't their choice. Yet this is where they have ended up. I have been honored to spend time with some of the most amazing people, who had been left with no choice but to leave Syria. Among them were English graduates, department-store buyers, teachers, doctors, and architects, and all of them had to start anew.

A lot of what I discovered in my research for this book made me cry. The most difficult: articles and footage about life inside Syria now and in refugee camps, interviews of children sharing their experiences of the bombings, the trauma, the bad dreams, and their hopes to live like other children. I spoke to many refugees, some who'd spent time in detention centers—often treated far worse than in this book. Although this book is set in 2015–2016, I chose to show the legal process in force during early 2015, before fast-track cases were ruled to be unfair, to show what it feels like to be detained for long periods. My research also revealed the everyday, happy lives of Syrians before they were so terribly affected by civil war. I watched videos online of Syrian teenagers chilling out in cafes, in schools, and on social media. I looked at photos shared by Damascenes on Instagram. I watched rap songs by Syrians on YouTube, in which they played basketball and dressed in chinos, blue oxfords, silk dresses. They were smiling, laughing, painting, swimming, fishing, horseback riding, cooking, studying at school, selling in shops, presenting on the radio, playing the violin, the drums, and, of course, football. These videos showed their normal, happy lives, which made me cry for what they'd lost. And then hearing it all in person from Syrian friends themselves made me even more passionate about challenging stereotypes and sharing another perspective to the well-known refugee "story."

Boy, Everywhere was further motivated by the stories of three Damascene refugees. Nawar Nemeh was a sixteen-year-old boy from an English- and French-speaking private school in Damascus, who escaped the war and eventually settled in San Diego, California, where he became a rising star in his high school. Razan Alsous was a Syrian mother of three who fled Damascus in 2012 when her husband's office block was blown up. Even though Razan had two degrees, she struggled to find work in the UK. But she didn't give up and established the multi-award-winning Dama Cheese Company, which has provided jobs to people in the UK. And then there was Ahmed, who featured in a CBBC documentary about four Syrian boys who had settled in the UK. Ahmed had four bedrooms in his house in Syria, yet now lived in just one room. He never went out because his parents were anxious about their new surroundings. I felt compelled to amplify the voices of boys like Ahmed.

My main aim for this book was always to convey the true lives of Damascenes—to show the color and richness of their lives before the civil war, in contrast to the gray rubble and dust that dominates TV footage. I wanted to challenge the narrative that refugees are needy and desperate and instead show the reality of their lives, the choices they're forced to make and also what and who they leave behind. I wanted this to be a universal story, in which my protagonist is a typical boy who loves cars, playing football, and his PlayStation. My hope is that this book helps to challenge stereotypes and break down barriers in our society. In a world where we are told to see refugees as the "other," I hope you will agree that "they" are also "us."

 Acknowledgments

LIKE MANY AUTHORS, WHEN I first started writing I thought I'd get published easily. (Boy, was I wrong!) They say it takes a village to make a book. I'd say it also takes a village to make a happy, productive writer. One of the best things I did as a novice writer was asking Sheena Dempsey to illustrate my draft picture book. She kindly explained the process and told me that I'd need an agent first; she recommended I join SCBWI and added me to a supportive Facebook group, through which I met the most wonderful, encouraging people, who I am proud to call my friends. I wouldn't be where I am in this long publishing journey without the following people.

I must start by thanking my incredible critique group who I met in 2015: Nicky Matthews Browne, Sue Wallman, Zena McFadzean, Annabel Harris, Camilla Chester, and Sarah Day. They saw this book develop slowly and read my very worst drafts. Through their patience each month, I learned how to show readers what was in my mind. I adore this phenomenal group of women who are always there for me.

I finished my manuscript because Jo Franklin set up the 29ers, a group to motivate friends to write "THE

END" by February 29, 2016 (a leap year). Jo and Nina Oaken encouraged me to keep on every time a book about Syrian refugees was announced. If it weren't for you, I would've taken longer to edit and send it out to agents.

In 2017, Writing East Midlands and We Need Diverse Books awarded me a mentorship. I am enormously grateful for the encouragement you gave me—a big thanks to Aimee Wilkinson, Henderson Mullin, Alex Sanchez, and Padma Venkatraman for seeing something in that submission and for selecting it out of the many you read. Padma, your wholehearted support to see this book published has meant so much to me.

I was delighted to meet my dear writing friends Philippa East and Maya Prasad who were in exactly the same position as me and just as passionate to get published. Thank you so much for listening to my drivel, for advising, and for patiently guiding me through my many editing crises. I couldn't have shared this journey with anyone better.

The biggest thanks of all must go to my mentor, my guide, my friend, Catherine Coe, who showed me that every book can be rescued and rewritten to reach its potential. You taught me so much and I am here because of you. You pushed me to challenge myself. Working with you has been inspiring and sometimes you just listening helped me fix my problems! I am so grateful to have you in my life.

Thank you to my agent, Jennifer Laughran, who loved the concept the moment we met in London and insisted I send my manuscript to her inbox before she landed in New York! Thank you for persisting and navigating UK and US publishing on my behalf, and for sincerely protecting me when offers of interest came in.

A big thank you to my incredible US publisher Lee & Low and superb editor Stacy Whitman, who loved this story and believed in me. Thank you for asking the perfect questions, for your support and visions for this book. I am *so* lucky I get to do this with you.

I am truly honored Zainab "Daby" Faidhi, an award-winning illustrator who worked on the film *The Breadwinner*, chose to work on my cover while she was busy on so many projects in LA. Thank you, it means the world and I love it.

Thank you to Alexandros Plasatis for all the helpful feedback you gave me, and for through your work introducing me to wonderful refugees such as Cloud and Jafor Chowdury, who shared their traumatic detention center experience with me. Also a big thanks to Sheila

Averbuch for reading my early draft, and Eiman Munro for telling me I'd pushed boundaries with it.

A huge thanks must also go to Nadine Kaadan, my favourite Damascene picture book author and illustrator. Thank you for telling me this book is important and needed and for supporting me. Your invaluable advice made Sami's story more authentic. Through you I met my dear friend in Damascus, Mayida Yord, who spent an unbelievable amount of time fact-checking my book. I will always treasure our friendship and look forward to the day we meet in Syria. Miss Majida is named after you! Thank you to student Mohamad Ghabash for telling me he felt Sami could be him, and Layla Jazairy for saying that through this book I'd expressed for you what you couldn't from Damascus.

Ahmad Al-Rashid and Ammar Alsaker, Emad, Rawaa, Maya, Mahmoud, and Abu Karim, you are the most inspiring people I have met. Thank you for sharing your stories of Syria with me and offering me support with this book. I am so glad you are able to show the world who you were and are. Emad, I hope you build houses again in Syria. Rawaa, I hope you work as a department-store buyer once more. Ammar, I can't wait to see your designs, I know you'll be famous. Ahmad, I still haven't read Chaucer, but will continue to tell everyone you have!

Thank you to all my writing friends who have cheered me on and celebrated each tiny step I've taken to get to this point: Kathryn Evans, Patrice Lawrence, Sarah Broadley, Claire Watts, Liz Flanagan, Kate Mallinder, Louise Cliffe-Minns, Julie Sullivan, Louisa Glancy, Kate Walker, Dawn Finch, Caroline Fielding, Joanna de Guia, Louie Stowell, Swapna Haddow, Rashmi Sirdeshpande, Catherine Emmett, Karen Ball, Kirsty Applebaum, Tracy Mathias, Tanya Landman, Bob Stone, Maisie Chan, Em Lynas, Alexandra Strick, Vanessa Harbour, Anna Orenstein, Kim Howard, Savita Kalhan, Beebee Taylor, Marie Basting, Nicky Schmidt, Candy Gourlay, Catherine Johnson, Nizrana Farook, and so many more I can't fit here. Also Sophie Wills, my superhero, for fitting in a last minute proofread. A BIG thank you to SCBWI for helping me to connect with you all.

Thank you also to superstar editors Sarah Odedina and Cheryl Klein for seeking me out and commissioning me to write for you. I am truly honored. You gave me much-needed confidence to believe maybe I could do this thing.

And now my darling family: my husband Imran and

children Mustafa, Ahmed, and Hana. I couldn't have done any of this without your beautiful, wholehearted support. Thank you for coming with me to events, staying home when I had to go alone, cheering me on, and seeing me as an author before I could. Mustafa, thank you for being my first child beta reader. You read it four times and gave me invaluable insights into a thirteen-year-old's mind. Hana, you read the book sweetly to me, aged nine, just because you wanted to. You made Sami's voice come alive, you should read for Audible! Ahmed, thank you for hand-selling my book to your school librarian and friends before it was even printed!

And finally, my mum. You taught me that everything I was blessed with was for a purpose, to help and serve others. You showed me that the sky was the limit and I could achieve anything if I put the work in. If it weren't for you, I wouldn't be where I am today.

Of course I mustn't forget God, thank you for blessing me with a supportive family, friends, a writing community, a computer, time, energy, and dedication to do something I not only enjoy, but also means the world to me.

This is a tribute to all of you. ♡

About the Author

A. M. DASSU IS A writer of both fiction and nonfiction books, based in the heart of England. She is the Deputy Editor of SCBWI-BI's *Words & Pictures* magazine and a Director of Inclusive Minds, a unique organization for people who are passionate about inclusion, diversity, equality, and accessibility in children's literature, and are committed to changing the face of children's books. Her work has been published by the *Huffington Post*, *Times Educational Supplement*, *SCOOP* magazine, Lee & Low Books, and DK Books. She won the international We Need Diverse Books (WNDB) mentorship award in 2017. A. M. Dassu has used her publishing advances for *Boy, Everywhere* to assist Syrian refugees in her city and set up a WNDB grant to support an unpublished refugee or immigrant writer. You can find her on Twitter @a_reflective or at amdassu.com.